ANNA HOPE studied at Oxford University and RADA. She is the internationally bestselling and award-winning author of *Wake* and *The Ballroom*. Her highly acclaimed contemporary fiction debut, *Expectation*, explores themes of love, lust, motherhood and feminism, while asking the greater question of what defines a generation. She lives in Sussex with her husband and young daughter.

Also by Anna Hope

Wake
The Ballroom

Praise for *Expectation*

'Profoundly intelligent and humane . . . Devastatingly perceptive
and emotionally wise, *Expectation* deser~~ves~~
~~to featu . . . . l . . . l~~
GUARDIAN

'One of the most intensely readable novels
I've encountered this year.'
METRO

'A quietly political story that suggests historic battles
have left women with new impossible burdens of expectation.
A marvellously tangy London novel.'
DAILY MAIL

'Compulsive and beautifully observed – an ode to twenty-first century
London and an examination of the pressures of modern society.'
IRISH TIMES BOOK OF THE YEAR

'I couldn't stop reading *Expectation*.
Such brilliant points on the feminist legacy.'
PROFESSOR KATE WILLIAMS

'Hope's writing is sublime and her characters so
well fleshed out they will feel like friends at the end.'
GOOD HOUSEKEEPING BOOK OF THE YEAR

'The real joy of this novel – while exploring just what
second-wave feminism has done for this generation of women –
is in its writing . . . It's the perfect summer reading.'
STYLIST MAGAZINE

'Absolutely encapsulates what it means to be a
young woman today, and beyond.'
GRAZIA

'Completely redefines the friendship novel.
I am in awe of the way Anna Hope captures what
it means to be a woman, right here, right now.'
RED MAGAZINE BOOK OF THE YEAR

'I loved it . . . 10 out of 10!'
BRYONY GORDON

Expectation

Anna Hope

BLACK SWAN

TRANSWORLD PUBLISHERS
61–63 Uxbridge Road, London W5 5SA
www.penguin.co.uk

Transworld is part of the Penguin Random House group of companies
whose addresses can be found at global.penguinrandomhouse.com

Penguin
Random House
UK

First published in Great Britain in 2019 by Doubleday
an imprint of Transworld Publishers
Black Swan edition published 2020

A CIP catalogue record for this book
is available from the British Library.

ISBN
9781784162801

Typeset in 10.81/14.94pt Minion Pro by Jouve (UK), Milton Keynes.
Printed and bound in Great Britain by Clays Ltd, Elcograf S.p.A.

Penguin Random House is committed to a sustainable
future for our business, our readers and our planet. This book
is made from Forest Stewardship Council® certified paper.

MIX
Paper from
responsible sources
FSC
www.fsc.org   FSC® C018179

1 3 5 7 9 10 8 6 4 2

For Bridie, when she's older,
and for Nimmi, who wove me back into the tale

You do not solve the problem or question of motherhood.
You enter, at whatever risk, into its space.

Jacqueline Rose, *Mothers:*
An Essay on Love and Cruelty

London Fields

2004

It is Saturday, which is market day. It is late spring, or early summer. It is mid-May, and the dog roses are in bloom in the tangled garden at the front of the house. It is still early, or early for the weekend – not yet nine o'clock, but Hannah and Cate are up already. They do not speak much to each other as they take turns at the kettle, making toast and tea. The sun slants into the room, lighting the shelves with the haphazard pans, the recipe books, the badly painted walls. When they moved in here two years ago they vowed to repaint the dreadful salmon colour of the kitchen, but they never got around to it. Now they like it. Like everything in this shabby, friendly house, it feels warm.

Upstairs, Lissa sleeps. She rarely rises before noon on the weekends. She has a job in a local pub and often goes out after work – a party at a flat in Dalston, one of the dives off Kingsland Road, or further afield, in the artists' studios of Hackney Wick.

They finish their toast and leave Lissa to sleep on, taking their faded canvas shopping bags from the rack on the back of the door and going out into the bright morning. They turn left and then right into Broadway Market, where the stalls are just getting set up. This is their favourite time – before the crowds arrive. They buy almond croissants from the baker at the top of the road. They buy strong Cheddar and a goat's cheese covered with ash. They buy good tomatoes and bread. They buy a newspaper from the huge pile outside the Turkish off-licence. They buy two bottles of wine for later. (Rioja. Always Rioja. They know nothing about wine but they know they like Rioja.) They amble further down the road to the other stalls, looking at knick-knacks and second-hand clothes. Outside the pubs there are people, in the manner of London markets, already clutching pints at nine o'clock.

Back in the house they lay out the food on the table in the kitchen, make a heroic pot of coffee, put on some music and open the window out on to the park, where the grass is filling with small clusters of people. Every so often one of those people will look up towards the house. They know what the person is thinking – how do you get to live in a house like that? How do you get to live in a three-storey Victorian townhouse on the edge of the best park in London? Luck is how. A friend of a friend of Lissa's offered her a room, and then, during the same year, two more rooms came up, and now they live in it together; the three of them. In all but deed the house is theirs. There is an agent somewhere in the far reaches of Stamford Hill, but they have a strong suspicion he does not know what is happening to the area, as their rent has remained stable for the last two years. They have a pact not to ask for anything, not to complain about the peeling lino or the stained carpets. These things do not matter, not when a house is so loved.

Sometime around eleven Lissa wakes and wanders downstairs. She drinks a pint of water and holds her head, then takes her coffee to the steps outside and rolls a cigarette and enjoys the morning sun, which is just starting to warm the lowest of the stone steps.

When coffee has been drunk and cigarettes smoked and

morning has become afternoon, they take plates and food and blankets out into the park, where they lie in the dappled shade of their favourite tree. They eat their picnic slowly. Hannah and Cate take turns to read the paper. Lissa shades her eyes with the arts pages and groans. A little later on they open the wine and drink it, and it is easy to drink. The afternoon deepens. The light grows viscous. The chatter in the park increases.

This is their life in 2004, in London Fields. They work hard. They go to the theatre. They go to galleries. They go to the gigs of friends' bands. They eat Vietnamese food in the restaurants on Mare Street and on Kingsland Road. They go to openings on Vyner Street on Thursdays, and they visit all the galleries and they drink the free beer and wine. They remember not to use plastic bags when they go to the corner shop, although sometimes they forget. They cycle everywhere, everywhere, all the time. They rarely wear helmets. They watch films at the Rio in Dalston, and then go to Turkish restaurants and eat pide and drink Turkish beer and eat those pickles that make your saliva flow. They go to Columbia Road flower market and buy flowers in the very early morning on Sundays. (Sometimes, if Lissa is coming home early from a party, she buys cheap flowers for the whole house – armfuls of gladioli and irises. Sometimes, because she is beautiful, she is given them for free.)

They go to the city farm on Hackney Road with hangovers, and they eat fried breakfasts in amongst the families and the screaming children, and they swear never to go there again on a Sunday morning until they have children of their own.

Sometimes on Sundays they walk; out along the Regent's Canal to Victoria Park, and beyond to the old Greenway, to

3

Three Mills Island, savouring the sideways slice of London that the canal offers up.

They are interested in the history of the East End. They buy books on psycho-geography from the bookshop at the bottom of the road. They try to read Iain Sinclair and fail at the first chapter but read other, more accessible books instead, about the successive waves of immigration that have characterized this part of the city: the Huguenots, the Jews, the Bengalis. They are aware that they too are part of a tide of immigration. If they are honest, they would like to halt this particular tide – they fear encroachment by those who resemble themselves.

They worry. They worry about climate change – about the rate of the melt of the permafrost in Siberia. They worry about the kids who live in the high-rises, right behind the deli where they buy their coffee and their tabbouleh. They worry about the life chances of these kids. They worry about their own relative privilege. They worry about knife crime and gun crime, then they read pieces which suggest the violence is only ever gang on gang and they feel relieved, then they feel guilty that they feel relieved. They worry about the tide of gentrification that is creeping up from the City of London and lapping at the edges of their park. Sometimes they feel they should worry more about these things, but at this moment in their lives they are happy, and so they do not.

They do not worry about nuclear war, or interest rates, or their fertility, or the welfare state, or ageing parents, or student debt.

They are twenty-nine years old. None of them has children. In any other generation in the history of humankind this fact would be remarkable. It is hardly remarked upon at all.

They are aware that this park – London Fields – this grass on which they lie, has always been common land, a place for people to pasture their cows and sheep. This fact pleases them; they believe it goes some way to explaining the pull of this small, patchy patch of green they like to feel they own. They feel like they own it because they do; it belongs to everyone.

They would like to pause time – just here, just now, in this park, this gorgeous afternoon light. They would like the house prices to remain affordable. They would like to smoke cigarettes and drink wine as though they are still young and they don't make any difference. They would like to burrow down, here, in the beauty of this warm May afternoon. They live in the best house on the best park in the best part of the best city on the planet. Much of their lives is still before them. They have made mistakes, but they are not fatal. They are no longer young, but they do not feel old. Life is still malleable and full of potential. The openings to the roads not taken have not yet sealed up.

They still have time to become who they are going to be.

Hannah

Hannah sits on the edge of the bed, holding the vials in their plastic case. She runs her thumbnail along the thin wrapper and brings out one of the tubes. It weighs almost nothing. A quick fit of the needle, one flick of her fingertip to release the bubbles – she knows what she's doing, she has done this before. Still. Perhaps she should mark the moment somehow.

The first time, two years ago, Nathan bent over her with the needle, kissing her belly each day as the injections went in.

He kissed her differently this morning.

Promise me, Hannah, after this, no more.

And she promised, because she knew after this there wouldn't need to be more.

She lifts her shirt and pinches her skin. A brief scratch and it is over. When she has finished she stands, straightens her clothes and heads out into the morning to work.

Lissa is not there when she arrives at the Rio, so Hannah gets a tea from the little bar and moves outside. It is September but still warm, and the small square beside the cinema is busy with people. Hannah spots Lissa's tall frame threading its way up the street from the station and lifts her hand to wave. Lissa is wearing a coat Hannah has not seen before; narrow at the shoulders, fuller below the waist. Her hair, as ever, is long and loose.

'I love this,' Hannah murmurs, as Lissa leans in to kiss hello, catching the rough linen lapel between finger and thumb.

'This?' Lissa looks down as though surprised to discover she's wearing it. 'I got it years ago. That charity shop on Mare Street. Remember?'

Never anywhere you might be able to go and get one for yourself, always a charity shop, or *that little stall in the market, you know, the man in Portobello?*

'Wine?' says Lissa.

Hannah wrinkles her nose. 'Can't.'

Lissa touches her arm. 'You've started again then?'

'This morning.'

'How are you feeling?'

'Fine. I'm feeling fine.'

Lissa takes her hand and squeezes it lightly. 'Won't be a sec.'

Hannah watches her friend weave over to the bar, watches the young man serving light up at her attention. A bright, shared laugh and Lissa is back outside in the sun, her red wine in a plastic cup. 'All right if I have a quick cig?'

Hannah holds the wine while Lissa rolls. 'When are you going to give that up?'

'Soon.' Lissa lights up and blows smoke over her shoulder.

'You've been saying that for fifteen years.'

'Have I? Oh well.' Lissa's bangles clink as she reaches back to take her wine. 'I had the recall,' she says.

'Oh?' It's terrible, but Hannah never remembers. There have been so many auditions. So many parts almost got.

'A fringe thing – but a good thing. A good director. The Polish woman.'

'Ah.' She remembers now. 'Chekhov?'

'Yeah. *Vanya*. Yelena.'

'So how did it go?'

Lissa shrugs. 'Good. In parts.' She takes a sip of wine. 'Who knows? She worked with me quite a bit on the speech.' And then she launches into an impression of the Polish director, replete with accents and mannerisms.

'Here, do it again. Make it real. None of this – how do you say it? Microwave emotion – put it on high. Two minutes. Ping! Tastes like shit.'

'Jesus,' says Hannah, laughing. It always astonishes her, the crap Lissa puts up with. 'Well, if you don't get the part, you could always do a one-woman show, *Directors I Have Known and Been Rejected By*.'

'Yeah, well, that'd be funny if it weren't true. No. It is funny. Just . . .' Lissa frowns, and throws her cigarette into the gutter. 'Don't say it again.'

'Not bad,' says Lissa, as they emerge from the cinema into the darkness of the street outside. 'Bit Chekhovy, actually.' She threads her arm through Hannah's. 'Not much happens for ever and then the big emotional punch. The Polish director would probably have loved it. Long though,' she continues, as they head down towards the market, 'and no decent parts for women.'

'No?' It hadn't occurred to Hannah, but now she thinks of it, it's true.

'Wouldn't pass the Bechdel test.'

8

'The Bechdel test?'

'Jesus, Han, call yourself a feminist?' Lissa steers her towards the crossing. 'You know – does a film have two women in it? Do they both have names? Do they have a conversation about something other than a man? This American writer came up with it. Loads of films fail it. Most of them.'

Hannah thinks. 'They did have that conversation,' she says. 'In the middle of the film. About the fish.'

They both snort with laughter, as arm in arm they cross the street.

'Speaking of fish,' says Lissa, 'you want to eat something? We could head down and get some noodles.'

Hannah pulls out her phone. 'I should get back. I've got a report due tomorrow.'

'Through the market then?'

'Sure.' This is their favoured route home. They weave their way past the shuttered-up fronts of the African hairdressers, past sliding piles of cardboard boxes, crates of too-ripe mangoes buzzing with flies. The blood-metal stink of the butchers' shops.

Halfway down the street a bar is open and a knot of young people stand outside, drinking lurid cocktails with retro umbrellas. There is a rackety, demob air to the throng; some of them still wearing sunglasses in the dusky light. At the sight of them Lissa hangs back, tugging on Hannah's arm. 'Come on – we could just have a little drink?'

But Hannah is suddenly tired – irritated by these young people laughing into the weekday night, by Lissa's spaciousness. What does she have to get up for in the morning? By her constant capacity for forgetting that, lately, Hannah does not drink.

'You go. I've got to be in early. I've got to do that report. I think I'll get the bus.'

'Oh, OK.' Lissa turns back. 'I guess I'll walk. It's such a lovely evening. Hey' – she brings her hands either side of Hannah's face – 'good luck.'

Cate

Someone is calling her. She follows the voice but it twists and echoes and will not be caught. She struggles upwards, breaks the surface, understands – it is her son crying, lying beside her in the bed. She brings him to her breast and gropes for her phone. The screen reads 3.13 – less than an hour since his last waking.

She had been dreaming again: the nightmare; broken streets, rubble and her with Tom in her arms, wandering, searching the burnt-out carcasses of buildings for something, for someone – but she did not recognize the streets, or the city, did not know where she was, and everything was over, everything destroyed.

Tom feeds, his grip slowly slackening, and she listens for the change in his breathing that signals the beginning of sleep. Then, with the barest of movements, she slides her nipple from his mouth, her arm from above him, turns on to her side and pulls the covers up over her ear. And she is falling, falling down into the pit of sleep and the sleep is water – but he is crying again, escalating now, announcing his distress, his indignation that she should fall like this away from him, and she hauls herself back awake.

Her tiny son is writhing beneath her in the gritty light. She lifts him and rubs his back. He gives a small belch and she puts him back on the breast, closing her eyes as he suckles and then bites. She cries out in pain and rolls away.

'*What?* What is it?' She pushes her fists into her eyes as Tom wails, hands and legs flailing, fists closing on nothing. 'Stop it, Tom. Please, please.'

On the other side of the thin wall there are low voices, the creak of a bed. She needs to pee. She moves her crying son into the middle of the bed and goes out towards the landing, where she hovers. To her right is the other bedroom, where Sam sleeps. Nothing wakes him. Downstairs is the narrow hallway, filled with piles of boxes, the lumped, heaped things she has not attended to since the move.

She could leave, leave this house, pull on her jeans and boots and walk away from here, away from this wailing creature that she cannot satisfy, from this husband wrapped in the interstellar blankness of his sleep. From herself. She would not be the first woman to do so. In the bedroom her son's cries grow louder – a small animal, afraid.

She hurries to the toilet and pisses quickly, then stumbles back to the bedroom, where Tom is howling. She lies beside him, pulls him back on to her breast. Of course she will not leave – it is the last – the very last – thing she would do – but her heart is beating strangely and her breath is ragged and perhaps she will have no choice, perhaps she will die – die like her mother before her, and leave her son to be brought up by his father and his family in this sterile house in the far reaches of Kent.

Tom flutters finally on her breast, slackens and sleeps. But she is wide awake now. She sits up in bed and pulls back the curtains. Through the window she can see the car park, where the cars sit in their neat, obedient rows, then the dark shape of the river, and beyond that the orange lights from the ring-road, where the traffic is already thickening; lorries moving out to the coast, or returning from the Channel ports, cars on their way to London, the great greased machine of it lumbering towards the light. She feels her heart, the adrenaline swill of her blood. The moon comes out from behind clouds, illuminating the room, the rucked duvet, her tiny son beside her, abandoned now to sleep, his arms flung wide. She wants to protect him. How can she protect him from all the things that might fall upon his unguarded head? She reaches out and touches his hair, and as she does so sees the picture tattooed on her wrist, silver in the moonlight. She brings back her hand, traces the image slowly with her opposite fingertip – a filigree spider, a filigree web – a relic, now, from a different life.

She wants to see someone. To speak to someone. Someone from another lifetime. Someone who made her feel safe.

She is sitting on her bench, facing the river, where a low mist is rising from the water and a tangle of nettles clogs the bank. There is movement on the towpath now, a thin stream of humanity; joggers, early-morning workers, heads down, heading towards town. Tom is calm at least, a warm weight on her chest, face framed by a little bear hat. He woke again at five or so this morning and would not be placated, so they came out here. Her phone tells her it is almost seven o'clock, which means the supermarket will be open soon, which means there is somewhere warm to go, at least, and so she stands and follows the banks of the little tributary, over the humped bridge, under the underpass and out by the car park. By the time she joins the small crowd outside the supermarket doors, it has begun to drizzle.

Tom grinches in the sling and Cate shushes him as a uniformed woman comes out and casts a look to the sky, then goes back inside, and the doors slide open. The people bestir themselves and follow, funnelled through the bakery aisle, where the heated air circulates the smell of sugar and yeast and dough. She makes for the baby section, filling her basket with several little foil packets. She bought these packets in ones or twos at first – always sure the next meal would be the one she prepared properly – now she buys them in bulk. Nappies too; at first she was sure she would use washables, but after the trauma of the birth she started on disposables and then came the move, and now here she is lifting huge packets of nappies into her basket, the sort guaranteed to take half a millennium to decompose.

It is a two-minute walk back home, past the trees encased in concrete and wire cages, the bin store with its padlocks, the car park with its barriers, the signs alerting you to the anti-climb paint on the walls. She reaches her front door and lets herself into the narrow kitchen, puts down the bag and lifts Tom from the sling and into his high chair. She selects one of the little foil packages – banana and blueberry – and Tom holds out his hands for it as she untwists the seal and holds the plastic teat to his lips. He sucks away happily, like a little astronaut with space food.

'Morning.' Sam wanders in, hair mussed from sleep. He looks as though he slept in the clothes he was wearing last

13

night – a faded band T-shirt and boxers. Straight to the kettle he goes, without looking up; hand out to test the temperature, switch flicked, used grounds dumped into the sink, the cafetière barely rinsed before the fresh grounds are shaken in. The swaddled luxury of the morning trance – no point in speaking till the caffeine has entered the blood.

'Morning,' she says.

Sam looks to her, eyes with an underwater glaze. 'Hey.' He raises a hand.

'What time did you get in?'

'Late,' he says with a shrug. 'Two-ish. We had some beers after the shift.'

'Sleep well?'

'Oh. OK.' He sighs, cricking his neck. 'Not great, but OK.'

How many hours straight through? Even a late night gives him, what? Six, maybe seven hours of uninterrupted sleep – the thought of it, of seven straight hours, of how it would feel. Despite this, he still looks tired, with heavy shadows beneath his eyes – the indoor pallor of the professional chef. He sleeps in the spare room, which is no longer, it seems, spare: it is his room now, just as the room that should be theirs is hers – hers and their son's, Tom's cot unused, a dumping ground for clothes, while Tom sleeps with Cate. Easier that way, for the many, many times Tom wakes.

He turns back to the coffee, plunges, pours. 'You want one?'

'Sure.'

He makes his way over to the fridge for milk. 'On an early one today,' he says. 'Doing lunch.'

He works as a sous in a restaurant in the centre of town. *Ten years behind London*, was what she heard him say on the

14

phone to a friend back in Hackney the other night, *but OK, you know, OK. Getting some input already.*

He was on the verge of opening a place in Hackney Wick, before the rents went crazy. Before she got pregnant. Before they moved out here.

He hands her her coffee, takes a sip of his own. 'Did you wash my whites?'

She looks around, sees the pile in the corner, three days' worth. 'Sorry, no.'

'Really? I left them in your way, so you wouldn't forget.' Sam goes over to the pile, lifts the least stained overall to the light, starts scrubbing it viciously with the scourer at the sink. Outside the drizzle is thickening into rain.

'What are you two up to today?' he says.

'Washing, I suppose. Unpacking.'

'What about that playgroup? The one Mum mentioned?' He nods to the brightly coloured flyer stuck up on the fridge, the flyer Alice brought around the other day. Alice, Sam's mother, with her concerned face, mouth pursed somewhere between a grimace and a smile. *It's a lovely little group, it really is. You might make some friends.* Alice, the mastermind of the plan to *buy a little house for you all. In Canterbury.* Alice, their saviour. Alice, who has a key to the lovely little house and likes to pop round unannounced.

'Yeah,' Cate says. 'Maybe.'

'And we've got that thing tonight,' Sam says, giving up on the scouring, hanging his overall on a chair to dry, 'don't forget. At Mark and Tamsin's.'

'I haven't forgotten.'

'I'll pick you up, shall I?'

'Sure.'

'But Cate?'

'Yes?'

'Try and get out today, won't you? Take Tom out?'

'I was out while you were still asleep. Buying nappies and food.'

'I mean out-out.'

'Define out,' she says under her breath.

Sam looks at the kitchen. 'You know,' he says, taking a tea towel and wiping down the counter. 'It's really easy to clean at the end of the day. You just do what chefs do and put the day's tea towel into the wash. Along with my whites.' He holds up the damp dirty cloth. 'Where's the washing basket?'

She looks up at him. 'I'm not sure.'

'You just need a system,' he says, shaking his head. 'A system is all you need.' He puts the cloth on the side, then leans in and scoops Tom out of the high chair, lifting him up above his head, and their baby squeals with delight, kicking his heels. The moment plays out, passes, and then Sam gives him back, dropping a hand on Cate's shoulder. 'Knackered,' he says, to no one in particular.

'Yeah,' she says. 'Me too.'

Lissa

It's at the Green Room, Wardour Street. Scene of too many castings to count. The receptionist is young and glossy and hardly looks up as Lissa gives her name.

'Lissa Dane. Sorry, I'm a bit—'

'It's fine. They're running late anyway.' Her name is ticked off a long list, and a clipboard and biro are handed over the counter. 'Take a seat. Fill in your details.'

Lissa nods, she knows the drill. A quick glance at the room: four men, two women, the women both in their thirties, one dark, one red-haired. The redhead is speaking on her phone, low and stressed and apologetic: 'No, no, I know I said half past, but they're running late. Not sure. Half an hour maybe. Maybe more. Do you mind? I can come round and fetch him from yours. Oh God, thank God, thanks, I owe you one, thanks, thanks.' The woman flicks off the phone and catches Lissa's eye. '*Forty fucking minutes*,' she whispers furiously.

Lissa pulls a sympathetic face. Not great, but not so bad. She's had worse – has waited for almost two hours to be seen. But then, she doesn't have kids at the school gate. She glances at the casting brief in her hands.

A PTA meeting, a teacher and two parents, both concerned about their son.

At the top of the page she recognizes the name of a well-known brand of chocolate cookie. Across from her a man is diligently marking and highlighting his piece of paper. She flicks to the second sheet and begins filling out her details.

Height. 5'7.

Weight. She pauses, can't remember the last time she was weighed. Sixty? She usually puts sixty. She scribbles it down.

Waist. 30.

Hips. 38.

She tries to tell the truth nowadays; it's not worth stretching it on these things. For a long time she put any old thing down, not lying, just being . . . inexact. But then she was caught out at that shoot in Berlin; that old flat with the hundreds of Japanese paper lanterns, the assistant bringing out outfit after outfit, none of which fitted the measurements she had scribbled down in the London casting a month before, as the little designer fussed around her, tutting his disapproval.

But you look so fet. So fet in these.

In the end, she had to borrow the costume assistant's trousers. In the end, she was cut out of the ad.

As she scrawls across the pages, Hannah's comment from last night comes back to her: *a one-woman show. Directors I Have Known and Been Rejected By.* It was funny, of course it was, but it had stung. She wouldn't make a comment like that about Hannah.

Hey! Han! What about *All the Times I've Tried IVF and It's Failed*. What about that? Wouldn't that be hil*arious*?

But of course the comparison doesn't stand. Because nothing beats Hannah's pain.

The casting director puts in an appearance, and the atmosphere lifts and sharpens. 'All right, folks. Running a bit late.'

He is tanned, meaty, running to fat. His face the face of a self-satisfied baby. But he gets her seen for these things often, and so Lissa smiles and laughs and flirts with him despite herself.

The red-haired woman is up. Lissa watches her seal away her fury and paint on a smile.

She gives a quick, reflexive glance to her phone. Still no news on the recall. The Chekhov. That in itself doesn't mean anything – you can wait weeks for these things and then be surprised, but she can feel hope begin its long, tidal ebb. By tomorrow, if she has still not heard anything, she will be twitchy; by the weekend, fractured and emotional; by the beginning of next week, defensive, patched up. She has become more, not less, thin-skinned as time has gone on.

She ignores the hat and glove measurements – sometimes it seems as though these forms haven't changed since the 1950s – puts down her shoe size, then stands and hands the paper back to the young woman behind the desk.

The young woman rises. She is tall and skinny and wearing black. She picks up the Polaroid camera before her and waves it languidly towards the blank wall.

Lissa sees the other women look up as she takes her place against the exposed brick, their quick assessment of her figure, her clothes. Looking for the shadows, the wrinkles, the greys.

She arranges her face.

She used not to go up for these things at all.

When she left drama school, her new agent, who met her sitting on a yoga block and ran briskly through her impressive client list, said she wouldn't put her up for commercials unless she really wanted her to.

And if you do, said her new agent, *then they'll only be for Europe. We wouldn't want you to be seen over here.*

They both laughed at that. *Hahaha.* That was when she used to go up for three movies a week. When the casting directors made sure you never crossed paths with anyone else up for the same part. When you waited in hushed anterooms clutching your script, a racehorse, primed and ready. When the director leaped up as you entered the room, holding out his hand (always his, never hers). *Thanks so much for coming in.*

The Polaroid clicks and whirrs.

'Thanks,' the young woman says, wafting the photograph dry. 'Take a seat.'

Lissa does not sit. Instead she makes her way down the line to the small bathroom to check her face. In the mirror she sees that her mascara has run and little black dots mark her under-eye. *Fuck*. She rubs at them with her thumb. No matter how good you feel. No matter how well you think you have pulled together an outfit, put your game face on, something always occurs to prick it.

You've just got to play the game, Lissa, her first agent's assistant had sighed down the phone to her once, when she had refused to buy a Wonderbra for an audition. *You know that. They said they wanted someone with bigger boobs.* The Wonderbra had been cited in the phone call in which the agent dropped her.

She makes her way back out to the waiting room, threads past the legs of the waiting actors, takes a seat and closes her eyes.

She has tried.

As time has passed, as her twenties have given way to her thirties with little to show for them, she has really tried to play the game. Has bumped down through three agents, each further down the food chain than the last. Has gone from never having commercial castings to having nothing else. From being protected from the scent of desperation to being sure that she gives it off, sweating from her pores, at castings, at parties, in the street.

Please. Give me a job. Any job. Please, please, please.

Like that programme her mother used to watch in the eighties. *Gis a job. Gis a job.*

20

'Lissa. Rod. Daniel.'

She snaps open her eyes. The casting director is back. It is her turn. She makes her way into the darkened box where two men sit on a sofa, scrolling idly through their phones. The air is stale, the table before them littered with coffee cups and half-eaten sushi and e-cigarettes. Neither of the men looks up from their screens.

She takes her spot on the X on the floor. The camera pans up and down her body. She says her name, says the name of her agent. Turns to the left. Turns to the right. Shows her hands to the camera.

When the men have done the same, the casting director claps his hands.

'OK, so, Lissa, you're the mum, Rod, you're the father. Dan, you're playing the teacher.'

Dan nods wildly. Lissa can see he read the brief last night, since he has come dressed for the part in a jacket with patches on the elbows, and a tie.

'So, Lissa, Rod, you sit here.' The casting director gestures to a couple of chairs behind a table. 'And Dan, you here on the other side. And here's the cookies.'

Lissa looks at where a plate of cookies sits on a stool, anaemic-looking in the fetid air.

'So yeah, why not just do a bit of improvising then?'

One of the men on the sofa glances briefly up at the monitor, then back down at his phone, as Dan leans forward, eager to begin.

'So – erm, Mrs . . . Lacey. Mr . . . Lacey, I'm a little, um, worried about . . . Josh.' He sits back, obviously pleased with this first sally.

'Oh?' The actor beside Lissa leans forward now. He is handsome in a bland sort of way. She can see his muscles tensed beneath the cotton of his shirt. 'That's very ... concerning.'

'*Look at me.*'

Lissa looks up, startled, to where the casting director is reading from a script in a gruff baritone.

'The cookies,' the casting director says to her, waving her gaze away, 'I'm the voice of the cookies. Look at the cookies, not at me.'

'Oh,' she says. 'Right.'

'*Look at me,*' he says again.

She looks down at the cookies.

'*You know you want to. Yeah. That's right. Come a little closer.*'

Lissa leans tentatively towards the plate.

'*Yeah.*' His voice drops another half an octave. Is he moving into an American accent? He sounds like Barry White.

The men on the sofa have both looked up now. She can see the monitor – a tight close-up of her face, her cheeks red, her expression confused.

'*Yeah,*' the casting director murmurs. He too is looking up at the monitor now, waiting.

Silence.

'Go on,' he says, in his normal voice.

'Sorry?' She can feel sweat spreading over her back. 'I'm a bit lost here.'

Dan leans forward, eager as ever. 'You're supposed to pick them up,' he says. 'It said in the brief. To *shove them in your mouth*.' He points to the paper. 'It says you can't concentrate on the teacher. On what the teacher's saying. Because of the cookies. You just can't help yourself.'

'Ah. I see.'

The men look at her: the two actors, the casting director, the cameraman, the men on the sofa. One of the sofa men marks something on a piece of paper. The other reads it, nods, looks back down at his phone.

The casting director sighs. 'Did you read the brief, Lissa?'

'Obviously not quite closely enough.'

'No.' He flicks the sofa men an apologetic look. 'Shall we go again? And Lissa, could you flirt a little more with the cookies this time?'

Oxford Street is a scrum of lunchtime shoppers. The entrance to the Tube gapes, but she walks past it. She doesn't want to go down, not home, not yet.

Fuck the cookies.

Fuck the fat casting director with his three holidays a year. Fuck those two directors sitting behind their monitors like bored teenagers. Fuck the camera that pans up and down your body more slowly than it does the men's. Fuck the scriptwriters for these fucking commercials. *You just can't help yourself.* Fuck the men that run this fucking show.

Without thinking, she heads north and east, picking up Goodge Street, emerging on to Tottenham Court Road and then Chenies Street, past the red door of her old drama school. Now Bloomsbury, past the gates of the British Museum, the lung of Russell Square; the relief of it, the green. She walks on, further north, through Gordon Square to the clamour of Euston Road, where she ducks into the courtyard of the British Library, opens her bag for the man on duty, stands in the hush and bustle.

How long since she has been in a library? She takes the escalator up to the first floor, where banks of people sit at chairs with small armrests as though they themselves are some sort of exhibition, some sort of display. But here – ah – here are the Reading Rooms. Rare Books. Humanities One. She pushes the heavy door open; perhaps she can sit here for a while, in Rare Books, and let the rare books calm her, bring her back to herself.

'May I see your card, madam?' A pleasant-faced guard has his hand out to stop her walking further. 'Your reader's card?'

'I don't . . . I'm sorry.'

There is someone behind her, tutting, his belongings in a see-through plastic bag, card held out already in one bristling fist.

'You need a card, madam, to enter the Reading Rooms,' says the guard, waving the man along.

'Oh, I see.' The world is full of spikes today. She turns, pushes back out towards the main concourse, where she sinks on to a nearby bench.

'Lissa? Liss?'

For a moment she doesn't recognize him, here, out of context, but then – of course – 'Nath!' She stands and they hug hello.

'What are you doing here?'

'I . . .' What is she doing here? 'I thought I'd do some reading for something,' she says.

'Oh?'

24

'Yeah – a . . . course I'm thinking of taking. But they won't let me in.'

'Oh? Well. They're funny like that in here.' He smiles, and she is glad of him. She needs someone familiar today. 'Listen' – he gestures behind him to the crowded restaurant – 'I'm just on a break. You fancy a coffee?'

As they queue she scans the crowd: people of all ages, clutching laptops beneath their arms, tapping away on phones, all with those same see-through bags. She orders her coffee and as Nathan orders himself a cappuccino, double shot, she thinks of Hannah – no coffee, no booze, not for years now. She used to wave the wine bottle in her face – *Go on, Han, surely a little won't hurt* – but by now she has learned not to. How many years have they been trying? Four? Five? She has lost count.

In the early days, when Hannah and Nathan first started trying and nothing was happening, she remembers Hannah weeping one evening. *But I've worked hard. I've worked so hard all my life.* And her saying something back, like, *Of course it'll happen. It has to. It's you two, isn't it?* as though the universe gave two shits whether or not you'd worked your arse off and paid your taxes and your TV licence fee, whether you were the deputy director of a large global charity and married to a lovely man who was a senior lecturer at a leading London university and put your hand up first in class. What she had wanted to say was, *Bad things happen to good people all the time. Every day. Do you watch the news?*

'So,' Nathan says, letting Lissa go first as they thread their way towards an empty table. 'What sort of course?' He sits down before her and she sees his eyes are tired. But he looks well, still has something of the boy in him, still wearing the same flannel shirts he wore twenty years ago, the sleeves rolled up to the elbows. Even his hair has hardly changed, thick and dark, cropped close to his head.

'Ah . . . well.' She takes a sip of her coffee. 'Um . . . film.'

'Film?'

'Yes – it's a . . . PhD.'

'A PhD? Blimey. Careful. You can cut yourself on those things.'

'Yeah. So I hear.'

Now she has lied she should feel worse, but she feels marginally better. Why not? Why not do something different? Why not change her life?

'Hannah didn't mention it,' says Nathan.

'No, well, it's quite a new idea.'

'So, tell me,' he says, his gaze levelling with hers.

'Um.' Lissa stirs sugar into her coffee. 'It's a sort of . . . feminist appraisal. Using the – you know, the Bechdel test . . . looking at films now and in the seventies, and . . . the forties. Comparing parts for women. How they've shrunk. Changed. *All About Eve, Network* . . .'

'*Network*. Isn't that the one where he dies on screen?'

'Yes. Yes! But Faye Dunaway in that – she's incredible, totally fierce, totally unlikeable. And all those pictures of the forties, the "women's pictures"' – she makes quote marks in the air with her fingers – 'they were actually pretty great. Bette Davis, Katharine Hepburn . . .'

'*Autumn Sonata*,' Nathan says, leaning forward.

'What's that?'

'You don't know it? Seriously? Liv Ullmann. Ingrid Bergman.

26

Two incredible parts for women. Fierce doesn't even cover it. I needed therapy after that film.'

'I'll watch it,' she says, laughing. 'Thanks.' She leans over and takes his pen, scribbles the title on to the back of her hand.

'Hey,' he says, 'maybe you should invest in a notebook, for this new academic career.'

'Yeah.' She hands him back his pen. 'Maybe I should.'

'How's the acting then?'

'Oh. You know.' She shrugs. 'Appalling. Humiliating. Ask me tomorrow.'

'Really? But I thought it was going OK. There was that thing . . . the Shakespeare. You were great.'

'That thing was three years ago, Nath.'

A fringe *King Lear* at the back of a pub in Peckham. Playing Regan for two hundred a week plus expenses. Raising her voice even louder when the racing was on in the bar.

'So how do you live? You don't still work in pubs?'

She pushes her cup away. 'I do shifts in a call centre. Raising money for charities. And I do the life modelling.'

'Still? Jesus, really?'

'Yeah. Well.' The look on his face pricks her. 'It's not so bad. They're good charities. And the life modelling's fine. I work at the Slade. It could be worse.'

'Yes, but surely there's something else. You're so bright.'

'Thanks, but it's not so easy to find a world-beating part-time job that lets me go to auditions at short notice.'

He nods, chastened.

'What about you, Nath?'

'What do you mean?'

27

'How are you doing?'

'Oh, OK. Overworked. Underpaid. Drowning in admin.'

I didn't mean that. I meant the baby stuff. The no-baby stuff. How are you doing with that?

'But, you know, we academics love to moan.'

As they stand to say their goodbyes her phone buzzes – her agent. She gestures to Nathan, who waves his hand for her to take the call.

'Lissa?'

She can tell by the tone it's good news. 'Yes?' She tries to keep the eagerness from her voice.

'They want you. The Chekhov. You're in.'

Cate

Sam is at the wheel as they drive westwards, through the terraces and pound shops of Wincheap, out to where the city thins and frays into the ribbons of A-roads that lead to London, to the coast. They are late. She and Tom were asleep when Sam came back from work, both of them sprawled together on the bed. Now Tom nods again in the car seat as they take the Ashford Road, passing garden centres, small industrial estates housing soft-play zones, motor-home dealers, stands of scrappy-looking trees.

She's wearing the first decent blouse she could find and her maternity jeans, the ones with the huge black waistband. An old cardigan on top. She could have done better. Should have done better. 'So is anyone else going to be there?'

'I don't think so. Just Tamsin and Mark.'

'What is it he does again?'

'He's got a company. Agricultural machinery. He's doing really well.' Sam turns to her. 'He might invest in a restaurant. He's got the cash. We've talked about it for years.'

She tries to remember Mark's face but cannot quite picture it. She's only met him once since the wedding, the time they came down to see the house. But everything then was a blur. 'How long have they been married?'

'Forever. They got together at school.' He turns to her, a small tightness at the edge of his mouth. 'They're lovely people. Really. Just stay away from politics and you'll be fine.'

She nods, smiles, circling the spider at her wrist with her finger and thumb.

They turn up a country lane with large houses on either side, past a huge fruit wholesaler where even at this time of the day forklifts roam around the forecourt. Pulling up at a wooden gate, Sam presses the button on an intercom. There is a buzz and the gate slides open. A black Land Rover Defender stands on the driveway. Sam parks beside it and lifts a sleeping Tom out of the car. In answer to the bell there is the tinny yap of dogs, the scuttle of claws on a wooden floor, footsteps.

'Sorry we're late,' says Sam, as his sister opens the door. 'We had to get Tom dressed. Then traffic.'

Tamsin is dressed in jeans, heels and a grey jumper. Sequins crust like icicles at her shoulders. She hugs them – brief, angular, fragrant – then shoos them through to the kitchen, where a vastness of shining floor is punctuated by a large granite island. Cate pulls her cardigan tighter around her while Sam hoists Tom and the car seat on to the dining table. Three large black pendant lights hang suspended above it. On the wall, a sign reads 'EAT' in large wooden letters, as though without it Mark and Tamsin and their two children might forget what this side of the room is for.

'They're here!' Tamsin calls to her husband, who emerges from a different room. Mark is tall, broad. His shirt hugs his frame. He looks like an advert for a certain sort of manhood, a certain sort of success. He kisses Cate, fist-pumps Sam. A watch the size of a small mammal grips his wrist.

'Would you like a drink?' Tamsin ushers Cate towards an armchair. 'Fizzy water?'

'Actually,' says Cate, 'I'd love some wine. A red wine. If that's OK?' Her voice sounds odd. She has hardly used it today. 'I'd love a small red wine,' she says again, giving each syllable equal weight, as though speaking a language that is new to her.

'Mark!' barks Tamsin. 'Glass of red for Cate.'

'Coming up.' Mark moves towards the kitchen counter, behind which cabinets are lit from within, and pours wine from an open bottle into a goblet. He looks like a mortician, standing behind his slab, dealing in blood.

'There,' Mark says, bringing it over and setting it on the glass table before her. 'Put some colour in your cheeks.' And he laughs. And Tamsin laughs. And Sam laughs. And Cate laughs too, though at what she is not quite sure. Both Tamsin and Mark are deeply tanned. Their teeth are extraordinarily white against their skin. She remembers now Sam telling her – they have recently been on holiday. She can bring it up later, when she is at a loss for something to say.

'Antipasti,' says Tamsin, lifting a plate where meats and cheese and olives glisten in the bluish light.

30

Cate takes an olive and rolls its saltiness on her tongue.

Outside is a large garden, laid to lawn; beyond it, a fold in the hills where the river runs. The Great Stour, the same river that runs behind their house – she knows this because they walked there together, she and Sam and Tamsin and Mark, when they came down the first time to *get a sense of the area*.

Let's walk through the orchard! Tamsin had said. And so they did, the route taking them over the lane, past the wholesaler, past the cabins with the numbers spray-painted on the sides housing the fruit pickers, the dartboards, the mothers on camping chairs with their babies in their laps, watching them warily, the radios, the sound of Russian being spoken, then the orchard, which was simply lines and lines of trees. It was summer and the trees stood penned, grafted on to wire, their arms stretched in supplication, or defeat. *It's not an orchard*, she wanted to say, *it's a factory farm*.

'So how was your holiday?' she asks, turning back to the room.

'Oh, amazing,' says Tamsin. 'We were in Turkey. All-inclusive. The kids loved it. They were gone from breakfast till dinner. Had the run of the place.'

'Where are they?' Cate has the sudden terrible thought that they have been left somewhere, forgotten.

'In the snug.' Tamsin gestures to a door half open, and she sees them, their son Jack, their daughter Milly, faces stunned and immobile in the blue TV light. 'Hey! You should come, next year. We should all go together. We could bring Alice too, a big family holiday – she's amazing with the kids. Wait – or Dubai. Christmas!' She claps her hands together. 'Mark! Tell them. Tell them they should come to Dubai.'

31

'You should come to Dubai,' says Mark, with an indulgent smile to his wife. 'We go every year. I do a bit of work, then we have a week at Atlantis. You seen it?'

Mark brings up pictures on his phone and they all crowd round. Cate sees a huge pink stone edifice, a strip of sand, the ocean beyond. 'It's a man-made island,' he says. 'They've got everything – Gordon Ramsay restaurants. An aqua park. The kids go mental for it.'

It looks terribly fragile, its hugeness, its hubris. 'Atlantis?' says Cate.

'Yeah.' Mark nods. 'Check it out.'

'Didn't Atlantis disappear in the flood?'

'Which flood?' Tamsin looks bewildered.

'The Bible.'

'Thanks,' says Sam hastily. 'But I don't think we can get away this year – maybe next time.'

Cate looks over to where Tom lies. He looks tiny there, vulnerable, a small craft floating on a sea of polished oak. He is so still.

'Excuse me.' She rises quickly, goes to him, puts her hand to his nose, feels the soft relief of his breath. Outside, beyond the glass doors, the hillside is turning russet in the last of the light. The lawn is mown to within a millimetre of its life.

Tamsin comes over and joins her. 'Gorgeous, aren't they, when they're asleep?' Her face, dusted with a light pink powder, shimmers in the overhead lights. 'So how's the house?' she says.

'Oh.' Cate shifts a little. 'It's good – it's great. We're so grateful.'

'When are you going to invite us round?'

'Soon. When we've unpacked.'

'You're kidding?' Tamsin laughs. 'You haven't unpacked yet?'

'Still a few boxes left to go.'

Tamsin's hand lands on her sleeve. 'You look tired,' she says. 'Sam says you're sleeping together?' Her voice drops to a whisper. 'You and Tom? In the same bed?'

'Yeah.'

'Are you sure that's a good idea?'

'It's just easier like that. For the night feeds. You know.'

'You should stop.' Tamsin is gripping her now. 'Get that baby off the boob. You know what? You should have some time off. One day a week. What do you say?'

'I—'

'Say yes! Alice will do it. She's desperate to spend some time with Tom. Hang on – Sam!' Tamsin turns to the men, clapping her hands. 'Sam! Cate's going to have a day off! We'll arrange it. Me and mum. Alice is *dying* to help.'

It is almost dark when they return. Tom stays asleep as she lifts him from the car seat and into her bed. She goes down to the living room, where Sam is lying on the sofa, plugged into his computer. He pulls his headphones off as she comes into the room and raises his beer. 'You want one?'

She shakes her head. He makes room for her to sit. 'That wasn't so bad, was it?'

'Why did you tell your sister I share a bed with Tom?'

'Because you do.'

'Don't you like it?'

'Well, I'd rather share a bed with you.'

She laughs. She cannot help it. The thought is too absurd.

'I'm worried about you, Cate.'

He looks genuinely concerned. Or perhaps it is not concern, perhaps it is disappointment – the disappointment of one who has bought something online and then, just when the warranty has run out, realizes that it is faulty in all sorts of hidden ways.

'Did you ask Tamsin to arrange a Tuesday with your mum?'

His face tells her.

'Did you not think of asking me first?'

'I thought it would be good for you. I thought you would be relieved.'

'I thought you might have the courtesy to check with me before you rearrange my life.'

'Wow. OK. I'm just trying to help. I thought that's what mothers needed.'

'This isn't help. It's an ambush.'

'Jesus Christ, Cate.' He holds up his hands.

She gets up and goes into the kitchen. She is shaking. She looks through to the living room, where Sam's back is to her. He has already clicked on to some computer game or other, put his headphones back over his ears.

This is the pattern of their evenings. A little passive-aggressive banter and then separate computers on separate chairs. If she is lucky, she gets the sofa. Then they go to bed. In separate beds. Repeat.

Her phone buzzes. A message from Hannah – a missed call. Her heart leaps. She can navigate by Hannah. Hannah is true north. She lifts the phone and calls her back.

'Cate?'

'Hey.'

'How are you? I've been trying to get in touch with you.'

'Sorry. I've been . . .' What has she been? She has no idea.

'How's Canterbury?'

'Funny,' she says.

'Funny how?'

'I don't know.' She thinks of how it's funny. Tries to frame a joke. 'We went to see Sam's sister. They want to take us to Dubai.'

'That sounds nice.'

'Seriously?'

A small sigh. 'I'm sure you'll get used to it. These things take time.'

Cate is silent.

'How's my godson?'

'He's good. Asleep.'

There is a pause, the sound of Hannah's computer keys in the background, of Hannah doing two things at once – the great world swirling around her, summoning her back.

'Han?' says Cate.

'Sorry, just catching up on work emails. Had to send that one.'

'Do you fancy meeting up? Next weekend? Saturday, maybe? I could bring Tom into town. We could go to the Heath? I haven't come in since we've been out here. He's growing so fast . . .'

Cate braces herself for the no, but then, 'Hang on,' says Hannah, 'let me check . . . Saturday? Yeah. Why not?'

They speak a little more, then Cate ends the call, and goes

over to the window. It has been six weeks since she moved to Kent. Gulls sleep on the pointed roofs of the flats opposite. A man is out there, climbing out of his car. Perhaps he is the one who lives on the other side of the wall, whose sleep is broken nightly by Tom.

The man looks up. Cate lifts her hand. He stares at her – a dark shape in the window – with a baffled look of incomprehension on his face, then looks away.

Abjections

1995

The seminar is called Feminisms. It is not full. There is a general feeling, in the popular culture, that feminism has done its work. It is the era of the Spice Girls. Of the ladette. Lissa, the daughter of a feminist, has taken it for granted that she is a feminist too. A wholly unexamined position. She chooses Feminisms because the other option is Science Fiction.

The reading list is daunting and mostly foreign. Lissa reads none of it in preparation for the course. No one really does the preparatory reading for courses in the English department. You just skim the books in the week you have to write about them. This, to Lissa, seems to be the main thing that university teaches you – how to bullshit convincingly. The better the university, the better the bullshit. She has expounded this theory regularly in the bed of her new boyfriend, a Mancunian drug dealer with a terraced house in Rusholme who walks like Liam Gallagher and has a way with a parka. He is dark and funny and clever and the sexiest thing she has ever seen.

The girl is sitting close to the front of the room, long hair almost hiding her face, small frame drowned by a baggy jumper, the cuffs pulled down over her thumbs. One of those long patchwork skirts, DM boots, a heavy hand with the eyeliner. She is of a type – suburban rebels, indie kids, packs of them roaming Manchester on a Saturday night. Flailing around the dance floor of the student union. Sitting Down to James. Lissa and the girl (who is called Hannah) are assigned to present together – Kristeva and the abject. Having not done the reading, Lissa has no idea what any of this means. Why don't you come to my room? Lissa asks Hannah. Tomorrow? Three o'clock?

Hannah turns up at Lissa's room on the dot of three. She carries several weighty books in her arms. She knocks on the door and pulls her cuffs over her bitten fingernails. So far, for Hannah, university is not what she had hoped. She has only come to Manchester because she did not get into Oxford and her second choice – Edinburgh – was full. And so, after a year out – which she spent, not 'travelling' like the majority of students she seems to meet, but working to save the money for clothes and books and anything extra she might need – here she is at university number three, still living at home in Burnage. Cheaper this way, so she doesn't have to pay for her accommodation in halls. And her parents are happy about it. And she pretends she is too, but really she is seething. Seething because she fudged a question about Keats in the Oxford interview. Seething because her best friend, Cate, got in. Seething because she didn't put somewhere far from home for her third choice. And, mostly, seething with the discovery that the city she has lived in all her life is infected by privileged students. For the last few months she has had a bar job in the student union, and she, who is naturally a watcher, has learned much. Forget Feminisms – she could already write a dissertation on class. There are the boarding-school kids, who wear their shirts with the collars up and play sports and roam in unadventurous, braying packs. The state-school kids, who occupy different tables but eye the rugby boys and match them pint for pint in the bar. The misfits, who wear their misfit status like a badge, thus signalling to the other misfits and forming misfit cliques. And then those like this blonde girl whose door she stands at now. These are the ones who trouble her: they are slippery, hard to categorize. And Hannah is fond of categorization. This girl sounds posh, but does not necessarily act it. Hannah has never seen her in the student union. She is beautiful, but careless with her beauty – at the eleven o'clock seminars, for instance, she often has last night's make-up crusted around her eyes. The tip of her index finger is stained orange from smoking. She barely seems to brush her hair. But this girl possesses something indefinable, something that, although she cannot name it, Hannah knows she wants desperately for herself.

The other girl opens the door and Hannah steps inside. The room is a mess. It smells of fags, and ashtrays overflow on every surface. There are half-full glasses of water in various places. An empty bottle of wine. The single bed is covered with an Indian throw. There is a collage on the wall – photographs of young people on a far-flung beach, Lissa sitting on a scooter, no helmet in sight, Lissa and a dark-haired young man in a nightclub, both with large pupils, faces crowded into the frame. So far, standard fare. But Hannah's eye is caught by a different picture, this one propped carelessly against the wall – an oil painting of a fair-haired girl curled into a chair, reading a book.

Is that you? she asks, kneeling before it.

Yeah, says Lissa carelessly. My mum did it. Years ago.

It's really good.

Lissa sits on her bed, watching, a little amused, as the dark-haired girl takes her hungry inventory of her possessions, then sits at the desk and opens the first of her books. The girl moves precisely. Her pencils are sharp.

These are the things that Lissa thinks she knows about university and Manchester and class: she is the daughter of a socialist. She went to a North London comprehensive. She would rather hang out with a drug dealer than a public schoolboy. There are far too many public schoolboys and girls in Manchester, but scratch its grimy post-industrial surface and the city waits. That Manchester is, at this point in its history – if, like Lissa, you are a fan of dance music and of ecstasy – possibly the greatest city on earth.

She is interested in this long-haired girl because she has a Mancunian accent – a rarity at the university. She likes Mancunians. And she likes her serious, slightly cross face. She enjoys hearing her spar with the other kids in the seminar group. Hannah is chippy and Lissa likes it. And she is also interested in her, this spring afternoon, because she thinks she might help her to get a good mark.

OK, says Hannah. The abject.

Hit me, says Lissa.

Hannah bends her head and reads, twisting the ends of her hair in her fingertips.

Abjection preserves what existed in the archaism of pre-objectal relationship, in the immemorial violence with which a body becomes separated from another body in order to be.

Immemorial violence, says Lissa. What does that mean?

Well, says Hannah, it's birth, isn't it? And infancy – before we enter the symbolic order. Language. All of that.

If you say so, says Lissa. Tell you what. She leans over and pulls a small bag of weed from a drawer in her cabinet. She has been given it this morning by her boyfriend.

But . . . Hannah feels a mild panic as she casts her hand over the ranged books. It's three o'clock. I mean – we've got to give a presentation tomorrow, haven't we?

I know, but this might help.

Lissa feels Hannah's eyes on her as she rolls the joint. She takes her time, enjoying her skill, finishing with a flourish before she opens the window and leans out of it, four floors up above Owens Park. Go on then, she says, lighting up.

Hannah sighs and reads on.

On the level of our individual psychosexual development, the abject marks the moment when we separated ourselves from the mother, when we began to recognize a boundary between me and other, between me and (m)other.

Lissa thinks of Sarah driving her up here last September, her mother's old Renault 5 packed high with her stuff. She took her out to lunch at a restaurant in town. Now, darling, she said over the pudding, you are on the Pill, aren't you? Then she gave her twenty pounds, a rather beautiful portrait of Lissa aged eight sitting in the flowered attic chair, a large packet of Drum tobacco, a brisk kiss on the cheek, and drove off back down the motorway to London. A separation which hardly seemed to bother Sarah at all.

. . . as in true theatre, Hannah reads on, without make-up or masks, refuse and corpses show me what I permanently thrust aside in order to live. These bodily fluids, this defilement, this shit are what life withstands . . .

Wait – does it really say that?

Yeah. Hannah looks up and smiles. It is the first time Lissa has seen her smile. She has a lovely smile. Interesting. All the better for not being easily won.

41

This shit . . . this shit are what life withstands, hardly and with difficulty, on the point of death. There, I am at the border of my condition as a living being.

Wow, says Lissa.

Yeah, says Hannah.

Lissa blows out smoke on the evening air. There is the sound of traffic on Wilmslow Road below, the hazy, blurred sounds of the tower block; Portishead, 'Glory Box', drifting out of some-one's nearby room.

So . . . says Hannah. The presentation?

Oh. Yeah. OK. How about, Lissa says, how about, for start-ers, we name all the sorts of abject we can come up with?

Why? says Hannah. She is not a fan of thinking around things. She has a linear mind.

Well, why not? Go on – Lissa waves the joint at Hannah – how many can you name?

Hannah scrunches her nose. Well, there's piss, obviously – urine. Shit. There's blood; two types of blood. Vein blood. Menstrual blood.

I'll bet there must be more types of blood than that.

There probably are.

That'll do for starters. Vomit. Snot. Earwax.

We need to write these down. Hannah snatches up her pen-cil and starts scribbling.

How many is that? says Lissa.

Seven so far.

What about eye gunk?

Definitely eye gunk. What's the right term for eye gunk?

I don't know. Here, don't you want some of this?

Hannah has only smoked a joint once before. It was at the

Ritz with Cate last summer, and it made her feel dizzy and ill. She is self-conscious as she makes her way over to the window. She takes the joint from Lissa – a short, exploratory drag. Lissa watches, amused, from the corner of her eye, then takes up the pad and pen.

Spit, says Hannah, taking a longer drag this time. Speaking of which, I might have made this a bit wet.

It's fine, says Lissa, keep going.

Phlegm, says Hannah.

OK. Don't say phlegm again.

Phlegm.

They both snort.

Dandruff?

Dandruff will do. Lissa stops scribbling and comes back to the window. They are close to each other. She catches Hannah's smell of incense and shampoo.

What about babies? says Lissa, taking back the spliff.

What about them?

Well, aren't they a form of abject in themselves?

Maybe. Hannah scrunches her nose. Or at least what's around them. What's it called? Some sort of fluid. Amniotic.

Yeah. That's it. We should form a band, says Lissa, giggling. The Amniotics. No – wait – the Abjections.

They are laughing properly now.

Oh God. We should. The Abjections. I love it.

They print out band T-shirts: black with hot-pink writing across the chest. The hot pink is allowed, they decide, as it is ironic. They name their Abjections, giving examples of each from their own life. They discuss whether a man's sperm leaving your body – leaving its trace on your knickers after sex – can be seen as an abjection in itself. (Having not yet had sex, Hannah lets Lissa do the talking here.) They declare there are many different types of vaginal discharge: the one that leaves a white crust, the one that leaves a yellow crust, the one that floods you when you're turned on. They discuss whether discharge – with its pejorative connotations – is itself a patriarchal term. They decide that there are as many different types of vaginal abject as Inuits have words for snow.

They watch with satisfaction as the boys cringe. They feel a new power. They become electric. They become friends.

Hannah

She waits in the queue for the fishmonger, hovering over the threshold, the sun strong in the window, the shouts and calls of the market behind her. It has been a warm day; the ice is melting and the remains of the day's catch are blood- and scale-streaked. Two young men in waders pass between the front and a chopping block at the back, where the fish are gutted and bagged.

Eight years ago, when she moved to the area, a Jamaican guy owned this place. It was painted the colours of the Jamaican flag. He sold fresh and salt fish and vegetables, and other bits and bobs in the back; incense, reggae on bootleg cassettes. He had the most beautiful face. There was a campaign to help when his shop was sold from underneath him to a property developer: articles in the *Guardian* by local writers, a sit-in in the premises of a cafe on the street – a place owned by the same developer. An angry meeting was called in the church hall, to which they all went along – Hannah remembers a guy in his fifties, face livid with anger, standing and shouting, *I remember when it was shit round here. It was much better then.*

But now the ripples have been smoothed over, now marble tiles and line-caught fish have replaced pineapples and salt cod and plantains. This fishmonger is no longer new. And, despite an occasional, residual queasiness, Hannah likes it, with its day boats and its flirty young men and its sense that the sea is still full of abundance – that all might yet be well with the world.

It is her turn at last, and she duly flirts a little as she buys medallions of monkfish, asks advice on what else she might add to the pot, buys saffron and samphire and stows them in her bag. She is sweating as she leaves the shop – the first sign of the hormonal dip. Her scalp is laced in it. This is the hard part, the part they don't tell you about, the *down-regulation*, the menopause brought about in three weeks, your hormones suppressed to ground zero: the day sweats, the night sweats, the constant urge to cry.

But she is good at not crying – has it down to a fine art. She does not cry when woman after woman at work announces her pregnancy. As day after day she takes her temperature and marks it on a graph. As month after month she bleeds. And when her oldest friend told her she was pregnant, Hannah held her very close, so Cate would not see the expression on her face.

Outside she weaves past the coffee shop with its inevitable buggies clogging the pavement, her gaze grazing the babies, the parents with their fists clutching cappuccinos and flat whites. (She is good, too, at not looking closely at the children, it is not wise to stare at a baby's plump arms, at a toddler hand in hand with its mother, a newborn slung across a father's chest.) But as she passes the flower stand, she stops, her eye caught by the display. The woman with the stall turns to her. 'What do you need?' she asks. She is in her late fifties or early sixties, her eyes are blue.

'I—' For a moment Hannah is taken aback. What does she need? 'What are these?' She gestures towards a tall spiked flower.

'Teasel. They came from my own garden, we had a bumper crop this year. And here,' – the woman bends to her buckets – 'these are Michaelmas daisies.'

'I'll take some of both.'

The woman ties the flowers loosely with twine, and as she hands them over, her rough knuckles brush Hannah's own. Hannah heads to the bottom of the market, where the crowd thins out, crosses the canal and turns right, through the estate, towards her flat, jostling her bags as she opens the unprepossessing metal street door, then climbs the external stairs to the third floor of a three-storey building, an old pub, converted and sold before it was even finished. They had to elbow their way round with twenty other couples, then send their offer in a sealed bid the following day. Before the decision to move to Canterbury, Cate would visit, stroking her bump, staring out at the view, wondering aloud at Hannah's luck.

It's not luck, Hannah wanted to say. *It's how life works. You work hard, you save throughout your twenties, and by the time you're in your thirties you have enough for a deposit. It's not magic, it's simple maths.*

And now here is Cate, living in the house that has been bought for her by her husband's parents, for which, it seems, she has to pay no money at all, with her healthy, beautiful son, conceived with the utmost of ease – here is Cate, unhappy again. Or at least so she sounded on the phone last night.

Hannah slides her purchases from her bag, places the fish and samphire and wine in the fridge, cuts the stems from the

47

flowers and arranges them in a vase, which she places in a long slant of afternoon light. The teasels are unexpected, their beauty severe, precise. Her laptop is open on the table, and as she goes to close it, she sees the report she was working on this morning, before the sun called her outside. She saves the document and shuts the lid.

She is sweating still, so goes to the sink to splash her face with water. It is the strangest feeling, as though her skull is being scraped out. The urge to cry is on her again. She wants Nathan here, beside her, wants to feel his arm steady on her back. But he is only at the library, only a cycle ride away, along the canal. He will be home soon. They will eat together. He will tell her about his day. She looks up, her gaze resting on the flowers, the table, the light.

This is the house that Hannah built.

Here is the table she found in a junk shop in an old railway arch and spent a weekend sanding herself.

Here is the framed photograph of the garden of the house in Cornwall where Nathan proposed, each blade of grass frosted, whole.

Here is the bookshelf along one wall, filled with poetry, with novels, with Nathan's journals. (She, who grew up in a house with no books, can spend minutes standing in front of it, letting it speak back to her, the spines arranged by author, alphabetical: Adiche, Eliot, Forster, Woolf.)

Here is the rug they bought on a weekend in Marrakesh. The night shopping in the souks, the haggling and then the final capitulation and the exorbitant price to take it back on the plane. But it is beautiful, Beni Ouarain – from the Atlas mountains. A thick cream wool. *It will bring you fortune*, said the seller, tracing the diamond patterns with his fingers, and was it her imagination or did his glance flicker to her womb as she took out her credit card and paid?

Here is the sofa they bought from a warehouse in Chelsea, and chose for its low mid-century lines, its dark slate-blue linen. The sofa on which she sat, two weeks after the first round of IVF, holding her test – the jubilation of those two clear pink lines. The sofa on which she sat cocooned in blankets while Nathan cooked – soups and risottos for his pregnant wife.

Here, a little way down the hall, is the bathroom. The white bevelled tiles. The lotions in their plain brown glass jars. Here is the place where, three weeks after that test, she writhed in pain, where after a day of bleeding she passed a clot. The fibrous sac which held the baby that did not live. That she and Nathan did not know how to dispose of. That, in the end, they took to the park late at night, where they dug a hole and buried it deep in the ground.

But wait, here – come, walk this way, down the hall to a little room – open the door and stand within, watch how the light falls, softer here, more diffuse. This room waits, nothing in it but a quiet sense of expectation.

This is the house that Hannah built, three floors above London, floating in light.

The stew is cooked and bubbling on the stove. There is crusty bread and a bowl of aioli. A bottle of white stands glistening on the counter and two glasses wait beside it. Hannah takes parsley and chops it, adding lemon and salt. She hears the front door and then Nathan is behind her, his hand on her

49

back. 'Hey.' She turns to him – a brief kiss on the mouth. 'How's the chapter going?' When he has writing to finish, her husband takes himself off to the British Library. He says he likes it there on weekends, when the Reading Rooms are quieter; says he finds it easier to work there than at home.

'Oh, you know. Getting there, slowly.'

She hands him a glass of wine which he takes gratefully, then ladles out stew, sprinkles parsley over the top, and hands Nathan his bowl. She takes her place at the table before her husband, aware of a slight sense of ceremony. It is Saturday; she is allowed to eat and drink what she likes. She sips the wine. It is clean and hard and bright and she could down it in one gulp, but she puts it back on the table beside her plate. Discipline. This is what she has always had, and this is what she has brought to bear on this situation. No caffeine. No alcohol. Apart from Saturday nights.

Nathan looks up at her, catches her watching, reaches his hand across the table and takes hers. 'This is delicious.'

'Thanks.'

'How about you? Did you work today?'

'A bit, this morning. And then it was too lovely, so I walked to the park.'

'Hey,' he says, 'I meant to tell you, I saw Lissa.'

'Lissa? Where?'

'At the library. Yesterday.'

'The library? What was she doing there?'

'She said she wants to do some reading, for a PhD.'

'That's funny. I'd never have imagined that.'

'Well. You know Lissa. She seemed a bit haphazard about it all.'

He reaches for the bottle. She watches as he pours himself another glass.

'Nath?' she says softly.

'What?'

'I thought . . . it's daft really, but I had this thought, earlier in the week, when I started the injections. When I was there with the syringes . . . I wondered about doing some sort of . . . ritual.' The word tastes strange. As she speaks, a fresh wave of sweat breaks on her forehead. She lifts her sleeve to dab it.

'What sort of ritual?' Nathan puts down his spoon, folds his hands in front of his chin. Rituals are what he teaches – they are his butter and his bread.

'I don't know.' She can feel herself begin to flush, the heat rising again. 'Something to mark it. I mean, if we did . . . If we did do something, how would we go about it, do you think? What could we do?'

'Well,' he smiles, 'you know, a ritual can be anything. It doesn't have to be serious, even. We can do something simple.' He reaches over and catches her hand. 'We could light a candle or . . .' Then, when she doesn't respond: 'Or we could just do nothing. We could just wait and see.'

'Yes,' she says, embarrassed now, releasing her hand from his. 'Yes. Let's just wait and see.'

Lissa

'Sweetheart.' Sarah opens the door, and immediately begins walking back into the darkness of the hall. 'Come in. Got something on the stove.'

Lissa follows her mother through the hall into the kitchen.

'I'm making soup, though God knows why. It's still so bloody hot. Want some?' Sarah goes over to the range and lifts the lid off a pan, giving it a stir. Her mother's long grey hair is twisted on top of her head, held in place by two Japanese combs. She is wearing her work apron, ancient and brown and covered in paint.

'Love some,' says Lissa. She never refuses a meal at Sarah's – her mother is a fantastic cook.

'Ten minutes,' says Sarah, putting the lid back on the pan. 'And I'll do a bit of salad to go with it.'

Lissa lifts the cat from one of the dining chairs and sits. The mess is, if anything, messier than usual: drifts of letters on the table, some opened, some not. Her mother's periodicals: the *New Statesman*, old editions of the *Guardian Review*; missives from charities: Greenpeace, Freedom from Torture. One official-looking envelope is unopened and being used to make a list, Sarah's elegant hand spidering across the paper.

Judy??
Cortisol? Ask Dr L.
Ruby – pills.

'What's wrong with Ruby?' Lissa looks up.

'Something with her tummy. Poor thing's been puking and shitting for days. That vet. You wait years for an appointment, you really do.'

'How's your hand?'

'Oh. You know.' Sarah flexes her fingers. 'OK.'

52

'This one looks important.' Lissa lifts a letter and waves it at her mother.

Sarah turns back to the stove, dismissing her daughter with an airy hand. 'Not really. You can tell by the envelope.'

'Really?'

'It's a charity asking for more money. Or someone wanting me to take out a credit card.' Sarah plucks tobacco from the pocket of her apron and rolls herself a cigarette. 'Cig?'

'Sure.'

Lissa takes the proffered packet, enjoying the sweetness of the sugared paper on her tongue as she rolls – always the same brand, always the same liquorice Rizla papers, her mother's fingertips, for as long as she can remember, orange-stained, her breath murky and low. Her mother is making work again, that much is clear; the apron, the mess, and a distant edge of manic energy to her, as though there is a gathering somewhere nearby, a better conversation happening in an adjacent room. Lissa knows enough not to ask, though, not this early in the game. Whatever Sarah is working on, it is new.

'Cumin.' Her mother is rattling in the cupboards. 'Needs cumin. Course it does. Bugger.'

Lissa tosses the envelope back on to the pile where it triggers a minor landslide across the table, only stopped in its tracks by the fruit bowl. If her mother isn't going to worry about unpaid bills, she isn't going to do it for her.

'Sweet paprika?' Sarah turns, herbs in hand.

'Whatever you think, Ma.'

'I think it'll have to do. It's just – cumin seeds. I'm never without them. It's odd.'

'Can I do anything?'

'I'm going to do something salady. You can chop if you like. Wait a bit, though. Here.' Her mother chucks a greasy box of Cook's Matches over to her, Lissa catches them and wanders over to the door, which is propped open to the late summer air.

The garden is the nicest thing about this place. Her mother is a fine gardener, and what feels like chaos inside the house makes sense when you step outside – her mother's sensibilities; everything poised just on the edge of wild. Lissa strikes a match and smokes. 'I got the part,' she says softly, to the lavender and the honeysuckle.

'Sorry, darling?' her mother calls from inside. 'What did you say?'

'That part.' She blows out smoke in a thin line, turns back to the kitchen. 'The one I told you about?'

'Tell me again.' Her mother's face is in shadow.

'Chekhov. Yelena.'

'Oh, wonderful. That's wonderful.' Her mother comes to embrace her and Lissa inhales her smell of paint and herbs, the dry crackle of her hair.

Lissa laughs, feeling again the bubble of excitement she has been carrying in her stomach since she heard the news. 'Thanks. It is. The director – she's a woman. She's good, I think. Tricky, they say, but good.'

'But how wonderful. We must celebrate!'

Before she can object, her mother is rooting in the cupboard where she keeps the booze. 'Hmm. White wine. Lidl Pouilly-Fuissé. Supposed to be OK. Not cold, though. Or there's a bit of Gordon's – what about a G and T? Hang on. Not sure I've got any ice. I can chip a bit off the roof of the freezer. Shall we start with that? See how we go?'

'Sure.'

'Chuck me a lemon then.'

Her mother hums as she pours out large measures of gin and splashes a bit of tonic on the top. 'Bit flat but it'll have to do. Here.' Sarah hands her the glass with a flourish. 'Come and sit in the garden. The salad can wait.'

Sarah leads the way down a crooked stone path, through lavender bushes, past tomatoes and squash and herbs to where a small weather-aged table and chairs stand beneath a wooden trellis.

'You've gone out, darling.' Her mother leans forward and re-lights Lissa's cigarette. 'Cheers. Goodness. Here's to you.' She raises her glass. 'Here's to Chekhov. So Yelena – that's . . .'

'*Vanya*.'

'*Vanya*. Marvellous. Hang on, remind me, is that the one with the gun?' Her mother picks a stray strand of tobacco from her lip.

Sarah taught English before she retired. English and Art at the local comp; a good North London school, the sort that middle-class parents fought with their elbows out to get their kids into.

'That's *The Seagull*.'

'Ah yes. *The Seagull*. The one with the failing young actress. So – *Vanya*?'

'He's the failed . . . well, he's just failed. Failed at life. They're all failing, aren't they? It's Chekhov.'

'And you're the wife of the . . .'

55

'Failed academic. Serebryakov.'

'That's right. Oh gosh, yes – I think I saw Glenda do it, back in the day.'

Glenda Jackson is her mother's touchstone for all things good and wholesome about the acting profession.

'Or no – wait, it was that gorgeous one – Greta something or other.'

'Scacchi?'

'That's it. She was wonderful. So will you be.' Sarah leans forward and grips Lissa's wrist. 'Goodness, well done, darling. A proper part. About time too. You should tell Laurie. She'll be thrilled.'

Laurie, her mother's oldest friend, who taught drama at Sarah's school, who gave up her time to coach Lissa to get her into drama school all those years ago.

'You tell her,' says Lissa.

'I will.' Her mother sits back and regards her through the smoke. Sarah's gaze. Nothing escapes it. How many hours has she suffered it? She used to model for her mother as a child – hours and hours for years and years of sitting in that battered old chair in the attic. Until one day she refused to do it any more.

'I must say,' says Sarah, 'it's wonderful you can pass for . . . whatever it is she's supposed to be. I mean, they're never more than thirty, are they, these women in these plays? Unless they're fifty. Or the maids. They shuffle on and off a bit, don't they, the maids?' She waves her cigarette in the air. 'Light a samovar or two.'

'Yes,' Lissa says, though to what she is saying yes she isn't quite sure. All of it, she supposes. Yes, it's wonderful she can pass for thirty. Yes, there's bugger all between thirty and fifty, not just in Chekhov, but in everything else. Perhaps in life. Perhaps this is it – Womanhood. The Wasteland Years.

'Gosh.' Her mother takes a healthy swig. 'This is fun, isn't it? Haven't drunk in the day for aeons. So who's the director then?'

'She's Polish. Klara.'

'I can't believe you didn't say anything.'

'I've stopped. I mean, it's hardly worth it, is it, any more?' She picks at a stray piece of skin on her thumb with her opposite nail.

'Oh no, don't say that. You must let me know, when things come up. I can wear my lucky earrings.'

'Yeah, well. I'm not sure they've been that helpful. In the grand scheme of things.'

'They helped when you got that telly part. And when you were ill.' Her mother points the cigarette reprovingly in Lissa's direction.

The sun rounds the corner of the wall and falls on to the grass beside them. Lissa angles her face towards it. The cat winds itself, mewling, against her mother's calves.

'So when do you start?'

'Week on Monday.'

'So soon? And how long do you have?'

'Four weeks.'

'That's decent then. And are they paying you well?'

'Not really. Enough.'

'Good,' says Sarah, putting her cigarette out in the nearest plant pot. 'Good.' She claps her hands together. 'Right. Hungry?'

'I'll help.' Lissa goes to stand, but her mother waves her away.

'You sit. Enjoy the sun. It's just coming round the house. Lovely this time of day.'

So she sits while her mother clatters in the kitchen. Sarah is singing snatches of opera. In the sky above, contrails purl and lace against the blue. It is hot. Lissa looks up at the house; three storeys of Victorian brick. She can see the window of the room that used to be her bedroom. The attic skylight. Her mother bought the house with the settlement from Lissa's father, thirty years ago now. She has never spent any money on it, never had any money to spend, only a teacher's salary, enough for good food, for paints and materials, a holiday now and then. If she sold this house, her mother would be rich.

'Salad's coming.' Sarah brings two steaming bowls to the table, heads back up the path and returns with a large wooden bowl. Bitter red leaves mixed in amongst the green, walnuts and goat's cheese crumbled on the top. There is olive oil in a separate bowl, with a pool of balsamic at the bottom. Good, chewy bread with salty butter. They eat for a while in silence, the sounds of the neighbourhood around them: kids in paddling pools, barbecues, people laughing, the dusty, easy end of the holidays; summer in the body, sun on the skin.

'And how's everything else?' says her mother when she has finished, pushing away her bowl, rolling and lighting up again. 'How's Hannah? How's Cate?'

'Cate's in Kent. I'm not sure, really. I haven't spoken to her for a while.'

'Why?'

'Oh, you know. It happens like that sometimes.'

'Like what?' Sarah's gaze is hawk-like.

Lissa shrugs. 'We've sort of lost touch.'

'You must keep hold of your friendships, Lissa. The women. They're the only thing that will save you in the end.'

'I'll remember that.'

'Do,' says Sarah. She regards Lissa through the smoke. 'I always admired Cate.'

'I know.'

'She has principles.'

'Really?' says Lissa. 'I suppose she does.'

'And Hannah?' Sarah says.

'Hannah's OK. I saw her the other night.'

'Is she still . . . ?'

'She's doing another round of IVF, yes.' Lissa presses a hunk of bread into the bottom of her bowl.

Her mother tuts. 'Poor Hannah.'

'Yes,' says Lissa.

'That poor woman,' Sarah says again.

'Hannah's not poor.'

'It's a figure of speech.'

'I know,' says Lissa, 'but it's an inaccurate one. She's pretty successful. She and Nathan. They've done pretty well.'

Her mother puts down her spoon. 'Goodness. You're testy suddenly, Melissa.'

'I'm not testy, I'm just – you might as well be accurate, if you're going to pass comment.'

'I say *poor Hannah*, because I know she's been trying to have a baby for years. Trying and failing to have a baby. And I can't think of anything worse.'

59

'Really? What about trying and failing to have a career?'

'What do you mean?'

'Nothing.'

'No, really.' Her mother's eyes are sharp now; she has caught the scent of something. 'What do you mean? Do you mean yourself? Is that how you feel, darling?'

'Yes. No. Actually, no. Forget it. Let's just forget it. Please. This is nice. Let's not spoil it.'

'All right.' Sarah reaches down, scoops Ruby on to her lap, strokes her skull with an absent hand. There is quiet, the sound of Ruby's motorboat purring. Lissa finishes the last of her food.

'Your generation,' her mother says quietly. 'Honestly. You baffle me, you really do.'

'And why is that?' Lissa pushes away her bowl.

'Well. You've had everything. The fruits of our labour. The fruits of our activism. Good God, we got out there and we changed the world for you. For our daughters. And what have you done with it?'

The question hangs heavy in the summer air. Sarah closes her eyes, as though summoning something from the depths.

'When I was at Greenham. Standing there with thousands of other women. Hand in hand around the base. You were there, beside me. Do you remember?'

'I remember.'

A dusty campsite. A fence, covered with children's toys. Other children who knew all the words to all the songs. Ruddy-faced women huddled beneath tarpaulins drinking endless cups of tea. Her mother's friends: Laurie and Ina and

60

Caro and Rose. No men. The only men the soldiers who patrolled on the other side of the wall, their guns held against their chests.

She remembers a terrible blue dawn when the police came and dragged her mother out of the tent by her hair. She remembers the fear that her mother would be shot.

She remembers crying, asking to go home. Sarah taking her to a phone box and calling Lissa's father, who came to get her in his black Volvo. She remembers the look on Sarah's face as her father drove away. The disappointment. As though she had expected more.

'We fought for you. We fought for you to be extraordinary. We changed the world for you and what have you done with it?'

Lissa stares at the wall where the wisteria fights for space with the ivy.

'I'm sorry,' she says, a tight, familiar feeling rising in her chest. 'If I let you down.'

'Oh God,' says Sarah, grinding out her cigarette in the remains of her lunch. 'Don't be so bloody dramatic. That's not what I meant at all.'

She takes the overground from Gospel Oak to Camden Road. It is full, this Saturday afternoon, packed with families heading home from the Heath. Children yowl and carp, their faces pink and smeared with the remains of sun cream and ice cream and crumbly bits of picnic, their parents harassed and rosy, a couple of bottles down. Women her age, fresh from the Ladies' Pond, the ends of their hair damp. At Camden she manages to find a seat. The heat is terrible, the day overdone. Beside her, a teenager, the whites of his eyes red, blasts music from his headphones.

The train empties out at Hackney Central and Lissa makes her way across the park. Here – the province of the young – things are just getting going, the barbecues cranking up, people in groups of five or ten or twenty, the drift of cigarette smoke and charcoal and weed and the undertow of booze and coke and the night to come. She passes two young women, skirts hitched to their waists, holding on to each other and cackling as they piss behind a tree.

Her flat is just adjacent to the park, in the basement of the old house. She moved down here when she was still with Declan, who gave her the money for the deposit and helped her with rent. Since the break-up she has managed to hang on to it through a precarious combination of her life modelling, the call-centre work, the occasional acting job and some tax credits to top it up. She has stumbled through, has survived. Just.

Inside it is mercifully cool, and she drops her bag in the tiny hall, goes into the kitchen, fills a glass, and drinks down water from the tap. On the other side of the garden wall someone is being sung to – *Happy Birthday*, sing the half-cut voices, *to youuuuuuuuu!!!*

She lies down in the bedroom and shuts her eyes. Her head hurts – from the alcohol, from her mother, from the sun. *We changed the world for you and what have you done with it?*

She knows what Sarah thinks. That she has wasted time – fumbled the baton in the intergenerational feminist relay.

What she should have said – *Our best. We're just doing our fucking best.*

The tinny blare of music from the park is irritating her and she goes next door to the living room, closing the blinds against the low sun.

She slides a DVD from her bag – *Autumn Sonata*. Sarah had a copy in the dusty TV room, a Bergman box set. The cover is an intense close-up of the two actresses. She weighs it for a moment in her hand, then takes it and her computer over to the couch and slides it in.

At first she is bored, put off by the simplistic, static camera work, the clunky monologues to camera, and considers turning it off, but then Ingrid Bergman sweeps in and the film ignites. It is like watching a boxing match between two heavyweights, evenly matched, round after round of brutal pummelling, as a mother and a daughter go head to head, raking over the bones of their relationship. Half an hour in and Lissa is aware she is holding her breath. By the end of the film she is a small tense ball, arms locked around her knees.

When it is finished, she gets up and walks around the living room, feeling the blood come painfully back into her limbs. She rolls herself a cigarette and pulls up the window, sitting on the sill as she smokes. It has grown dark outside, and the night air lifts her skin in her vest top. The smell of petrol mingles with the smell of fried food, the charcoal of the barbecues drifting from the park.

She thinks of Nathan, of his face in the library. *I needed therapy after that film.* The sort of thing that most men don't say. But then, Nathan has never been most men.

It was down to Sarah that she met him. The first time was just after she turned twelve, when she refused to sit for her mother any more, and since Saturdays were Sarah's painting day, Sarah found herself a different model and Lissa was left to herself.

After a few weeks of watching crappy Saturday-morning telly, she began leaving the house and walking down the hill to Camden without telling Sarah where she was going. Kids not much older than her were hanging out in groups on the canal. She took to buying a Coke from a newsagent's and then sitting on the bridge to watch them. Nathan was one of those kids. No particular tribe, just a North London teenager who hung out and smoked weed on a Saturday afternoon on the canal.

Once, on a chill afternoon, he came over to her. *Are you all right? You look cold.* She admitted she was and he lent her his jumper. It was big and warm and he had done that teenage thing of making holes for his thumbs, and they shared a can of cider. He gave her her first cigarette.

A few years later they would see each other at Camden Palace. They would hug each other – the way you did then, with your whole wide self – you could tell each other you loved each other and mean it, high and platonic in your tracksuit on a Friday night. Then he went off to university and she never had his number and she didn't see him for years, until that night at Sarah's opening, bumping into him just after graduation, introducing him to Hannah. When she was already with Declan.

He must be nearly forty now.

She takes out her phone and composes a text.

Bergman slayed me. Thank you, I think.

She puts a kiss. Takes it away. Adds it again. Deletes the text. Writes another.

How did you know?

Deletes it. Puts down her phone.
How did you know? Did you know? Did you know it would make me feel like this? Can I call you? I need to speak.
She picks up her phone again and writes:

Thanks for the Bergman. Loved it. Liss. X

Soulmates

2008–9

The night of Hannah's wedding Cate has sex with the only other single person on her table, one of Nathan's cousins, a thirty-eight-year-old banker in the City. They get slaughtered on cava during the reception and fuck in the toilets at the Pub on the Park. After that she meets him quite often. He calls her sometimes at eleven o'clock at night and she goes over to his house. He owns a whole house to himself, which he lives in alone, on the far reaches of London Fields, over towards Queensbridge Road. He has already flipped a house in Dalston. He has a kitchen with a huge range on which he never seems to cook, as there are always takeaway packets filling up the bin.

Mostly they have sex there, in his house, but sometimes, if he is away on business, which he often is, they meet in hotels in Manchester or Birmingham or Newcastle, rooms of featureless luxury. They watch porn together. Having rarely watched porn before, she is surprised by how much she enjoys it. Once, they have sex in front of his computer in front of another couple who are having sex in their room in front of their computer somewhere in the southern states of the USA. It definitely turns her on.

This arrangement continues for several months. They never meet in the daytime. He never asks her to a gallery, or out for dinner. He is her secret. She feels shame when she thinks of him. Sometimes he goes quiet for a few weeks and she knows he is having sex with someone else. Sometimes she wants to hate him for not being someone else. But he is not a bad man. He is not a wanker. He has many good qualities. He just does not want her to be his girlfriend and, in truth, she does not want him to be her boyfriend either.

One day he stops calling. She tries him a couple of times, then waits for the text that will signal he is ready to resume intimacy. Instead she receives a short, polite message that tells her he has met someone and is getting engaged.

She is thirty-three years old. She understands that this man has taken up a space in her life, space that could have been filled by a proper partner. She has not had a proper partner since she left Lucy, in a forest in Oregon, almost ten years ago. But then, in the intervening years, she has come to suspect that Lucy was never really hers.

She is seized by a sense of desperation. She will do Guardian Soulmates. *It is the only sensible option. She chooses a photograph of herself from Hannah's hen do in Greece. It is taken from a distance and she is sitting on a wall and she doesn't look too fat. The drop-down option gives her pause:*

Women seeking Men.

Men seeking Women.

Women seeking Women.

Men seeking Men.

For simplicity's sake, she chooses number one. She calls herself LitChick, talks about her love of books, of politics, of Modernist writers, of the history of the East End.

She goes on a date with a guy who is in a band. He is skinny and short and Scottish and wearing black jeans. He has no bottom. His eyes scope the room behind her while he speaks.

After one beer he gets a text and stands up. Gotta go, he says, and leans over to kiss her on the cheek.

She travels to Covent Garden, to a huge outdoor pub in the plaza that is full of tourists. She meets a man in a suit who looks shifty and depressed. He is recently divorced, he tells her. His wife wants custody of the kids. When she is with him she feels as though she can't breathe. She excuses herself to go to the toilet and walks quickly out of the pub towards the Tube.

She carries on, more dates, more men, aware that this is not good for her – that it hurts her – but like gambling, like an addiction, she is compelled to carry on.

In despair, one afternoon, she goes downstairs to Lissa's flat.

She is nervous as she knocks. I wouldn't have come, she wants to say, unless I was desperate. I know you don't want to see me. I know you're still angry.

But Lissa, when she opens her door, is pleasant enough.

She shows Lissa her profile. Jesus, says Lissa. Do yourself a favour. With Lissa's help she chooses another picture – one closer up, of her laughing.

And boobs, says Lissa.

Really?

Definitely a bit of boob.

They craft a different profile, one that sounds less serious. You want to sound as though you're OK without a partner, says Lissa. Nothing scares them off like need.

She wonders when and where Lissa learned these rules.

This time she is more successful. Lots of men seem to want to date her. She meets a man – good-looking in an unobtrusive way. He has ginger hair and glasses. Her heart rises when she meets him. They have a drink and then they go to a restaurant.

They argue about Philip Roth. He writes freelance book reviews while temping. He takes his glasses off and wipes them quite often. It is a tic she decides is endearing. He is small, but she doesn't mind. They finish dinner and pay half each. They kiss lightly on the lips – the tiniest bit of tongue – and say how great it was and go their separate ways. She hears nothing from him. She checks her computer constantly. She sends him a message. Another one. She starts to feel she might be going mad. After a while she sees he is active on there. He has changed his profile. Changed his picture. He says he would like to meet someone who likes books.

In these moods everything is black. In these moods all men are damaged monsters. As is she. Everyone tells her that everyone meets online nowadays, cheering her on from the sidelines, but in these moods she knows it is just the leftovers. The leavings. She cannot imagine Lissa, for instance, ever going on there to find a man.

She shows Lissa the pictures of the men. These leavings. These leftovers. Listen, says Lissa. You're going for the wrong ones. They're all too skinny. Too cerebral. What you want is a bear. What about him? She points to a man with a beard and bags underneath his eyes. He looks kind. Or him? She leans forward and clicks the profile of a tattooed man with a baseball cap. There you go, she says. Try him.

They meet in the Dove on Broadway Market. They drink ale and talk about music and food. He is a chef. He knows nothing about politics or books. He has no A levels. He left school to go to catering college and he has lived in Paris and Marseilles and speaks fluent French. She feels she has been waiting her whole life to meet a man with no A levels who speaks fluent, backstreet Marseilles slang. He does not flirt. When he takes off his cap she sees that he is starting to go bald. She sees his small reflexive flinch as he monitors her reaction. But now, two hours into their date and several pints down, she has no reaction to monitor because by now she has decided that he could have lost all of his hair and she would not mind. He tells her that one day he would like to own a restaurant. No pretensions, simple cooking, local food. He asks her about herself. She tells him about her job, working for a small company, pairing community projects with big banks. The office on the edge of Canary Wharf. Queuing on her lunch break with all the suits. She makes it sound funny. She tells him about a five-a-side football match between local kids and a German bank. How the kids thrashed them. How pleased she was. He likes this story, as she hoped he would. About the Bengali women's group she took to a meeting this morning at the Bank of America, nervously fluttering in their saris like beautiful birds.

That's good, he says. That's good work. Those bankers. You should take that lot of bastards for whatever you can.

Yeah, she smiles, I'll drink to that.

When he goes up to get more drinks she sees that he is trying to hold his stomach in. By the end of the third pint he has stopped trying. They kiss on the street outside, their hands in each other's hair.

They go back to his. It is a large studio in a run-down block overlooking the canal. He has a futon and a wall of records. He plays her vintage reggae and opens a bottle of wine. The bed is messy and he hastily covers it with a throw.

I wasn't expecting anyone back here, he says. She believes him, and she likes him even more. They are hungry and he says

71

he will cook. She watches him chop vegetables with startling efficiency. He must be drunk but his knife does not slip. His tattoos. His wide forearms. Lissa was right. What she needed was a bear.

He cooks pasta with capers and chilli and fresh tomatoes. It is unbelievably delicious. When they have eaten they have sex on the unmade bed. She is astonished by how lovely he is to fuck.

In the morning the sun rises over the gas tower, over the canal. She counts his tattoos; he tells her the story of each one.

And what's this? he says, catching her wrist, tracing her spider with his fingertip.

Oh, that? she says, pulling her hand away. Just a nineties thing.

Three months later she is pregnant. Nine months later they are married. Seventeen months later she is living in Canterbury.

It is as though life has decided for her. Has picked her up and turned her round and deposited her a long, long way from home.

Cate

'Come on,' she says brightly to Tom in his high chair, where he sits solemnly eating a banana. 'We're going on a trip today. To see Hannah!'

Sam looks up from his phone. 'It's Saturday,' he says.

'I know.'

'Saturday is my day.'

'I know,' she says. 'But I want to see Hannah and she works in the week. I thought you'd be pleased. You can go back to bed.'

'I mean . . .' He pushes his baseball cap back on his head. 'I was going to go to Mum's, but if you're sure. Where are you meeting her?'

'In Hampstead. On the Heath.'

'*London?*' He stares at her, uncomprehending. 'Why?'

'Because I miss her. I miss London. And Tom's growing so much, and she misses him and . . .'

'Really?'

'What?'

'Well, I mean, with everything . . . I just – can't imagine that's true.'

'What do you mean?'

'Well – if you were Hannah, would you miss Tom?'

73

She looks down at her hands, takes a breath. 'He's her god-son. And yes, I think I might. They say being around babies is good for women trying to conceive.'

Tom giggles and she looks up. He is grinning at them both, clapping his hands together, his latest trick.

She sources those little Tupperware cartons she bought, back when she thought she was going to mash and purée and blend his food herself, finds them at the back of the cupboard, stacks two with apple slices, rice cakes, fills his sippy cup with water, the changing bag with nappies, gathers the sling, a change of clothes, bundles Tom into his coat, grabs her wallet and makes for the door. Sam rises to open it, staring sceptically at the world outside. 'What shall I tell my mum?' he says, scratching his beard.

'Tell her I had to see Hannah. Tell her we'll see her next week. Tuesday. Tamsin's arranging it. Remember?'

'Oh. Yeah. Cool.' He leans in, high-fives Tom, gives her a brief kiss on the cheek. 'Look after yourselves. You sure you're going to be all right?'

'We'll be fine!' The brightness in her voice makes her wince.

She pounds down the road, past the scrubby patch of grass with its one tree, past the supermarket, down the underpass and out at the crumbled edges of the city walls. If she keeps going like this, she might outpace her tiredness. Sun strikes off flint, but it is chilly. The season is turning; the air here has a bracing twist that she doesn't remember feeling for years. The sea – it must be something to do with proximity to the sea. She is wearing only a thin jacket. She thinks about returning to the house, but to do so would be to risk defeat – if she does so, she might pluck Tom from the buggy and give up. And he is happy enough, kicking his legs, looking from left to right, practising his wave on the dogs and the passers-by.

He is good on the train too, standing on her thigh and bouncing, trying his legs out for size as the flat estuary lands of England pass by. Her phone buzzes. Hannah.

You still OK for this morning?
Yes!

She adds a smiley face, something she would have avoided in the past, but today, for the sake of speed and this new primary-coloured brightness she feels, it seems appropriate.

But by the time the train is slowing for London, Tom is tired and fractious and has missed the window for his nap. He protests when she tries to get him into the buggy on the platform, bucking and twisting away from the straps. She bends down and rummages through her bag for the Tupperware, but the bag, large and voluminous and many-pocketed, is reluctant to give it up. She locates it eventually, takes out a rice cake and brandishes it towards Tom. 'Here! Here, darling.'

He is crying properly now, real tears on his cheeks. He doesn't want a rice cake. He probably wants a feed. She kneels before the buggy. 'Just – hold on. Please. You can sleep soon.'

She pushes the buggy a little way down the platform, but Tom is beside himself and so she stops and takes out the thinner of the two slings, the one she has used since he was tiny, the one Sam would put him in and sing to him. Sam. She would put up with any number of his comments and sideswipes to have him here beside her. But he's not here. There is no cavalry, no *deus ex machina*. She is the grown-up now.

'Hang on,' she says, her voice getting tighter, as people cast quick, worried looks towards her. 'Hang on, darling.' She slots the sling in place, ties its origami folds tightly and manages to get Tom into it. It is like wrestling an octopus. He twists against her chest, but finally the crying eases and soothes and they both breathe together.

'OK?' she says, stroking his back through the sling. 'OK. OK?'

He is drifting into sleep. Now. She can either pace up and down the platform until he sleeps more deeply, or walk on, to the Tube, and risk him waking up. After a look at her watch she decides on the latter.

The Tube is loud, louder than she can ever remember it being, but Tom, mercifully, stays sleeping, his head on her chest. People look and smile, and she smiles back, but her heart is clanging. What if something were to happen – an attack of some sort? It just feels entirely wrong to have this tiny, sleeping infant in this carriage, this metal carriage in which it feels as if death could come in so many guises – which is tunnelling past the heaped bones of the dead, past the hungry ghosts of the city, and under the river – *the river* – which in and of itself must be dangerous, must it not? How has she not considered these things before?

She should never have left the house.

Tom sleeps on but she is a tight knot of worry now, her hand rigid against his back. *Please. Please don't wake. Not now. Not yet. Not till we're there.*

And he doesn't, the movement of the train keeping him

rocked and unconscious – he sleeps still as she wrangles the buggy on to the escalator, leaving the Underground at Camden, as she walks to the overground, as she takes the train to Gospel Oak, and it is only as she is rounding the gates of the Heath that he lifts his lovely sleepy head and looks around.

'Oh, hello! Hello, darling!' She is jubilant, on the verge of tears, she is so relieved. 'Look! Look at all the trees. The leaves! Can you see? Can you see?'

It is a beautiful morning. The broad swathe of Highgate Hill in the distance is alight with reds and golds and browns. There are runners, dog walkers; elegant couples in matching down jackets gesticulate as they talk in French, Italian, Arabic. It is the Great World and she is a part of it. 'Isn't it lovely?' she says, taking him out of the sling and strapping him into the buggy, then making her way to the cafe at the bottom of Parliament Hill, the cheap one, their favourite, the old Italian where you can still get ice-cream sandwiches and scrambled eggs on toast. She sees Hannah before she has been seen herself, sitting alone at a table outside.

'Hey! Hey, Hannah!'

She is shouting, sweaty and shouting, but she doesn't seem able to lose this terrible jaunty tone. Hannah looks up.

Hannah stands, a hug – the scent on her neck of something expensive and restrained – and then she bends to Tom. 'Hey, little one.'

Hannah is dressed in a sleek woollen winter coat; her hair looks as though it has recently been attended to by a very good hairdresser.

'You look nice,' says Cate, gathering her breath.

'Thanks.'

Cate searches Hannah's face for signs of stress, but can see none, finds rather that her gaze falls off it, as though Hannah is coated in something smooth and impenetrable, a rock face with no hand- or footholds, while she feels porous. More than. It is as though there are great gaping holes in her that anyone might be able to see into, poke around in and pass judgement upon the mess within. She is sweating, and Tom, when she lifts him out, is sweating too.

'Oh,' says Hannah, staring at Tom. 'He's wet.'

'It's just sweat.'

Hannah nods. 'But his chest, it's soaked. It's quite chilly, isn't it?'

Hannah is right. He has drooled all over himself. He is teething and she should have brought a dribble bib. Why didn't she bring a bib? His chest is covered with sweat and drool and he is tiny and he is teething and Hannah is right, it is not warm – the season has changed while she was hiding inside the house. 'Here, just a sec.' She thrusts him at Hannah, who takes him and puts him on her knee.

'Hey, Mister.' Tom twists round and stares at Hannah doubtfully, and Cate can see the momentary flash of panic on Hannah's face.

'He's fine. He's just woken—'

'Don't worry.' Hannah lifts her hand. 'We're cool.'

Cate bends to the buggy, rummages for his change of clothes. The bag again. The fucking bag is terrorizing her. 'Here!' She has a clean jumper in her hands. She holds it up to Hannah, who nods and smiles. It is impossible to convey the sense of achievement inherent in this find, so Cate says nothing. Instead she begins to wrest the jumper over Tom's head, then thrusts him a rice cake, which he takes happily as she shoves a hat on his head.

Breathe. Breathe. Breathe.

'Will you be OK with him if I go and get a coffee?'

'Sure. We'll be great, won't we, Tom?'

Tom kicks his feet and grins.

'You want anything?'

'No. Really, I'm fine.'

Cate stands, makes her way into the cafe and joins the queue at the counter, casting frequent looks back towards where Hannah and Tom sit, Hannah with her hand raised, pointing to something just out of sight. She scans the herbal teas, decides against them, orders a cappuccino and a pastry, dumps two sugars into the coffee and carries them back out into the morning.

Breathe.

'Tell me what's happening then.' Cate puts down her coffee and sits.

'There's really nothing much to tell. I'm having a menopause right now. I'm sweating. I'm irritable. It's pretty horrible, but it won't last long.'

'But you look great!' cries Cate, and she reaches out and touches Hannah's sleeve. A strange, reflexive action – she wants something of that sleekness for herself. Hannah's hand comes down on her own.

'And you?'

'I'm fine,' says Cate.

I think I might be losing my mind.

There is a pause. Cate blows on her coffee while Tom chirrups on Hannah's lap, and she stares at her lovely child in the arms of her oldest friend and feels sudden, stupid tears in her eyes. She bends to wipe them before Hannah sees. But she has seen, of course she has.

'Hey, you're crying.'

Cate nods. The tears are streaming now. 'I'm OK. I promise. It's just—'

There is snot; there is nothing to deal with the snot, only a small, thin napkin on the side of her coffee, beneath the plastic-wrapped biscuit. She blows her nose and the napkin dissolves in her hands.

'Here.' Hannah reaches into her bag for tissues and Cate takes a tissue from the packet and blows her nose. 'You look tired.'

'I am tired. Tom wakes so often to feed in the night.'

'That's tough.' Hannah nods. She leans in to Tom and whispers in his ear. 'Hey. Listen, you. You give your mum a break. She needs to sleep.'

'You watch,' Cate says. 'When you have this baby, you'll have a sleeper. You'll have it on a routine from day one.'

Hannah laughs. 'Yeah, well, let's see. How's Sam?'

'He's OK. Well, maybe he's OK. I'm not sure. They offered to take Tom for me, one day a week. Tamsin, Sam's sister, and Sam's mum.'

'But that's great!' says Hannah. 'Free childcare. Isn't that part of why you moved out there?'

'I suppose it is.' Cate looks at Tom, who is flapping his arms with great enthusiasm at a nearby dog. 'But what if he turns out like them?'

'What do you mean?'

She shakes her head. 'I'm sorry. I don't really mean that. I just—'

'What?'

'Sometimes I feel I failed.'

'At what?'

'Everything.' She lifts the balled-up tissue in her fist. 'I didn't even have tissues today. My mum always had tissues. That's just what mums do. And I'm scared.'

'What of?'

'Everything. The future. Climate change. War. I keep thinking what sort of world it will be, when he's our age.' She circles her hand with her opposite wrist, her thumb touching the spider, just hidden from sight. 'And I keep thinking about Lucy. About where she is.'

'Lucy? Really?' Hannah's expression darkens. 'I'm sure wherever she is she's fine. Come on, Cate, you've got Tom. You've got Sam. You've got your life.'

'But what if it's not my life?'

'What on earth does that mean?'

'I just feel—'

'What? What do you feel?'

Lonelylonelylonelyallthefuckingtime.

'Sometimes I feel . . .'

'What?'

'That maybe it was irresponsible. Having a child at all.'

And just like that she feels Hannah detach – arms folded, head turned. Feels the morning, with all its promise, drain away from her, drain from them all.

'Cate,' says Hannah, her voice tight, 'listen to me. Take the offer of childcare. Have a day a week to yourself. Sleep. And I think you should see someone. A doctor.'

'A doctor?'

'If you're depressed,' says Hannah slowly, 'there are things you can do. You've been here before. Go and see the doctor. Take some pills. Get better. Please.' She lifts Tom, places him back on Cate's lap. 'Come on, Cate, nip it in the bud. For Tom, if not yourself. And he's cold,' she says. 'Tom's cold. Let's go inside.'

Lissa

The first day of rehearsal is a crisp, early autumn day and Lissa rises early. In the shower she hums, sounding out her voice, running her tongue round her jaw. She chooses her outfit with care: a loose cotton shirt open at the neck, jeans and a necklace of red beads. No make-up other than a touch of mascara. She pins up her hair, shrugs on a man's oversized jacket and winds a light scarf around her neck. She is nervous, but it is a manageable feeling, a sharpening, a slight fizz at the edge of things as she walks across the park, enjoying the pull of the morning tide, the fast pace of the walkers, the bikes. The air is clean, the leaves of the plane trees catch the early sun.

As she walks she speaks to herself in a low voice, running over the speeches she has half memorised; they are using the Michael Frayn version, and she is coming to know it well already, to internalise its cadences, imagining herself into the part: Yelena, the young wife of an old man, buried in her marriage and thirsty for life.

Yelena: You know what that means, having talent? It means being a free spirit, it means having boldness and wide horizons . . . he plants a sapling, and he has some notion of what will become of it in a thousand years' time; he already has some glimpse of the millennium. Such people are rare. They must be loved . . .

She is interested to see who is playing Astrov, the doctor with whom her Yelena will fall in love. Interested to see who is playing all of the parts she has been reading to herself over and over for the last three weeks.

She arrives fifteen minutes early at the address written on the front of her script, a basement studio in Dalston tucked away on a side street between two Turkish restaurants, their fronts shuttered up against the morning. The director, Klara, is there already, in a corner of the room, speaking to someone who can only be the designer, their heads bent to a scale model of the set. She is shorter than Lissa remembered, dumpy even, grey hair in a dandelion frizz around her head. Ten or so chairs are set out in a circle for the actors, another row behind them for the technical staff. On a small side table a kettle steams into the bright air. A clear-faced young woman comes up, pumps Lissa's hand and introduces herself as Poppy, the ASM. 'Great to meet you! There's coffee, pastries, help yourself.'

Lissa drops her bag by a chair and wanders over to the table.

'Might as well take advantage of the hospitality.'

She turns to the voice and sees a man about her height standing beside her.

'God knows when we'll see its like again.' There's a faint northern accent to the bass growl. Scouse? He is clean-shaven, fifty or so, with grey in amongst the brown of his hair, which is longish, falling past his ears. His eyes are the most extraordinary blue. She knows him from somewhere. She must have seen him on stage but she cannot remember when. She goes to say something back, but he has turned and gone already, croissant in hand, over to his seat.

'Lissa?'

She turns to see a much younger man this time, thin-faced with wide-set eyes and thick lips. She meets his proffered hand. Does she know him?

'Lissa Dane, isn't it?'

'Yes. I'm sorry, I—'

The young man laughs. 'I just recognize your face. From pictures.'

'Really?'

'Didn't you use to go out with Declan Randall?'

'Oh. Yes, I did.'

'I love his work.'

She nods. 'Well, he's a talented man.'

'That last film – the one in the prison. The French director? Awesome.'

'I haven't seen it,' she says.

'You're kidding.' He shakes his head. 'If I could have anyone's career, it would be his.'

She nods, finds her gaze sliding out to where the older actor is sitting. It is bugging her. His face. Where does she know it from?

'So you're not together any more?'

'No,' she says. 'Not for a couple of years. He dumped me. For a make-up girl.'

'Jesus,' he says, shaking his head. 'That's harsh.'

'Yeah, well. He was an egotistical monster. So, you know.' She picks up her coffee. 'Silver linings and all that.'

The room is filling up now, the hubbub around the coffee table increasing, the knot of actors spilling out into the room. The assistant stage manager is clapping her hands and gathering everyone together. Lissa and the young man, who tells her his name is Michael, wander over to the circle, where she takes her seat beside the older actor, who acknowledges her with a slight nod of the head.

All of the chairs are taken. Klara makes her way to her place but stays standing, her gaze sweeping the circle as one by one her actors fall silent. She lets the silence swell until it fills the room, then touches her hand to her heart. 'Here you are,' she says. 'Here you all are. And who are you? Tell us. Johnny.' She nods to the man beside Lissa. 'You begin.'

'Johnny, Vanya.'

A young, intense-looking woman in black jeans and a polo neck speaks next. 'Helen, Sonya.'

One by one they speak – *Richard, Serebryakov*; *Greg, Astrov* – and as they do so, the play populates itself: the elegant older woman playing Maria, Yelena's mother-in-law; the woman who looks to be in her seventies playing Marina the nurse. Lissa watches Klara watch her actors – they all watch each other with wariness, with excitement, until the circle is complete and it is Lissa's turn. 'Lissa,' she says, 'Yelena.'

'So,' Klara says, 'let us read this brilliant play.'

As Johnny bends to the black leather bag at his feet and fishes out his script, it comes to Lissa where she knows him from – the call centre. She can picture him there now, sitting in the grotty break room with the same faintly disdainful look on his face. Something regal about him. Something tragic. Dressed all in black, with the same black leather briefcase at his feet.

Hannah

They have been told to report to the hospital early, and she and Nathan sit silently, side by side on hard plastic chairs nailed to the floor, as dawn breaks over London.

Nathan scrolls through work emails on his phone as Hannah counts the couples. Seven of them. She knows the statistics: 24 per cent of those in her age bracket will conceive, 15 per cent of those older than her, slightly higher for those under thirty-five. She watches faces, guesses ages, tries to do the maths. How many of those sitting here will be lucky? One couple? Two?

The women's names are called and they rise, their small bags in their hands, saying goodbye to their partners. Nathan stands before Hannah and presses his forehead against hers.

Then the women are taken away through swinging double doors, to a waiting room where a television is playing – the gaudy blare of morning TV. It scratches at Hannah's nerves and she does not want to watch it or listen to it, so she pulls out her book and tries to read, wishing she had brought headphones. Her name is halfway down the list that is pinned to the wall.

They are given hospital gowns to wear – strange garments, open at the back. They sit so their knickers are not on show.

The morning passes like this. There is weak squash to drink. One by one the women leave and Hannah watches them go – each with their precious cargo, full of hope. She tries to read their faces, their bodies, as though she might see their destiny written there – which one of them will have the longed-for child. As though if they win, then she loses. As though fertility were a zero-sum game.

She thinks of Cate. *Sometimes I feel I was irresponsible, having a child at all.*

The carelessness of her comment. The luxury of a gift that came so easily.

In truth, her words had made Hannah furious, but she'd said nothing, packing away the anger she has no spare energy to feel.

The woman beside her is nervous. She keeps getting up to go to the toilet. It is making Hannah nervous too.

'Is it your first time?' asks Hannah, when she returns.

The woman nods. 'You?'

'Third.'

'Really?' The woman looks unhappy to hear this, and Hannah wishes she had kept quiet.

'I don't like anaesthetic,' the woman says. 'Don't like being knocked out.' Her face is ashy in the hospital light.

By the time Hannah's turn comes, she too has grown nervous. How many eggs will there be? The more she has, the higher her chances. It looked like eleven on the monitor, when she had the last scan, but sometimes they are just empty sacs.

'Hannah Grey? Follow me.'

She pads after the nurse into the small cupboard-like anaesthetic room, where she climbs on to the table.

'OK there?' The anaesthetist shoots her a quick look.

Her hand is taken, the anaesthetist asks her to count backwards, and Hannah does and . . .

'Thirteen,' she says to Nathan, in the recovery room. 'I got thirteen.' She is dizzy, jubilant.

'Blimey.' He reaches over to kiss her. 'Aren't you clever?'

'How was yours?'

'Fine.' He grins. 'It was funny, though, they had the same magazines in the drawer they had last time.'

'You're kidding.'

'I'm not!'

'Do you think they disinfect them? Do you think that's someone's job?'

'I've no idea.'

They are laughing and she is light, sitting here, high on hospital tea in the wipe-clean recovery chair. Other women sit opposite her. Some look happy, some less so. And she knows. She knows this is their time.

It is still early afternoon. They walk home, through the back streets, over the park, where leaves spin and fall in golden light. The flat has the calm, clandestine feeling of a midweek afternoon and they are playing truant, together. They open the windows and let in the day, and then, for the first time in weeks, they lie on their bed and make love.

She wakes early. She has been dreaming but she is not sure of what.

Beside her, Nathan sleeps on. She stands softly, pulls a blanket from the bed and goes into the kitchen, where she makes herself camomile tea and then takes out her laptop, wondering if she should distract herself with a movie, but there is nothing she wants to watch, so she clicks through some other pages, the IVF message boards – the thousands of women posting their queries, and the thousands who answer them – the pastel-hued sorority of anxiety and reassurance. She cannot bear these message boards and yet they call her, again and again, with their siren, sister song.

After a while she casts the computer aside, takes the blanket and goes over to the window, looking out over the park to the city beyond. She thinks of those embryos, tinier than sight. How many of them have fertilized? How many of them pulse now with the smallest possible pulse of life? She wants to be near them. To walk back to the hospital and find the room where they lie and sit beside them. To watch over them in these long, small hours before the dawn. She is their mother, after all.

They call her the next morning while she is at work. As soon as she sees the unknown number on her phone she jumps up and takes the call in the corridor. 'Eleven have fertilized,' the nurse tells her, and she feels her heart leap.

She tries to call Nathan, but his phone rings and rings and she gets his voicemail. A text comes through. *In a meeting. All OK?*

Eleven, she writes, and he sends back one word. *Great!*

Now she must wait.

*

There is no news the next day. Nathan is working late, and the flat feels large. She opens the door of the little room. This small room faces west, towards the hospital. She slides down to the carpet and sits there in silence. After a while she lifts her phone and calls her parents' house. Her father answers.

'Hi, Dad.'

'Hannah. How're you doing, love?'

'I'm good.'

'Glad to hear it.'

'How're you?'

'Grand.'

Have they ever said more than this to each other on the phone?

'Hang on a sec, love. I'll just get your mum.'

'Thanks, Dad.'

His soft call. She sits in the dusk of her empty room and imagines her mother getting up from whatever she is doing, watching telly most probably, feet up on the low table in front of her. Wearing the slippers Hannah bought for her from the catalogue last Christmas. Here she comes, padding into the hall. Shooing the dog away from the little armchair by the telephone table.

'Hannah, love.'

The soft vowels.

'Hiya, Mum. Did I disturb you?'

'No, love. Not at all. Just catching up with a bit of *Strictly*. Hang on a sec, I'll just get comfy.' She can hear her mother settle further into the chair. 'How're you? Have you had the thingy?'

'Yes.'

90

'And how did it go?'

'Well, I think.'

She doesn't go into details. Her mother's concept of IVF is hazy at best.

'Oh, that's good, love. You know, I saw Dot the other day. Her daughter's little one is one now.' The talismanic properties of Dot and her daughter's daughter – conceived by IVF and born last year – are strong. They were wheeled out last Christmas, all three generations, invited over for an awkward cup of tea.

'One?' says Hannah into the darkness. 'That went quickly.'

'Such a poppet.'

'How's Jim?' she asks.

'Good. They've exchanged on the house. They're moving in a week or so. Just in time for the birth.'

'Hayley must be getting close now.'

'She is. She's big all right. You'll be an aunty soon.'

'That's good,' says Hannah.

'How's work?'

'Quiet.'

'Well, that's a blessing. And Nathan?'

'He's . . . good.'

'Well, that's grand, love.'

She closes her eyes. She wants to be up in Manchester in her parents' little living room, watching *Strictly* with her mum with the gas fire turned up too high.

'I'll pray for you, love,' her mum says.

'Thanks,' says Hannah. She never knows what to say in response to this.

Thanks, Mum, but there's no such thing as God.

'I'd better go. Leave you to your telly.'

'All right. If you're sure?'

'Nathan's got something on the stove,' she lies.

'Oh good, well, you give him our love, won't you?'

'I will. Bye, Mum. Love you.'

'Love you too, Han.'

The next day, early, there is a call from the hospital.

'The embryologist would like to do the transfer today.'

She thanks them, and goes into the bathroom, where Nathan is brushing his teeth.

'They want to do it today.'

He spits, rinses his mouth. 'Did they say anything else?'

'It was just a receptionist. They must not look good, the embryos.' The smallest flickering pulse.

'I'm sure it's fine, Han. It's just – science.'

She fiddles with a bit of toilet roll.

'Hey. Hey, Han.' His hand on hers.

They are shown into a tiny, dimly lit anteroom. She is told to take off her clothes from the waist down and given a gown to wear.

The room is dark but for small lowlights set in the wall. There is a nurse. A doctor. Her on the gurney. Her feet in stirrups. The monitor beside her. Her heart. Her heart. Nathan's hand, steady on her arm. The embryologist appears. 'Ms Grey? Mr Blake?'

She nods.

'Well, the thirteen eggs that were taken three days ago have been watched closely. There were seven still developing last night.'

She nods.

'There are three that look viable. One is excellent. A 3.5. The others are a 2.5 and a 2.'

'And the others?' asks Nathan.

'Less viable. Our recommendation is to transfer the top two.'

'Yes,' says Nathan. 'Of course.'

The ceiling has small pinpricks of light, like stars.

'Han?'

'Shall we proceed?' says the voice of the doctor.

'Yes.'

She lies back, gasps at the chill of metal as a speculum is inserted. There is a deep, strange almost-pain as her cervix is stretched wide.

'Now, just watch the screen.'

Nathan grasps her hand.

'There we are,' the doctor says. 'There they go.'

Two points of light appear in the darkness of her womb.

She looks at them.

'Here,' the doctor says kindly, reaching down and tearing off a printout. 'Would you like this to take with you?'

'Thank you.' Hannah stares down at the photograph, at those two smeared points of light. She looks. She looks and looks and looks.

Resistance

1998

Cate puts her full stop on her final finals paper (Greek Myth in Spenser's Epithalamium*) and steps out into the mild May sun, where she is duly pelted with flour and rice by a small cluster of waiting friends, with whom she drinks a bottle of champagne in the cobbled street. Then she goes to the pub and drinks pints of lager in the beer garden until the ground is tipping, when she goes to the toilets and is sick.*

The next morning she wakes late and sits and stares at the wall, which is peppered with Post-it notes, quotes by Spenser, Rochester, Congreve, Donne. She takes them down one by one and puts them in the bin. She has to be out of this room on Monday. It is over. She has limped to the finish line, patched up on Prozac, pills she has been taking since the end of her second year, when, quite suddenly, standing in the college quad, her mind began to fracture. Grief, was what the college counsellor said to her. Delayed grief, agreed the doctor, writing out his prescription. And of course, he went on, Oxford can be very stressful in itself.

She took a year out. Went back to Manchester. Stayed in her father's house.

She knows she will not finish first or last, but somewhere in between. From her mullioned window she can see hungover students stumbling to the shop for soft drinks and cigarettes.

To her right, just visible, the ghoul masks of the Sheldonian Theatre. The Bodleian beyond. She will never set foot in the library again. She has packing to do. She wonders what it was all for.

There is nowhere to go home to. Her mother is dead and her father is in Spain. Her sister is in Canada. So she goes to stay with Hannah, who is living in a small flat on the edge of Kentish Town, walking distance up a long hill from where Lissa lives with her mother. Cate sleeps on the sofa in the living room of Hannah's flat. Hannah has a new boyfriend, a man called Nathan. She met him through Lissa (of course.) He is tall and handsome and gentle, and walks with a slight stoop, as though apologizing for his height. In all other respects, though, he seems like a winner in life. Nathan spends nights there, in the small Camden flat. Sometimes, waking in the darkness, Cate hears them through the walls.

They talk, just once, she and Hannah, about Hannah's new job – entry level in a management training firm.

Why would you want to do that? Cate asks her.

It's not for ever, says Hannah. But I need money. I want it. I'm sick of not having it. I'll do it for a bit and then I'll do something worthwhile.

But what about Patti Smith? Cate wants to say. And Emma Bovary? And the Pixies? But she says nothing, only nods.

So, what are you going to do? asks Hannah of Cate. And Cate has no answer to that at all.

She doesn't like London. The transport system alone makes her head hurt. Hannah leaves copies of Loot on the kitchen table, drops hints about people who might have a spare room going, but Cate follows up no leads. She is ill at ease with

Hannah and Lissa, a friendship that has grown and eclipsed her own. Ill at ease when they go out to dinner together with Nathan and Declan, Lissa's boyfriend, a laughably good-looking Irish actor, to a restaurant Lissa knows, an Ethiopian place where food is served without cutlery on sour flatbread, which they all tear into with their fingers and dip in sauces with equal alacrity, and drink coffee which is brought to the table and roasted on the spot. They talk emphatically at these meals, using their hands as they speak, they seem certain about all sorts of things, like which films to see, and which books to read, and who they are and what they are going to be.

Cate herself is certain of nothing. Life seems at once becalmed and full of danger, as though a wave could come at any moment, rising out of the still waters, a great towering wave, and take her down.

She receives her finals results. She has scraped a first. She tells Hannah, who looks shocked. It was an accident, says Cate hurriedly. And then hates herself for saying it. Still, she thinks, it was an accident. She never expected that.

Her tutor calls to congratulate her. So what are you going to do? he says.

She can only think that she would like to tell her mum. To give her the good news.

She gets an email from Hesther, a friend from Oxford who is living in Brighton, inviting her down for the day. There is a room going in her house.

As she steps off the London train, Cate can smell the sea. She walks down to the seafront and stands on the pebbled beach and stares out at the pale horizon. She walks through the city to Hesther's house. Brighton seems appealingly ramshackle, human-sized. The room is cheap and small with a window that lets in good light. She takes it. She buys herself some furniture from the charity shops on the Lewes Road.

The other room is occupied by a woman called Lucy. Lucy wears combat trousers and vests and boots with strong soles, as though she is a foot soldier in an unnamed war. She has thick dreadlocks that hang down her back, and her face is small and fine. She is studying for a Master's in International Development at the University of Sussex. She is half American – grew up between Devon and Massachusetts, and her accent is deliciously confused. Two summers ago Lucy lived up a tree in Newbury, sleeping on a wooden platform a hundred feet above the earth, protesting the destruction of ancient woodland for the building of a bypass road.

Lucy teaches Cate how to use a drill, how to put up shelves in her room. She has a light cloud of armpit hair and does not use deodorant. When they stand close, Cate catches her musky scent. Walking around the city with Lucy is an education – she has a scavenger's eye: wood for the wood burner, wine crates for shelves, just-out-of-date food from supermarket skips. Lucy carries herself lightly, as though she still walks in the forest. As though at any moment she might be predator or prey.

A rhythm establishes itself. Once a fortnight Cate signs on at the job centre, and once a month money lands in her account. It is not much, but enough to cover the small bedroom, and to buy cheap food – enough to allow her to breathe. She is pleased to find her needs are few. Hesther tells her there is a job going in the cafe in which she works, a cycle ride away, on the other side of town. Cate takes the job. At the end of her first shift she is paid money from the till in cash. The first time is hard – she feels like a cheat. She tells Hesther this, and Hesther tuts. You know how much the British government spends on weapons? Besides, it's just till you get sorted, till you get on your feet.

It is easier after that.

At the weekend they go down to the seafront and drink cider and watch the sunset, watch the starlings stream in to roost on the skeleton of the West Pier, watch them cast themselves in great clouds of murmuration against the evening sky.

Lucy and Hesther are part of a group of young people who like to gather together at the house and talk – about capitalism, about hierarchies, about horizontal power and the potential for change. They plan actions. Cate has no idea what an action is until, one dawn in late summer, Lucy knocks on the door of her room and tells her to get out of bed. Cate pulls on her sweater and tracksuit bottoms and they drive out along the High Street, where Lucy stops the van and instructs Cate to sit in the driver's seat. Which she does, nerves jangling, as Lucy covers her face with a bandana and neatly spray-paints the word SLAVERY – the V made by the swoosh of Nike – on the front of a trainer shop. Lucy jumps back in the van and shouts at Cate to drive. Which she does – giddy and fast. She feels like Bonnie, or Clyde.

She begins to read again, different books: Chomsky and Klein and E. P. Thompson. She starts to join the discussions. At first it is odd to hear her voice in a group – it has been so long since she felt she had anything to say. She begins to think that Oxford, that place of power – that place she hoped would confer power on to her – robbed her of her voice, or rather, that *she gave it away. Or perhaps, she thinks, it was only hidden. Perhaps she had only to follow the trail of breadcrumbs to find it again.*

She and Lucy and Hesther go up to London and they march in the streets. They dress up in costumes which they run up on sewing machines; they don fat suits with pinstripes to protest at the fat cats in the City. There are bicycles everywhere. There are solar-powered sound systems blowing bubbles into the crowd. Passers-by stop and shake their hips.

She goes to dance classes on a Monday morning, where the teacher plays loud music and people of all ages throw themselves around the room and sweat and shout as though possessed. Sometimes in these classes, when the music is at its height, she screams. No one takes any notice, for this is what you are supposed to do. She realizes that she is angry. Very, very angry indeed.

On the other side of her anger is something else.

One morning, in Cate's room, Lucy finds her anti-depressants.

What do you want these for?

I had a breakdown, says Cate. At uni. I've been taking them since then.

You don't need anti-depressants, says Lucy, looking up at her with a smile. You just need better friends.

She throws away her pills, waits for the crash that she fears will come – but feels only relief at the ebbing of the fog.

She is aware, somewhere at the back of her mind, what Hannah would say if she could see her, how easy all of this would be to parody, this benefit fraud and cider drinking and dancing and horizon watching. But she is starting not to care.

She writes Hannah a postcard, an old-fashioned picture of an old woman with her skirts hitched up and her ankles in the sea – *Come on in, it says, the water's lovely*.

Lucy and Hesther both have vans and with her small savings Cate buys one too – a decommissioned ambulance which she parks at a cement works outside the city and, over the winter, with a little help from Lucy and a small Makita drill, converts herself. Tongue-and-groove cladding inside, a bed made from sawn plywood, shelves above and drawers beneath. It is ready by spring, and when it is finished she thinks she has never been prouder of anything in her life.

There is an album they all listen to, all autumn, winter, spring. Clandestino, *by Manu Chao. There is a song, 'Minha Galera', that Cate loves above all.*

Oh my waterfall.

Oh my girl.

My Romany girl.

She plays it over and over, and when she listens to it she thinks of Lucy.

Summer comes. They stock up on muesli and coffee and rice from the local wholesaler and take to the road. They drive west. They swim naked in rivers, emerging jubilant, silver-backed. They go to small festivals tucked into folds in the green hills.

Cate comes to recognize some of the faces around the evening fires: young people like themselves, and older people; people whose faces tell stories, of weather and work and lives lived outside. At night, with tea and whisky, these older people loosen *their tongues – they speak of Enclosure, of the Commons, of an older, wilder Britain, of gentle and of not so gentle defiance of the status quo. Cate thinks she can touch it, this life-giving current, ribboning out into the clear western night.*

And then they dance.

One black night, at one small gathering, in high summer, when the air is still warm at midnight, where there are no lights, when there is no moon, Cate loses Lucy. She wanders around for hours, searching, feeling panic bite at the edges of her. She finds her again as dawn begins to break, sitting in the middle of a pile of people, naked from the waist up, her nipples painted gold.

Lucy holds out her arms for Cate and Cate steps into them and then, filled with love and relief and a desire to claim, she bends her head to Lucy's golden nipple and takes it into her mouth. It tastes of salt and metal and earth.

Soon after, as the sun presses itself against the windows of her van, Cate slides her fingers into the slick warmth of Lucy and encounters no resistance. She watches Lucy buck and arch beneath her, her eyes half closed. She sees a tattoo on Lucy's inner thigh, a filigree spider, a filigree web, and she puts her mouth on it, kisses it. She herself is shivering with desire – she doesn't even need to be touched to come.

Cate

Mid-morning and Tom is sleeping. Cate sits at the kitchen table, the bag of pills beside her.

Come on, Cate, nip it in the bud.

As though it were that easy.

This morning she went to the doctor, as Hannah suggested. The doctor was nice, was kind; she asked about Cate's eating, sleeping, libido. She asked about the manner of the birth and Cate told her.

Caesarean section.

And was that hard?

She thought about the fear – for her child, for herself. The confusion. The knives and numbness, the smell of burning flesh.

Yes. I suppose it was.

The doctor asked about whether she thought of hurting herself, hurting her son. *No*, said Cate. *Not that*.

The doctor said that yes, she thought Cate was depressed. She said there was CBT, but a long waiting list, or anti-depressants. But if she took anti-depressants, she would have to wean her son. She asked if Cate had ever been on anti-depressants before.

Yes, Prozac. At university.

Good, said the doctor. *Well, perhaps we'll start with that.*

Cate reaches for the packet of pills, pops one from its packaging and holds it in her palm. The innocuous white and hospital green. They used to make her head fizz. If she drank while she was on them she would black out.

She puts the pill down on the table and brings her computer towards her, searches 'breastfeeding anti-depressants' and reads that the amount of medication that gets to the breastfed baby is usually less than 10 per cent of the amount found in the mother's blood. Which still sounds like an awful lot.

You don't need anti-depressants. You just need better friends.

Her fingers hover over the keys, then she types 'Lucy Skein' into Google, feels her heartbeat increase. Several pictures appear, but none that resembles Lucy, although she would be older now of course, much older. She was four years older than Cate, so forty now, or nearly so. Perhaps Lucy Skein was never even her real name.

They parted in the States. They had gone there to Seattle, to take part in the protests against the WTO. Had locked themselves into Perspex pipes and shut down the city. Had watched the police on their horses, their black uniforms, their masked faces, like a scene from a fairy tale, good against evil, light against dark. Had sat and chanted with thousands of other protestors as they were sprayed with CS gas till they were burning and almost blind. She remembers the pain, the inrush of feeling – the ecstatic logic of the binary. Of black and of white. Of being right.

After Seattle they went down to Eugene, Oregon, and lived

in a squatted warehouse for a couple of months with ten other activists, and that was where Lucy heard about the protest camps by Mount Hood – loggers cutting down ancient trees. They caught a ride out there together, walked out into the forest on a crisp November morning, the mountain rearing before them, the tang of earth and resin and snow in the air. They reached the camp, and there were the trees, and the people in those trees, their shouts and whistles as they moved about in nets high above their heads. And Cate saw the look on Lucy's face, and watched, helpless, as Lucy pulled out her ropes and strapped herself on, and then she was climbing away from her, and Cate stood earthbound, leaden-hearted, as Lucy climbed up into green and light.

They rode back to Eugene. Cate's visa was running out. Lucy didn't need one. They went to a tattoo parlour downtown, where Cate sat while Lucy held her hand, as an unsmiling man leaned over her arm and drew a filigree spider in a silver web. She flew home, determined to fly back again as soon as she could. She went down to the internet cafe every day to check her email, but there was never a word. Those first weeks, as the tattoo scabbed and healed, when missing Lucy grew too much she would press her fingernail into it, would lift the scab to feel that pain again.

She went back to her job in the cafe, signed on, trying to save for another flight, waiting for word, but no word came. Spring came and went, and brought nothing from Lucy. Then in the early summer, an email – a few words.

Some of us in the camp have been arrested. They say we're terrorists. I won't use this account any more.

Spin always.
Weave always.
Love always.
L. X

And then nothing. Severance. Free fall.

Years. Years in which Cate thought she saw her constantly, on the beach in Brighton, or cycling through the city, her long hair down her back. Years in which Cate stayed working at the cafe, still watching the door, waiting for Lucy to walk back in.

It was Hannah who finally walked through the door. Hannah who came down to Brighton one day, who stood in her smart work clothes and looked around the cafe – at the cakes on their cake stands and the menu chalked up on to the board, the pitta and hummus and the bean burgers and soya lattes, and said, *You have a first-class degree from Oxford University. What the hell are you still doing working here?*

It was Hannah who told her about the room in the house Lissa had found in London Fields. Cheap rent. On the park. A chance to start again. And because she knew she was rotting behind that counter, corroded with waiting, Cate took it.

She stares back at the pictures on her computer screen, feels the old twist of loss.

She could have searched harder. Could have gone back to the States, could have found her. Could have claimed her, claimed that part of herself.

And then a thought comes to her – Hesther. Perhaps there are pictures of Lucy in Hesther's feed – perhaps they have stayed in touch. She searches for Hesther, finds her profile, the pictures of her family, her Georgian house in Bristol, her high ceilings and her lovely kitchen. Clicks back and back and back. There are a few photographs from the Brighton days but none of Lucy.

She clicks on Hesther's name.

Hey Hesther, long time. Hope all is well.
Just thinking about some old friends today. Wondered if you had Lucy Skein's contact details?
Much love
Cate.

She presses send.
Fuck.

There is a knock at the door. Cate stays where she is, but the knock comes again, imperious this time, and then the sound of a key turning in the lock. Horrified, she goes out into the hall where she sees Alice coming through the door.

'I thought you might need a hand.' Sam's mother is brisk, dressed in a scarf and padded gilet, her cheeks rosy. A bulging bag stands at her feet. 'So I brought some help.' She lifts the bag, which is bristling with lurid plastic bottles. 'Shall I come in?'

Cate steps back as Alice passes her into the kitchen. The pills are still on the table, next to the computer, open to a series of photographs of women's faces. Cate moves, putting herself between the table and Alice, her heart beating wildly.

'Still haven't unpacked those?' Alice takes off her gilet and hangs it on the back of a chair, then points to the tower of boxes behind the door.

'Not yet. I mean – I've been waiting to borrow a car, for a charity-shop run.'

'You can borrow Terry's,' says Alice, taking a crisp, ironed apron from the bag and tying it around her waist. She lifts bottles from the bag. 'I thought we could tackle the kitchen and bathrooms then go for a bit of tea and cake. Get you both out of the house.'

Cate eyes the bottles. Alice's cleaning cupboard is a temple to carcinogens in all their many varieties. 'Oh, well, that's so lovely of you, Alice.' She turns around, gathers her computer and the pills and brings them all into the safety of her cardigan. 'The thing is . . .'

'Yes?'

'I'm actually just heading out.'

'Out?' Alice's head is cocked; she appears to be sniffing the air for untruths.

'Yes. To playgroup.'

'Playgroup?'

'The one you recommended.' Cate nods at the flyer on the fridge. 'I've just been waiting for Tom to wake up. I'm just going to check on him now. Excuse me a sec.'

She races upstairs to the bedroom, where Tom is fast asleep, his arms flung out at right angles on the duvet. She shoves the pill back in the packet, puts the packet in the paper bag and the bag at the very back of the bathroom cupboard, covered with a towel, scrubs her face with a flannel, returns to the bedroom, pulls a jumper over Tom's Babygro, pulls on the sling and manoeuvres him swiftly into it, then makes her way downstairs as he begins to properly stir.

'There we are,' she says, snatching the playgroup flyer from the fridge and one of the space-food packets from the cupboard. 'I'm really sorry to miss you, Alice. And I'm so grateful for your help.'

Alice stands in the middle of the room. 'Well, all right then. But don't forget Tuesday.'

'Tuesday?'

'Tuesday, my grandson and I have a *date*!'

The address on the flyer is a low, unprepossessing municipal building. She walks quickly past, further up the hill, then curves back around the block, in sight of the hall once more.

She need not actually go to playgroup at all. She could take Tom and go somewhere else, perhaps to a cafe, one with wifi, drink coffee and jitter through the morning, spending her finite energies on more fruitless internet searches, but it is starting to rain, and Tom is grizzling and here she is. She crosses the street, over the threshold, coming into a hallway which is a chaos of buggies and shoes and coats. She lifts Tom from the sling and gives her name to the woman at reception. A tidal roar comes from behind double glass doors.

'It's five pounds for the session,' says the woman, 'but you can pay three. It started an hour ago.'

Cate pulls some coins from her wallet and tosses them down. Inside she is greeted by a thrashing sea of children and plastic toys. She grips on to Tom, who grips back, his head turning this way and that. There seems to be no safe harbour anywhere. Her heart is thumping, sweat breaking on her back.

'It's circle time now.'

Cate turns to see a brisk, grey-haired woman standing beside her.

'There's a baby mat over there for when we're done.' The woman points into the far corner and claps her hands. 'Circle time!' she calls in a sing-song voice, and Cate watches as the hordes form themselves into a ragged approximation of a circle. 'Come on,' says the grey-haired woman to Cate, in a tone that brooks no opposition. 'Come and join in.'

The woman launches into a joyless version of 'The Wheels on the Bus'. Larger children practise commando crawling across the space, and Cate shields Tom between her legs. Here, amongst the older children, he seems terribly small.

When do we get off the bus? Cate wants to ask, as the grey-haired woman grinds on. *When does the bus actually stop?* The last time she sat on a mat like this was when she was a child herself. *Miss? Miss? Are we nearly there yet? Please, Miss, I want to get down.*

Eventually the bus judders to a halt, and after a few rounds of 'Twinkle, Twinkle' and 'Wind the Bobbin Up' the woman claps her hands. 'All right, children. It's free play!'

There's general screaming as the larger children dive towards racks of dressing-up clothes. A girl emerges from the melee in a fireman's suit; her hijab-wearing mother grins back at her and gives the thumbs-up. Superheroes twist and flail across the room. Cate retreats to the corner, to the baby mat, where a scattering of toys have been put out.

'Jesus Christ, it's like World War Three in here.'

She looks up to see a woman standing close to her, a baby around the same age as Tom in her arms. 'I was told it was OK for little ones.'

'I know. I think perhaps you have to keep to the corner.' Cate gestures to the mat beneath her.

'Really?' The woman looks cross. 'Well, what's the bloody point in that?'

The woman's baby has seen Tom and is reaching out for him. The mother notices, amused. 'You want to get down?' She kneels and puts her child on the mat. The baby is dressed in a hand-knitted, haphazard style. She wears a home-spun bonnet which gives her the look of a small mushroom, or a Bruegel peasant. The woman plucks her daughter's hat from her head and black curls spring forth, then throws off her own cardigan. She is small, with a gentle intensity to her features, short brown hair, an angular fringe.

On the mat, their children are groping for each other. Their hands touch and they both scream in delight. The woman laughs. 'Who's this then?'

'This is Tom,' says Cate.

'This is Nora,' says the woman.

'That's a good name.'

'You think? My partner decided on it. All the ones I wanted had some sort of tragedy attached to them. Antigone. Iphigenia.'

Is she joking? Cate can't tell, but the woman catches her eye and smiles. She sits back and blows her fringe from her forehead. 'Where's the Tom from then?'

'Oh, well, we just liked it, I suppose.'

'Fair enough.' The woman reaches out and places a toy in front of Nora. It has lots of buttons which Nora presses in turn, blaring out Americanized versions of nursery rhymes.

'Oh, nonononononono.' The woman leans in and turns the

111

sound off. 'We've had quite enough of that for one morning.' Nora presses the buttons a few more times, but when they yield nothing, loses interest and crawls over to where Tom is bashing a block against the side of a table. 'I like the Babygro,' says the woman, gesturing to him.

'Oh.' Cate can feel herself colour. 'We were late, and he was sleeping, so—'

'I'd wear one myself if I could. Can you imagine, someone putting you in a Babygro and tucking you in? Letting you sleep? Heaven.' The woman closes her eyes, and for a moment exhaustion takes over her features, until there is a cry and she snaps them open again. Nora is reaching for the wisps of hair on Tom's head. 'Oh, no no, we don't grab, darling,' says the woman, lifting her child away and on to her lap as Nora's fingers clutch on air.

'Nora Barnacle!' says Cate. 'Joyce.' She has spoken before she has thought.

The woman looks up. 'Yeah.' She grins. 'That's right. She's certainly growing into the Barnacle bit. Crusty and clinging. Here, poppet.' She reaches down with her sleeve and swipes at her daughter's nose. 'My partner's writing about Joyce,' she says. 'I'm Dea.' The woman looks up, smiling. 'So, what happens next?'

Lissa

Her head hurts and her tongue feels swollen. The pint glass beside her bed is empty – she must have woken and drunk it all at some point during the night. She didn't eat after rehearsals, going straight to the pub with the other actors, and

112

was three glasses of wine down before realizing how hungry she was. By then the pub kitchen was closed, so she had two packets of crisps for her dinner.

From her bed she can see through the window, out to where rain falls dully on to the sodden garden. There must have been a strong wind as the trees have lost many of their leaves. At least the park on the other side of the wall is quiet – you can usually hear the chatter from early on a Saturday, but today the weather has obviously kept the crowds at bay.

She hauls herself out of bed, pulls on her old dressing gown and pads through to the kitchen, filling the glass from the tap and drinking it straight down. She rummages in the cupboard for ibuprofen but finds only an empty packet. A further search turns up a couple of paracetamol, which she swallows gratefully. The fridge yields a lump of Cheddar, badly wrapped and hard, and a bit of butter, knife-gouged and jam-stained. She takes the cheese and nibbles on it, staring out at the rain.

When Declan used to visit, it would send him mad, this habit of hers, of not replacing things, not using things up properly, or putting lids back on empty jars. Once, during the last stint of his living here, she came home from work to find five almost-empty Marmite jars piled up on the little kitchen table with a note beside them: *See what I mean?*

It was a strange thing about Declan – how he came across as so easy when you met him, loose-limbed and wolf-grinned, happy to sink several Guinnesses in the pub with you, to sit up polishing off a wrap of cocaine, but it was always she somehow that was the messy one – always she that drank more than him and didn't remember the night before. He would be up and out and running around the park, even on a few hours' sleep. He liked discipline, did Declan. He liked a clean kitchen. He liked a hairless vagina. He had a streak of cruelty which cut through the craic and kept you in your place. She thinks of Michael, that conversation on the first day of rehearsal – *If I could have anyone's career, it would be his.*

She'd lied. Of course she'd seen the film. She's watched them all. Several times. Declan's a brilliant actor. He makes clever choices. He works with who he wants. He's such a good actor she can watch his films and forget who it is and forget that she hates him for a while.

She pulls up the hood on her dressing gown and rolls herself a cigarette, lights it at the table, takes two puffs and puts it out in disgust.

She wants to be touched. When was the last time anyone touched her? When was the last time she had sex? She doesn't even want sex. She just wants to be touched. She might wither if she isn't touched soon. She's no good at being single. Good single people plan for the weekend – they know the wretchedness of this ambush and head it off at the pass with yoga and brunch dates and exhibitions and dinners – but she has nothing planned, only a hangover and her own company and the long day ahead.

She considers going back to bed and attempting sleep again, but that feels even more depressing, so she makes herself some tea and brings it into the living room. The blinds are drawn and she leaves them that way.

Her eye falls on the Bergman DVD and she remembers Nathan's face in the library cafe, laughing at her as she scrawled on her hand with his pen.

Do they discuss her together – he and Hannah?

Lissa's thinking of doing a PhD. Oh hahahahahahahaaa.

She takes out her phone and scrolls back to the brief text exchange.

Thanks for the Bergman. Loved it. Liss. X
I'm glad. Hope you got yourself a notebook. See you in the library sometime. Nx

Since then she has been back to the library a couple of times, got herself a reader's card, ordered up some books on Russian history. She likes it there, likes putting her possessions in the locker, likes drinking good coffee in the cafe. She looks for him, often, but has not seen him there again.

Her bag is on the sofa beside her, contents spilling out: script, scarf, tobacco, phone. She pulls the script towards her. It is folded open at the scene they were working on yesterday, she and Johnny, the scene where Yelena berates Vanya on behalf of all men: *You recklessly destroy forests, all of you, and soon there won't be anything left standing on the face of the earth.*

It is only the end of the first week and yet there is already an atmosphere in the rehearsal room. Klara is prone to outbursts, flying off the handle at the slightest provocation. Greg, the actor playing Astrov, was half an hour late on Thursday, a doctor's appointment for his son having overrun. He was screamed at and told he would be sacked if it happened again.

Usually, by this stage, at the end of the first week, there is a sense of how things are going, but this time she cannot tell – yesterday, for instance, when she was working through Yelena's monologue, the director's expression was one of barely contained disdain, ultimately erupting in her banging the table. 'Stop this microwaved emotion!'

Microwaved emotion, it is rapidly becoming clear, is Klara's favourite phrase. They went on to try the monologue several different ways but each time Klara shook her head, muttering under her breath. Yet when it came to Johnny's turn, Vanya's speech to Yelena – *You're my happiness, my life, you're my youth . . . let me look at you, let me listen to your voice* – Klara sat back, nodding, murmuring her assent. If she were a cat, she would have purred.

There is no denying that Johnny is a superb actor. Last night she heard Greg raving to Michael in the pub about a performance he'd seen Johnny give twenty years ago in Liverpool – *Best Hamlet of his generation. Made me want to be an actor. Total fucking tragedy he's not a star.*

Despite the fact that most of the men and most of the women in the cast seem to seek his approval in some unspoken way, Johnny keeps himself to himself. He didn't stay long at the pub last night, just the one pint, which he drank at the bar in the company of Richard, the older actor playing Sereb-ryakov. He is careful with his energies, unlike the others, who spill over already into easy intimacies, into kisses and hugs and the swapping of tales. As he left she overheard him telling Richard that he had his kids this weekend. *They always want to go to soft play – it's hell on earth with a hangover.*

She has no idea what Johnny thinks of her. His expression is unreadable. Yesterday, when she was rehearsing alone with Klara, she saw Johnny slip quietly into the room. He stayed at the back silently watching her – those blue eyes, the calm intensity of his gaze.

116

A thought comes to her, and as it does she slides down further on the sofa, opens her dressing gown, reaches into her knickers and puts her hand to her crotch. She closes her eyes and thinks of herself standing there, alone on the stage, and of Johnny watching her, of taking off her clothes for him, one slow layer at a time. And his face, his blue eyes, the way he watches, the way he wants her – and then it is not Johnny, it is Nathan, Nathan sitting in Johnny's place, at the back of the room, watching her, wanting her, and her standing naked now, and she is coming, coming into her hand.

She lies there, gathering her breath, staring up at the ceiling.

Then she curls over herself, groans and pushes her head into the cushion with shame.

Hannah

'Shall we do something this weekend?'

Nathan is standing in the shower. It is the second day after the transfer. The door to the terrace is open, and autumn sunshine streams into the flat.

'Like what?' he calls over the water.

'Like – I don't know – get out of London? Go to the countryside. The sea.'

'Yeah, why not? Oh, wait . . .' He turns off the shower and reaches for a towel. 'I've got that paper to turn around for publication.'

She watches him towel himself dry, stretch in a shaft of sun. He comes towards her. 'You look well,' he says.

'I feel it.'

117

He tastes of coffee and toothpaste and soap.

'But you should,' he calls behind him, as he goes into the bedroom and pulls out a pair of boxers and jeans from the chest of drawers. 'Get out, I mean. Why don't you go and see someone? See Cate? Go to Canterbury? Or – what's that place by the sea? Nearby? The one with the oysters?'

'Whitstable.'

'Yeah, that's it.' He comes back over towards her, buttoning up his jeans. 'Why not go there?'

'Maybe.'

'Wait. Can you eat oysters? If you're—?'

'Oh. No,' she says, closing her eyes, warmth inside, warmth without. 'No, I don't think you can.'

In the end she does nothing – finding that she does not want to stray far from home after all. But as she goes about her weekend, she thinks of the embryos inside her. Often, she takes out the photograph and stares at it, tracing them with her finger, those two points of light, surrounded by an immensity of dark.

On Monday, the fourth day, they call. She is in a meeting, and feels her phone buzz in her bag. She excuses herself, goes out into the corridor and answers.

'I'm sorry,' the nurse says. 'Nothing has been frozen. The other embryos were not doing well.'

'Oh,' says Hannah. 'Thank you.'

The pulse, the flicker of life. Gone out.

'What happens?' she says softly. 'To the other embryos? Can you tell me?'

'I . . .' The nurse falters. She sounds very young. 'They're . . . disposed of, I imagine. I'm sorry, no one's ever—'

'It's OK,' says Hannah. 'Thanks.'

On the sixth day, a Wednesday, she goes to meet Lissa at the theatre. She gets out of the Tube at Embankment and walks slowly over Hungerford Bridge, where dusk is falling and the lights are jaunty in the river.

The clear days have continued and the nights are crisp. She pulls her coat tighter around her, weaving around the buskers, finding a pound for a young girl who sits at the top of the stairs. She tries to remember what play they are going to see. A family drama. Lissa's choice. Theatre rather than cinema this time. In truth, she does not want to go inside. She would like to keep walking, this clear autumn evening, carefully, carefully along the river – a pilgrim, carrying her lights inside her. How long would it take to reach the sea?

The Long Bar is thronged. A jazz band plays in the corner. Hannah scans the space for Lissa, and finds her eventually, tucked away on a leather bench by the picture window, the remains of an espresso on the table in front of her. Her head is bent over a script, her pencil poised, her mouth moving soundlessly. Hannah touches her shoulder and she jumps. 'Oh, hey.' Lissa rises and kisses her cheek. She is wearing a little more make-up than usual; her long hair is pinned on top of her head with Japanese combs. She looks extraordinarily like her mother. Hannah perches beside her on the bench.

'Did you have the thingy?' says Lissa.

'The transfer. Yes.'

'And how did it go?'

'Good, I think. I hope. Is this your script? How's it going?'

'Oh, OK,' says Lissa, frowning, folding the script in half and putting it in her bag. 'She's tough. The director. I mean, I knew she was going to be, but she really is. I'm not sure she thinks I'm any good.'

Hannah looks past Lissa, to the wide river outside, the winking lights.

'It's just so . . . gladiatorial,' Lissa is saying. 'Having to prove yourself every minute, every day. There's nowhere to hide. And the guy playing Vanya. He's brilliant – but I just don't know where I am with him.'

Oh Lissa, she wants to say. *You chose this. Are actors never happy?*

What she says is, 'Sure, I understand.'

The bell rings for the performance. Lissa lifts the tickets from her bag and Hannah follows her into the dark mouth of the theatre.

The play is long, the cast large, the tickets cheap and the seats far from the stage. Hannah can't keep track of who is who, and the action seems to be happening in a little box very far away.

In the interval they go outside and wander without speaking over to the river wall.

Lissa takes out her pouch of tobacco. 'Do you mind?'

Hannah shakes her head. Lissa rolls and lights up and blows the smoke away from them both. They fall silent, watching the water. Beneath them the small beach has appeared, its sand and rocks glistening in the half-light. Hannah breathes in the tang of mud and salt and dirt.

'I'm thinking of studying,' Lissa says, 'thinking of making some changes in my life.'

'Oh?' Hannah brings herself back. She remembers then. 'Didn't you see Nath at the library? A few weeks ago? I'm sure he mentioned something about it.'

Lissa nods as a thin stream of smoke leaves her mouth.

'Something about a PhD?'

'Yeah. Maybe.'

'What would you want to do with it?'

Lissa shrugs. 'I'm not sure. I've been doing some reading.'

'Really, Liss?' Hannah pulls her coat close around her. 'If I had a fiver for every overqualified person with a PhD who applies for an internship . . .'

Lissa gives a brief laugh. 'You'd be rich. I know.' She turns to where the interval crowds are making their way back inside. 'We should go back.'

'Would you mind . . . ?' says Hannah. 'I'm really tired. Do you mind if I don't?' She wants to go home, to keep herself close, she doesn't want to spill a drop.

Lissa takes a quick last drag, then chucks her cigarette over the wall. 'Sure,' she says. She leans in, a quick hug. 'You look after yourself, Han.'

Hannah walks towards the steps, up to Waterloo Bridge. She waits for her bus. Thinks of the river beneath her, fast-flowing, thinks of its course – out through Wapping, out beyond the Thames Barrier, out, out, salt and sweet water swirling as its wide mouth meets the sea.

As the days go on she can feel it, she is sure of it. Traction. A catching. The points of light have buried themselves inside her and taken root. Her breasts are heavier. There is a fullness inside her that was not there before.

'It's happening,' she says to Nathan over breakfast, on the morning of the eighth day.

He reaches over and takes her hand. He is smiling, but it does not reach his eyes.

'What?' says Hannah. 'What's wrong?'

'Nothing's wrong, I just – don't want to get my hopes up.'

'Really? Why?'

'Hannah, please.'

'I'm telling you.' She grips his hand. 'I can feel it. It's happening. I *know*.'

On the afternoon of the eleventh day, when she goes to the toilet at work, there is a trace of blood in her knickers, tiny, but there.

She looks away. Looks back again. She wants to scream but she tries to breathe.

It is nothing. It is normal. She goes back to her desk and googles 'blood post IVF'. Her search leads her to the message boards, where she reads the blood could be a good thing – *implantation bleeding*. Meaning she is right, and they are burying themselves inside her, those twin points of light.

She does not visit the toilet again. She holds on for the rest of the day. She works on a report. She takes a conference call with the States during which she smiles and nods and takes diligent, copious notes. There will be no more blood. It is nothing, it is normal, it has worked. Everything is fine. *Itisnothingitisnormalithasworkedeverythingisfine.*

On the Tube journey home every bump of the carriage makes her wince, and there is pain now, deep in her abdomen, a claw tracing its way along her womb. By the time she reaches home she can hold off no longer. Her knickers are soaked with blood. It is over. It is done.

She is curled up on their bed when Nathan returns from work.

'Hey.' He kisses her.

'I'm bleeding,' she says to him.

'What? Oh God. Oh Han, I'm sorry.' He does not sound surprised.

'You're sorry?' Her voice is dull. 'Who for? For me? For you? For our child? Who doesn't exist?'

'All of it. You, mostly, Han.' He lies on the bed behind her, fits himself to her back, laces his arm around her waist. 'Are you OK? How long have you been here?'

'An hour. Or two.'

'You're cold,' he says, holding her closer.

And she is aware of her body suddenly, of how he is right – how cold she is, how it has grown cold.

'Oh, Hannah.' He puts his cheek on her shoulder. 'Oh Han, my love.'

The next morning she is hunched at her computer before Nathan wakes.

'What's going on?' he says, coming into the room, dropping a kiss on her head.

'I've found a clinic. Harley Street.'

She feels his fingers grip her shoulders. 'Hannah—'

'Please,' she says. 'Just look.' She gestures to the pictures of babies on the screen.

'No.' He moves away, over to the window.

'Nathan—'

'*No*, Hannah. You promised. You promised this would be the last time.'

'This man is the best. He's—'

'Hannah. I'm not listening to this.'

'Why?' She is standing, fists clenched. 'Why?'

'Hannah? Can't you just . . . Just let me . . . Can I hug you? Please?'

'Why? Why do you want to hug me?'

'Hannah. God, Han. Why do you think?'

'I'm going,' she says. 'I've made an appointment. I'll pay for it. Come with me. Please. Just – come.'

True North

1987–92

They are suspicious of each other. They know of each other's existence because they got the first and second highest marks in English last year, and these things are talked about. But they have not shared any classes together, until now. And here they are in the same classroom. Top set English, Miss Riley. They are twelve years old.

Miss Riley has long curly hair and glasses like Su Pollard from Hi-de-Hi! She passes round a poem by Thomas Hardy. Who would like to read first? She looks over the faces. They are in one of those prefab classrooms, the mouldy ones built after the war.

Hannah and Cate do not, this first day, put up their hands. They watch each other like snipers, each waiting for the other to make the first move. When the poem has been (badly, haltingly) read out loud by someone else Miss Riley lifts her face to her class.

Right then. Cate? Can you tell me what this poem is about?

She is not particularly pretty, Hannah thinks, this girl who got a full 5 per cent more than her or anyone in the English exam – 97 per cent. She has a round face. In an era in which girls wear their socks ruched around their ankles and hoist their skirts above the regulation height, Cate wears her skirt at the ordinary length. Her hair is cut to just above her shoulders and she is a little bit overweight. But she has something about her that Hannah doesn't have the words for, something going on under the surface, some force.

It's about love, says Cate. And losing that love. He loves his wife and she's gone.

Good. Anyone else?

Hannah raises her hand. Her hand feels hot.

Yes, Hannah?

She's dead, she says.

How can you tell?

She's dissolved to wan wistlessness. Heard no more again far or near. She's a ghost.

Yes.

But he's feeling bad. He's feeling guilty about something. You can tell by the metre, by the way it stumbles, changes in the last stanza. It doesn't end well.

Excellent! Miss Riley beams.

And Cate, from the other side of the room, stares at this triumphant girl, her long dark hair, her eyes intent, like a bird's.

The game is on: from that day forth they are locked in vicious, ecstatic rivalry.

After a certain time has elapsed – half a year or so – they go on a school trip together and end up sitting side by side in the coach on the way to Styal Mill. They get along surprisingly well. The next weekend Hannah stuns Cate with an invitation to tea, and Cate surprises Hannah by accepting.

Hannah's house is small, a semi on a council estate off the Parrs Wood Road. It has a long garden out the back. It still has a hatch between the tiny kitchen and the dining room, through which Hannah's mum passes oven chips and Angel Delight.

Hannah's room is tiny – smaller than her brother James's, even though he is younger. The injustice of this makes Hannah fulminate.

Her parents go to church and Hannah is expected to go too, every Sunday morning. She often takes books to read in the sermon. After she tells Cate this, Cate lends her a copy of Forever by Judy Blume, backed in William Morris wallpaper and made to look like an innocuous book of poems. I've turned down the corners of the good bits, she says.

Next Sunday, while the vicar drones on, Hannah opens it and reads:

He rolled over on top of me and we moved together again and again and it felt so good I didn't ever want to stop until I came.

Hannah grins, and begins to understand that the force she saw running beneath Cate's mild exterior, although she does not have the words for it yet, is subversion. She is a girl with a rebel heart.

Cate's house is an Edwardian semi in Didsbury, on the other side of the Parrs Wood Road, with four big bedrooms and a garden. She has a mum and dad and an older sister, Vicky, who is seventeen and stalks the landing like a wrathful deity.

Cate's mum is a nurse, pretty and round. She has long red hair which falls around her face and freckles scattered over her nose. She laughs a lot. She makes her own bread. Hannah has never eaten homemade bread before. Cate's dad is tall and has a beard, and when he is around he plays music in the living room; he has a collection of old vinyl and plays Bob Dylan and Paul Simon and Cat Stevens. Sometimes, after tea, they put on music and dance in the kitchen. Cate's mum is a really good dancer. So is her dad. Sometimes they dance close to each other, sometimes they laugh and kiss. Hannah has never seen parents touch each other before. Cate's sister, if she ever witnesses this display, rolls her eyes. For fuck's sake, she says. Leave it out.

Compared to her own parents, Cate's mum and dad seem young.

Cate's family vote Labour. Hannah's vote Conservative.

Cate's family have Zola and Updike. Hannah's have Reader's Digest and the Encyclopaedia Britannica.

Cate's dad does something to do with engineering. Hannah's dad works at Christie Hospital as a porter.

Cate's family have olive oil. Hannah's have salad cream.

When they are thirteen Cate's mum becomes ill. She loses weight and loses her hair and experiments with scarves. Sometimes she comes to pick Cate up at the school gate but Cate wishes she wouldn't. She wishes she could walk straight past the strange thin woman with the headscarf and the earrings and the lipstick, who is trying too hard, whose teeth are too big in her face.

After a while, though, her mother gets better. Her hair grows back, though a little differently, a little more thinly than before. Cate's dad still plays music, but they don't dance in the kitchen any more.

When they are sixteen Cate puts a picture of Patti Smith on her wall, a life-sized poster of the cover of Horses. She got it at the Corn Exchange in town. They go to Affleck's Palace and search the musty rails for jackets like Patti's. Hannah actually suits the look better, as she has no breasts to speak of yet. All that summer, on Monday nights they tell Hannah's mum she *is having a sleepover at Cate's and they take the bus into town to the Ritz, where they jump up and down on the bouncy dance floor to the Pixies and Nirvana and R.E.M. Cate wears tutus and DM boots and stripy tops with frayed edges. Hannah wears long patchwork skirts and DMs. If she pushed it any further, her mum would have a heart attack. As it is, when she applies kohl pencil her mum nearly has a fit.*

They go to a small town to the west of Paris on their French exchange and come back speaking halfway decent French. They walk on Saturdays, arm in arm in Fletcher Moss Park, where they practise speaking French in loud voices. They test each other on past exam questions.

How is Emma Bovary responsible for her own downfall? Or do the nature of provincial society and the people around her make her unhappiness inevitable?

Their English teacher that year is a dedicated, energetic woman who believes in social mobility, in empowering girls. She suggests that they both apply for Oxford and she puts in extra time in the evenings, tutoring them both for the exam. They enter a new era of competition, spurring each other on.

One Saturday morning Cate's mother falls, crumpled over herself in the cereal aisle in Asda. She goes back into hospital and Cate stays at Hannah's, on a camp bed in Hannah's room. At night, when Hannah is asleep, Cate lies beneath the duvet and looks at Hannah, cocooned in her sleep, in her security, and feels horror waiting for her in the dark.

She goes to see her mum in the hospice the week before she dies. Her mum's eyes are enormous. She seems to take up so little room on the bed. The room smells sharp and thick at the same time. Oh, her mother says, when Cate comes into the room. It sounds as if someone is pressing her stomach, letting out all the air. Cate walks slowly towards her. She thinks this is probably the last time she will see her mother. Part of her wants to laugh; she puts her hand to her mouth and presses it to stop the laugh from coming out.

Here you are, says her mother as she gathers Cate to her. Here you are.

After the funeral Cate's sister Vicky moves into her boyfriend's house. And now it is just Cate and her father, rattling around at home. Her father gives up cooking, and Cate often forgets to eat. She stops writing essays for the extra Oxford classes. Hannah is simultaneously horrified, appalled for her friend and, in a small uncharitable place, relieved.

They apply for their colleges. Since neither they nor their teacher know anything about the university, they choose them randomly – Hannah hers because it looks the most beautiful, Cate hers because it says it takes the largest number of state-school pupils each year. They take the exam. They are both invited up for interview, one dank weekend in November. Hannah is given a room looking over a quadrangle, which is misted in the morning and makes her heart rise with the beautiful future that seems to breathe from its walls. Cate is in modern accommodation round the back of the dining hall. Her window backs on to a ventilation shaft and the smell of cooking infuses her room.

They get their letters a month later, just at the start of the Christmas holidays. They call each other, as they have arranged they will. They open the letters. Hannah looks down at hers in disbelief.

Cate looks at hers. Shit, she says. Oh shit.

Cate

'Morning, my little soldier!'

Despite the early hour, Alice is her usual immaculate self: gilet, hair, ironed jeans. 'How's my little soldier doing today? Are you ready for our date?!'

Tom grins and flaps his hands and makes eyes. 'Good,' Cate says. 'He's good. We're good.'

'Have you got a kiss?' Alice swoops on Tom. 'Have you got a kiss for Grandma?'

Tom lunges delightedly for his grandmother. 'Terry's in the garden.' Alice takes Tom into her arms. 'Terrible wind last night.' She nods through the window to where Sam's father is wrestling gamely with a leaf blower. The three of them regard him for a moment in silence. Terry seems to be creating as much mess as he is managing to contain.

'I never know quite what they do,' Cate ventures. 'Those things.'

'They clean up the leaves,' says Alice.

'Ah. Yes.'

Terry looks up, sees them and manages a wild wave, while Tom kicks and bucks in Alice's arms. 'He wants to be with the big boys,' says Alice. 'I'll take him out for a bit. And we'll see you later.'

Cate swallows down her horror; her tiny son, that stupid machine. 'Whatever you think.'

'I think,' says Alice crisply, 'that it will do him good.'

Cate waits at the bus stop but no bus comes, and so she walks down the hill into town, the cathedral ahead of her. She has five hours to fill – five hours in which she can do anything, within reason. She could take the train to Charing Cross, go to the National Portrait Gallery. Look at the Sickerts. The Vanessa Bells. Walk up St Martin's Lane, through Covent Garden, go to the Oxfam bookshop at the bottom of Gower Street, buy a cheap paperback and sit in one of the squares with it, begin to feel the old contours of herself.

She knows what she should do – go home, wash tea towels and Babygros and chef's whites. Fold clothes. Unpack boxes. Finish moving into her house. But she does none of these things – instead she walks, her feet finding the old Pilgrims' Way, in through the city walls, down Northgate, Palace Street.

At the cathedral entrance the inevitable line of foreign students and international Christians wait to go inside. Cate ducks into Pret, where she buys a coffee and a pastry and sits in the window looking out at the half-timbered heart of the city. There are stalls selling tourist tat, baseball caps with LONDON emblazoned on them. Sweet shops selling gobstoppers and rhubarb and custards with 1950s lettering over their fronts. Red-jacketed young men cruise the crowd, selling punting trips, touting for business. All the ersatz thrills of Merrie twenty-first-century England.

Her eyes are caught by a small stall amidst the throng, a banner along the front reading: PROTEST TUITION FEE HIKES. VOTE 10TH DECEMBER.

A young woman stands in front of it, handing out leaflets, her hair long and dyed pink. Cate watches the way she talks to passers-by. Her small frame wrapped in a large jumper. The animation on her face. She reminds her of Lucy.

Despite checking her emails almost hourly, Cate has heard nothing back from Hesther yet.

When she has finished her coffee, Cate goes outside, approaching the stall shyly.

'May I have one?' she says to the young woman with the pink hair, pointing to the leaflets.

'Of course,' smiles the young woman, taking one and pressing it into Cate's hand. 'Do you want to sign the petition too?'

'Sure.' Cate leans in and does so, and then, suddenly self-conscious, and with no real idea of what to do next, mumbles a goodbye and moves away, joining the queue for the cathedral. It is ten pounds to go inside. She baulks, but pulls out her wallet and pays with her card. A cobbled road leads to the cathedral entrance and the building itself rears ahead. She goes inside, to the nave, where the roof soars above her and sweet-faced tabard-wearing guides stand selling guidebooks. She moves away, past the racks of candles, over to the far wall, reading the inscriptions on tombs set into the stone. They are a maudlin scrapbook of colonial misadventure: young men dead at Waterloo, in India, in West and South Africa, all the way up to the greatest hits of the First and Second World Wars. Tattered black flags hang from the walls. Somewhere in the distance is the sound of an organ. She stops before an oval-shaped monument, tomb of a certain Robert Macpherson Cairnes, Major of Royal Horse Artillery, 'taken from this sublunary scene June the 18th 1815 aged 30'.

This humble monument
erected by the hand of friendship
is a faithful, but very inadequate, testimony
of affection, and grief which no language can express,
of affection which lives beyond the tomb,
of grief which will never terminate
till those who now deplore his loss
shall rejoin him
in the blest realms
of
everlasting peace.

All these boys. All these mothers. All that grief. And here, no apology for any of it. It would be nice if somewhere, even on a tiny little plaque, it read: *Sorry. We got it wrong. All that colonialism and empire and slaying our children. All that God. Lands grabbed. Resources plundered. Patriarchy upheld. Church and military hand in hand.*

Who's a little soldier then?

She wants her son back. Wants to run up the hill to Harbledown and snatch him from his grandmother's arms. It is suddenly difficult to breathe. She hurries out through the side door into the cloisters, where the wind bites and the grass of the quadrangle is a deep green. She sinks to a stone bench carved into the wall and takes great gulps of air. And it comes to her, why she doesn't like this city: it reminds her of Oxford – the churches, the tourists, the grass on which you cannot walk. Even down to the punts, generations of students taking to the river, grasping for the *Brideshead* dream.

Evelyn Waugh was a fascist and a sentimentalist. Discuss.

She hated that fucking book.

There are footsteps on the flagstones. Cate looks up, sees a figure moving towards her, walking quickly. She is wearing a large man's coat, a beanie hat pushed down on her head, but Cate recognizes her from the playgroup and pulls back against the stone wall – she does not want to be seen today, but it is too late.

'Oh,' says Dea. 'Hey, hi! Cate, isn't it?' She smiles, stretches out a gloved hand. Her face is tired, wind-blown. 'I didn't recognize you at first. Without the baby. Where is he today?'

'With my mother-in-law. In Harbledown.'

'That's good.' Dea puts her head on one side. 'You don't look sure. Is that good?'

'Oh, no – it is. It's just the first time that I've left him. It's all a bit strange.'

'I know what you mean,' says Dea, nodding. 'I have the day to myself on Tuesdays. I look forward to it all week, and I'm supposed to be working, but I just . . .' She pulls a face.

'What's your work?'

'Church art. I'm writing a book. But it's taking me forever.'

'What sort of church art?'

'Some of it right here.' Dea points to the roof and Cate

looks up. At first she doesn't know what she is looking at but then, 'Here' – Dea takes her by the elbow – 'see that Green Man? And the mermaid?'

It is hard to see at first, but as Cate looks closer the details emerge – not just Green Men, but coiled dragons, lizards, shepherds with pipes. 'Oh,' she says. 'Yes. You'd never know they were there.'

'Exactly! I like to think of them as little nodes of subversion. Pagan deities holding up the buttresses of the established church.' Dea looks back. 'Did I actually just say that? Sorry.' She gives a rueful smile.

A chill wind is funnelling around the cloisters. 'It's cold,' says Dea. 'Shall we go back to mine? It's just around the corner. We can have some tea.'

'Sure.'

They walk out of the cathedral, past the stall manned by the students, where Dea stops for a second to speak to the pink-haired girl. Cate hangs back, watching as the girl proudly shows Dea the list of signatures.

'She's one of my students, or she was before I took maternity leave,' says Dea as she rejoins Cate. 'We're asking our Vice Chancellor to speak out about the tuition fees, but I don't think she will. It's interesting, though – all these kids. They're really taking a stand. I'm proud.'

Dea's house is close, just off the high street – tucked in a terrace of similar small houses. The front door is painted a muted grey-green; beside it, a window box blooms with late crimson flowers. The narrow hall is a tangle of coats and scarves. Dea leads her through into a kitchen at the back, where the house opens up and becomes light-filled and welcoming. A tall black woman with a loose Afro stands at the stove.

'Hey, Zo.' Dea unwinds her scarf. 'This is Cate. I met her at Playmaggedon. That terrible group I told you about. And I just bumped into her in the cathedral.'

The woman turns. Everything about her is long: long limbs, long neck, long fingers laced around a mug. She is surpassingly beautiful. 'Nice to meet you, Cate, I'm Zoe.' Her accent is American; Cate thinks she hears the sounds of the south. Dea wanders over to the stove and kisses Zoe. Cate watches Zoe's hand briefly linger on Dea's back.

'Take a seat, Cate,' says Zoe. 'Excuse the mess.'

Cate perches on the seat of a battered sofa, which is covered with throws and cushions. Sunlight slants in from the window behind, warming her back. Kilner jars compete for shelf space with books and toys and bottles, glinting in the sunlight. More books lie in piles on every other surface. A biography of Louise Bourgeois is being used as a plant stand. There is dust on the dado rails and the floorboards are scuffed. Washing-up is piled in the sink. The sight of the dirty plates invokes in Cate a mild but profound sense of relief. 'Have you lived here long?' she asks.

'Five years.' Dea shakes herbs into a pot. 'We were in the States before that. I was teaching at a university out there, which is where we met. But I'm a Kent girl. I grew up just outside the city. What about you? Have you been in Canterbury a while?'

'Almost two months. We moved when Tom was five months old.'

'That can't have been easy.'

'It was OK,' Cate lies.

'Where are you living?'

'Over the other side of town. Wincheap way.'

'I know it over there,' says Dea. 'We have an allotment, round the back of Toddler's Cove.'

'Well, lovely to meet you, Cate,' says Zoe. 'I'm just off to do a little work while Nora naps.'

'Oh, the spacious joys of a funded PhD.'

'Oh, the joys of fully paid maternity leave,' says Zoe, blowing Dea a kiss. 'Hey,' she says, turning at the door. 'You should set something up, you two. Something chilled. Something where mothers get together.'

'We're doing it.' Dea walks over with a cup of tea and hands it to Cate. 'Aren't we, Cate? This is it. This is our group. Right here. Right now.'

'Er . . . yeah, I guess so,' says Cate. She lifts her tea – it is pale yellow and gently fragrant. Small flowers float on the surface.

Dea slides herself on to the sofa beside Cate. 'Mum Club. The only rule of Mum Club is that we don't talk about Mum Club. Right?'

Zoe laughs and rolls her eyes. 'I'll leave you two to it,' she says with a wave.

When Zoe has gone, Dea turns to Cate. 'Chocolate biscuit? I've got a stash.'

'Um. Sure.'

Dea reaches into the cupboard behind her and takes out a tin. 'Amazing the stuff you find yourself buying when you become a mum. I'd forgotten how delicious chocolate fingers are.' Cate leans in and takes one.

'So . . .' says Dea. 'How are you doing, Cate?'

'I'm . . .' Cate falters, taken aback, her mouth full of biscuit. 'I'm OK,' she says.

'We tell the truth in Mum Club,' says Dea reprovingly. 'I'll go first. Ask me. Ask me how I'm doing.'

'Um . . . how are you doing, Dea?'

'Hmm. Let's see.' Dea closes her eyes for a moment. 'Well, I sleep on average five hours a night. I used to be a person that slept for eight or more. If I didn't get my sleep I would freak out. I'm still that person, somewhere inside, but I don't think I've completed a full sleep cycle since my daughter was born. My knee has flared up. It's an old injury, exacerbated by lugging my daughter in a sling, which seemed like the best and most wonderful thing to do when she was three weeks old and now is feeling like a less good idea. But it's the only place that she'll sleep. So. My boobs are enormous. I was told they would go down. They haven't gone down. My left shoulder has seized up. I'm assailed night and day by visions of horrors: my daughter falling, my daughter hurting herself, someone hurting her. I can't listen to the news without crying or switching it off. I haven't had sex since my daughter was born.'

Cate smiles.

'You think it's funny?'

Dea sips her tea. The chocolate fills Cate's mouth with sweetness.

'There's more, but – you know. I can keep it till next time. Now,' Dea says, turning to Cate. 'Tell me. How are you?'

She has made pasta and tomatoes; olive oil, a little bit of chilli. A knuckle of Parmesan she forgot she had at the back of the fridge is grated over the top. A portion for Tom in his little green bowl is ready to go, and a bottle of red is open on the table.

The door goes and she hears Sam hang up his coat in the hall. 'Hey.' He sniffs the air. 'Something smells good.'

'I thought I'd make some food.' She scoops Tom up from where he has been playing on the floor. 'C'mon, poppet. Come and try some pasta.'

The pasta is rather successful. Tom proves surprisingly adept at fingering farfalle and sucking off the sauce. When the meal is finished, when she and Sam have both had a glass and a half of wine each, Sam offers to give Tom his bath and Cate sits at the table, listening to them giggling and singing together. When the bath is done Sam brings him back down, his hair curly and wet, and she kisses his forehead. 'Who's my boy?' she says. 'Who's my lovely boy?'

'Shall I get him in his PJs?' says Sam.

'Yes, please.'

When she collected Tom from Alice's he was happy and calm.

She rises and does the washing-up, wipes down the table, and pours herself another half glass of wine.

The truth?

Yeah. We tell the truth.

The way Dea had said it, as though she wanted to hear the answer. As though anything other than the truth would not be good enough.

The truth is I'm scared too.

Go on. What of?

Of everything. All the time. I'm lonely. I'm in pain. I still can't

140

deal with the fact that they sliced me open. I feel like a failure. As a woman. As a mother. I get everything wrong. My mother isn't here. I miss her. I realize I've always missed her. She didn't prepare me at all. I'm angry that she left me on my own. I'm not coping. Not coping. No one told me it would be like this.

I think I married the wrong person.

She didn't say the last bit, but she said all the rest. Once it started, it didn't stop. And Dea sat there, listening – the simple, heady oxygen of being listened to.

So. Same time next week? Mum Club?

Yeah. Same time next week.

'Hey.' Sam comes into the room. 'Tom seems on good form. Did it go well with Mum then?'

'Oh,' says Cate. 'Yeah.' She drains her glass. 'I think it's going to work.'

Lissa

They are going to play a game, Klara says. Although it is a serious game, a *technique*, a technique for getting *out of the skin*. They need this technique because they are stiff. They are stiff in an English way. Not like the Russians. The Russians are not stiff, not at all. They have vodka and grief and the blood of the land in their veins, and the English have weak tea and the damp.

So.

The director stares around the room – her cast is assembled before her, a full roll call. It is first thing Monday morning, the beginning of the third week.

'Leesa.' She narrows her eyes. 'You are stiff. Always you are stiff. See how you sit? What does Vanya say about Yelena?' She turns to Johnny. 'About the way she is?'

'*If you could see the way you look*,' says Johnny, fixing Lissa with his eyes. '*The way you move. The indolence of your life. The sheer indolence of it.*'

'Thank you, Johnny. So, Leesa – does Yelena sit like this?' She crosses her hands over her lap in imitation of Lissa's posture. 'No. You are English. You are all wrong. Why did I choose English people to interpret this Russian play? I am crazy. Never again. Leesa – do you know the Meisner technique?'

Lissa nods; she does. 'We did it at drama school. Although it's years since—'

'Good. Sit here, please.'

A chair is produced and Lissa dutifully makes her way into the middle of the space and sits upon it. 'And you' – Klara turns on her heel and points to Michael – 'you are also stiff. You are only on stage for five minutes but you are stiff. It is horrible. Come here.'

Michael stands, runs his hand through his hair. He is grinning. 'Great,' he says. 'Nice one.'

'Michael, do you know this technique?'

Michael shakes his head.

'Leesa. Describe it to Michael, please.'

Lissa crosses her legs at the ankle, then uncrosses them. 'So . . . as far as I can remember . . . it starts by one or other of us noticing something about the other person. I will notice something about you, something on the surface at first. It may be what you are wearing. I might say, *You are wearing a*

142

blue top. And you repeat it back to me. *I am wearing a blue top*. We do that for a bit, and then we go deeper—'

'Stop!' Klara slaps the desk. 'Enough explanation. Begin.'

Michael gives a quick barking laugh. Lissa takes a breath.

'Your hair,' she says, 'is . . . shaped like a quiff.'

Michael smiles. 'My hair is shaped like a quiff?' he says, giving the word a little upward tick.

'STOP.'

Michael turns towards the director.

'No *acting*.' Klara bangs the table and Poppy the ASM jumps. 'You are acting. If this is your acting, I am glad you have no lines in this play. The point is *not to act*.'

Chastened, Michael turns back to Lissa, who shoots him a compassionate look, and they begin again.

'You look pale,' says Lissa.

'I look pale.'

'You look pale.'

'I look pale.'

She can see he is frozen now, too frightened to make a move.

She remembers her teacher at drama school, a small intense man who believed passionately in this way of working. *Call what you see*, was what he always said when they used the Meisner technique. *Put your attention on the other person, look closely, and call what you see.* 'You look scared,' she says to Michael.

'I look scared,' Michael agrees.

'You look scared.'

The game stumbles on limply as Klara hisses and tuts and shakes her head.

143

'STOP. This is terrible. Terrible.' She waves Michael off the stage with a vicious hand.

'*Je–sus*,' he says under his breath, as he stands and hitches his jeans. 'Good luck.'

'You.' Klara twitches her head towards where Johnny sits. 'Johnny. Your turn.'

Johnny rises silently and comes to take Michael's place.

He is still, very still, for a long while, watching her. His gaze is soft. She feels it brush her shoulders, her stomach, her feet, her breasts. She is aware of her legs, tightly crossed again – when did that happen? – the position of her hands. Aware of the heat in her palms, under her armpits. She is aware of the balance of power, of how it belongs to him. Then, 'You look sad,' he says.

'I look sad,' repeats Lissa, surprised.

'You look sad.'

'I look sad.'

'You look sad.'

'I look sad.'

'You're turning red.'

'I'm turning red.'

'You're turning red.'

'I'm turning red.'

'You're upset.'

'I'm upset.'

'I've upset you.'

'I've upset you, no' – she stumbles – 'you've upset me.'

'I've upset you.'

She can feel her cheeks flaming. 'You – have a black shirt,' she says.

144

Johnny raises an eyebrow. 'I have a black shirt,' he repeats.

'STOP.' They turn to Klara, who is out of her chair now, incandescent.

'Why did you do this? Why did you talk about his *shirt*? Something was *happening*. Something was starting to happen for the first time in this stinking fucking room and you talk about his *shirt*? No. Now. Go again.'

Johnny turns back slowly, smiles at her. It is the smile of an assassin. His blue eyes barely blink. 'You're uncomfortable,' he says.

'I'm uncomfortable.'

'You're uncomfortable.'

'I'm uncomfortable.'

'I make you uncomfortable.'

'You make me uncomfortable.'

'I make you uncomfortable.'

'You make me uncomfortable.'

'You look sad.'

'I look sad.'

'You look sad.'

'I look sad.'

'You have a sad face.'

'I have a sad face.'

Her throat is tightening. There is no time to recover from the last blow before he is on to the next.

'You've lost something.'

'I've lost something.'

She can feel it – the other members of the cast, sitting forward in their seats. As the ranged faces become an audience,

145

the invisible filaments between her and them tightening, something is happening.

'You're crying.'

'I'm crying.'

'You're crying.'

'I'm crying.'

'Good!' Klara is hopping. 'Now. *Now*. Begin your scene.'

She needs fresh air. She pushes her way outside and stands in the grotty stairwell, staring up at the sky.

Michael is out there already. 'Fuck,' he says. 'That was harsh. But electric.'

Lissa says nothing.

Behind her, Johnny appears.

'Fucking electric, mate,' says Michael. Johnny ignores him. Michael nods to himself. 'Electric,' he says, into the void.

'That was rather good,' says Johnny to Lissa. 'You could be a much better actor, you know, than you allow yourself to be. If you just let go.'

She has the afternoon to herself. She does not wish to go home. Nor does she wish to stay any longer in the room and watch the rest of the day's rehearsal, and so she climbs on the rackety old bus into town: Kingsland Road, Shoreditch, Old Street, Angel, King's Cross. The sky is low and yellow, and it is starting to rain as she descends at the library. She stows her coat and bag in the lockers, flashes her reader's card at the guard on the door of Rare Books, finds a seat and sits down. In the hush she closes her eyes.

She is hollow; there is nothing inside her, nothing tethering her, not talent, not success. Johnny is right – she has lost something. Or many things. Or she never had them. She is the sum total only of her failures. She is so hollow she could float up over these people, their heads bent in industry, up and out over this city, this city that she has loved but which does not love her back, which does not give her what she needs to live, only to survive.

She is going to go downstairs and get her stuff and call her agent and tell her she is pulling out of the play, that she is giving up this excuse of a career.

She goes down to the cloakroom and collects her coat and bag, walks out across the echoing foyer towards the doors, and then she sees him. She knows it is him even though he is facing away from her. He is hunched and he is not speaking but it is clear that whoever is on the other end of the phone is speaking a great deal. Lissa hangs back, hands in the pockets of her coat. After a short time he turns off his phone and she sees him stand, perfectly still for a couple of seconds, and then look up. She goes to him and touches him on the arm. Nathan jumps.

'Lissa. Hey.'

'You OK?'

He pushes his hands through his hair. His eyes look wild. 'I just need to . . . Cigarette. Have you got one?'

'Sure.'

They make their way past the security guards, out to the

small overhang that offers a little shelter from the rain, which is falling in earnest now. She hands him the tobacco, stands back while he rolls.

'Sorry,' he says, as he puts the cigarette to his mouth.

'For what?'

He looks up at her and his eyes are startled. 'I don't know. I'm just – used to saying sorry, I suppose. Sorry for smoking. I shouldn't be smoking.'

She hands him a lighter and he flicks it gratefully, leaning his head back with the release of smoke. She takes the leather pouch from him and rolls one of her own, and their smoke mingles in the damp air. On the concourse, people hurry over concrete, which is rain-slicked now, carrying their bags and their books. 'Have you eaten?' he says.

'No.'

'There's a pub somewhere around here. Does . . . tapas or something.'

Something about the way he says 'tapas' makes her smile.

He looks disoriented as they cross the road, and she has to fight the urge to put a hand on to his arm and steer him through the traffic to safety.

'It's round here somewhere,' he says, leading her through the redbrick flats that lie to the south of the Euston Road, along a wide Georgian terrace to a dark-looking corner pub. 'I think this is it. It'll do, anyway.' He holds the door open for her. 'Drink? I'm going to have a pint. And a whisky. You want a whisky?'

There is no further mention of food. She looks at the clock above the bar – two forty-five.

'Sure,' she says. 'Why not?'

She finds them a table in the corner of the bar, tucked away from the window. He comes back with two pints of Guinness and two glasses of whisky. 'Your health.' He gulps the whisky down, chases it with a healthy swig of Guinness. Then, as though he notices her presence properly for the first time, 'How was your day?' he says.

'Awful.'

He nods grimly.

'You?' she says.

'You don't want to know.' He lifts his head to her and she sees his despair. 'It didn't work. The IVF. The last go.'

She is not surprised. She wishes she were but she is not.

'I'm lost,' he says. 'We're lost. In all of it.' He looks away to where rain has begun to dapple the window, and downs the rest of his Guinness in three open-throated gulps. 'I'm going to get another drink. You want one? Another whisky?'

'Sure.'

She fiddles with her phone when he has gone. Turns it on. Turns it off again. It is strange, she thinks, that Hannah has said nothing to her of this news. She finishes her whisky. Sips her pint.

There are two more Guinnesses when he returns, and two whiskies. 'I'll drink it, if you can't.' He gives a small smile as he slides them over the table towards her. 'So go on then, why was your day so bad? Hannah says you're in a play?'

She wants to tell him that it doesn't matter. That she doesn't want to talk about herself. 'Yes,' she says. 'I am.'

'Something Russian?'

She nods. '*Uncle Vanya*. Chekhov.'

'How's it going?'

'It's OK.'

He leans forward. 'OK? That doesn't sound too good.'

'It is. It's just . . .' She gives a small laugh. 'I don't know. I'm doubting everything today.'

'I could have said that.'

'Really?' She is silent, waiting for him to go on, watching his hands around the pint glass. His eyes – the thin skin beneath them, the curled edge of his mouth. *Call what you see.*

You're sad.

You're angry.

'I don't know.' His fingers drum the stained wood of the table. 'I just – I can't even remember why we are doing this, this thing that our lives have become. Hannah. This *constraint*. Every. Single. Fucking. Thing. Regimented. Policed. Whatever I put in my body. I see her, hovering. Watching the coffee I drink. Asking me how many drinks I've had if I go out after work. Counting. Always counting. She's become a policewoman.'

He falls silent.

'She's just trying to have a child,' says Lissa softly.

'Don't you think I know that?' He is furious now. 'But that's all she's become. She has become a creature that is trying to have a child. And it's not fucking *working*. Shouldn't a child be conceived from love? And abandon? And good sex? Not a timetable. A spreadsheet. *A graph.*'

He has said too much. She sees him step back from his words.

He looks up at her. 'Did you never want kids?' he says, in a low voice.

'I – no. Once. I mean, I was pregnant once.'

'Really?'

'Yeah.' A blurred shape on a scan photograph at the Marie Stopes clinic in Fitzrovia. The end of the first year of drama school.

'What happened?'

'I had a termination.'

'I'm sorry.'

'Don't be. Here.' She lifts her whisky to his. '*Sláinte*.' It burns her throat. 'Cigarette?' she says.

'You read my mind.'

They step outside, huddling in the doorway, taking it in turns to roll.

'Go on then,' he says again, when they are both lit. 'You still haven't told me why your day was so shit.'

'Someone . . . criticized my acting. I took it badly, I suppose.' She tries to find an anchor – the rain, the cars with their lights on. The people manoeuvring their umbrellas. She is veering rapidly towards being drunk.

'Sometimes . . . I don't feel real.' She turns to him. He is watching her. He is close. He shakes his head.

'What?' she says.

'It's just so strange to me, to hear you speak that way.'

'Why?'

'Because I always saw you as so vivid. More than real.'

She gives a small laugh.

'I remember the first time I saw you. You just – you shone. And then those parties. When we were older. That gorgeous thrift-shop raver.'

'Yeah. What was I thinking?'

'They were good, weren't they, those days? We didn't care, did we? We were free.'

He leans forward, catching her wrist in his hand. She looks down, sees his fingers, the nails trimmed haphazardly, feels a pulse in her heart, her wrist, her crotch.

'I miss that,' he says.

Call what you see.

You want me.

'Who?' she says to him, looking back up into his face. 'Who am I? To you?'

'You're beautiful, you're bright, you're wild, Lissa. You're real.' And he lifts his hands to her face, her face towards his, brings his lips to hers.

The surprise.

The lack of surprise.

Her lips parting for him. The taste of his tongue.

'Sorry,' he says, pulling away.

'No,' she says.

'I shouldn't have done that.'

'It's OK. It didn't happen.'

He shakes his head. 'Hannah,' he says, and his voice is strangled.

'It didn't happen, Nath.'

He passes his hand over his face. 'Not that. It's just – she wants to do it again. The IVF. Wants to go to another clinic. On Harley Street.'

'That must be thousands.'

'And the rest.'

'So what are you going to do?'

'I don't know.' And the despair is back, cloaking him. He looks up at her. 'What would you do?'

'Oh God.' She laughs softly. 'Don't ask me.'

'But I am,' he says. 'I am asking you. You're the first person I've managed to talk to about this. You don't know how good it is to talk. Liss. Tell me,' he pleads. 'Please. What would you do?'

'I wouldn't do it,' she says, pulling her cardigan around her, staring out at the rain-washed street. 'I'd say no.'

Hannah

They come out of the Tube at Regent's Park, walk past the cream colonnaded buildings, then along the Marylebone Road before turning into Harley Street. She walks quickly, as if by hurrying – by ushering Nathan past these mini mansions, past the huge cars disgorging skinny, headscarfed women, past the elderly ladies carrying their tiny dogs in their arms – he might not register where they are.

She rings the bell of a three-storey house, mercifully slightly less grand than those that surround it. The buzzer admits them and they step into a black-and-white flagged entrance hall, where pictures of smiling babies decorate the walls and the slim curve of a Regency staircase stretches upwards towards the light. They give their names and are shown into a waiting room the size of their flat. Squashy sofas face each other over angular tables and magazines are arranged in tight-cornered piles. A couple sit on a sofa, twenty feet away. They eye Hannah and Nathan across the room.

Nathan sits, his ankle crossed over his knee. His trainers are scuffed. His leg jiggles on the deep pile carpet. In the corner, a coffee machine gurgles. 'I'm going to get a drink,' he says, jumping up again. 'You want one?'

'No, thanks.' Hannah leans down to the table: *Tatler, Harper's Bazaar, Country Living, Elle*. She slides out *Elle* and flicks through it, aware her breath is shallow and short.

Nathan comes over with a small white plastic cup.

'This coffee's terrible,' he says accusingly. 'How much do they charge?'

'Seven thousand.' She speaks quietly, but precisely. He knows this. She knows he knows this.

'Wonder what the rent is on this place?' His voice is a little too loud. The couple on the other side of the room lift their heads. The receptionist puts her head round the door.

'Dr Gilani will see you now.'

Hannah stands, smoothing down her skirt. 'Thank you.'

Nathan follows her up the stairs. 'Nice paintings,' he says, as they pass a series of lurid abstracts.

Dr Gilani sits behind a broad desk in a huge room. He is a large, smiling bear of a man. He leans forward to greet them, grasping their hands in his paws. 'Good to meet you,' he says, and looks as though he means it. 'Please, sit down.'

'So,' he says, as they sit. 'I've been reading through your notes. As you know, Hannah, there are a large proportion of women like yourself for whom there is no known cause of infertility.'

Hannah nods.

'And the fact that you have been pregnant once already, despite the miscarriage, is a good thing. The good news is that you might still conceive at any time. The bad news is that there is nothing, other than the usual, that we can tell you to do to help. But' – he smiles – 'we are very well equipped here.'

Nathan looks around the room, as though scanning it for equipment, but the room, despite its vast size, looks empty.

Dr Gilani runs through the treatments he can offer that the NHS cannot: the time-lapse cameras, the frequent scans, the womb scraping, the egg transfers at the weekend. All of it adding up to success rates in the 30 per cent range, for patients of Hannah's age.

'What's womb scraping?' says Nathan. 'It sounds barbaric.'

'It's a technique,' says Dr Gilani, 'that has been shown to help with implantation. Here.' He passes a piece of paper over the desk. He has underlined the numbers: 32 per cent pregnancy, ages 35–38. The live birth rates that follow are lower. The fee is in small figures at the bottom of the page.

'Can you give me an idea,' says Nathan. 'A breakdown of the costs?'

Dr Gilani's smile is immovable. 'Of course, I can have my secretary prepare it.'

'It's just – it's an awful lot of money,' says Nathan. 'Isn't it? For something that is seventy per cent likely to fail.'

Hannah presses the nail of her thumb into the palm of her opposite hand.

'I understand.' Dr Gilani gives the smallest of glances to the clock on the wall. 'Many of our patients use their insurance to cover—'

'We don't have insurance,' says Nathan. 'We believe in the National Health Service.'

Hannah leans over Nathan, sweeps the paper into her bag. 'Thank you,' she says.

'So – if you decide to go ahead, please make an appointment with my secretary and we can get you started straight away.'

'Wait,' says Nathan. 'Han – don't you need time? To recover? Hannah's just had a round of IVF. She's exhausted.'

'I'm fine,' says Hannah. 'And I can speak for myself.'

'Of course' – Dr Gilani spreads his large hands – 'if you'd rather wait. But every month that you wait, of course, is a month that—'

'No,' says Hannah. 'I'd rather not wait.'

Nathan is looking out of the window, his jaw clenched. 'Thank you, Dr Gilani. You've been very helpful.'

Dr Gilani presses their hands in his.

Nathan walks in front of her down the staircase, but does not stop at the receptionist's desk. Instead he pushes his way out on to the street. By the time Hannah catches up with him he is round the corner, halfway through rolling a cigarette.

'When did you start smoking?'

'Recently. And I haven't started smoking.'

'What's this then?'

'A cigarette.'

'Were you smoking? Last cycle?'

'No, Hannah. I wasn't. But now I'd quite like a cigarette.' He lights up. She stares at him. The traffic roars. It is a grey, polluted day.

'I can't believe you,' she says.

'What can't you *believe*, Hannah?'

She casts her hand towards him.

'Oh. I disgust you, do I? Well, this' – he waves his cigarette

156

at their surroundings – 'disgusts me. All these doctors making thousands, *millions*, out of people's desperation. This is a street of quacks. You might as well go and chuck seven thousand pounds down a wishing well for all the good it will do.'

'Really?'

'Really. They're fucking faith healers, Han.'

'What about the children on that wall? They exist. Because of this doctor.'

'They might have existed anyway.'

'You don't know that.'

'No, I don't. I don't know anything. Neither do you. Neither does Doctor fucking Gilani. No one does. Because the human body is a mystery. Because fertility is a fucking *mystery*, Han.'

'There are things you can do . . .'

'We've been doing them. We've been doing every single one of those things, Hannah. For months. For years. We still don't have a baby.'

'I've been doing them. *I've* been doing those things. What have you done, Nath? Tell me. What?'

He looks at her, takes a deep drag of his cigarette. 'I'm sorry, Hannah, I really am. I want you to know that I love you, but I can't do this any more.'

'What? What can't you do?'

'This,' says Nathan.

'What does *this* mean?'

He throws the cigarette out into the street, where cars growl at the traffic lights, and shakes his head.

*

Her father meets her on the platform at Stockport. She sees him through the window before he sees her – always the momentary shock at his hesitancy, the white of his hair. As she gets down she sees his head twisting this way and that, searching for her.

'Dad,' she calls, and he turns towards her, holding out his arms.

He smells of soap and the sharpness of her mum's washing powder.

'Let me take that.' He moves for her suitcase.

'It's fine. It's not heavy.'

'Shush. Give it here. Got your ticket? There's barriers at the back now.'

The car is parked where it always is. 'Now,' he lifts her case into the boot, 'your mother's made shepherd's pie. She's worried about you, love.'

It is raining, a light drizzle. The leaves are brown; autumn is already making itself felt up here. Her mother is in the kitchen when they arrive, the windows steamed up, the dog jumping up to say hello.

'Come here.' Her mum presses her to her chest. 'You've lost weight,' she says, tutting as she hugs her.

They eat the shepherd's pie and broccoli, then fruit and cream for pudding, and after they eat they go into the living room and sit in front of the telly.

'What would you like to watch?' Her father turns on the TV, hands her the three remote controls with a small flourish. 'You decide.'

'I don't mind, really. What would you normally watch now?'

She sits beside her mother. They watch an episode of a costume drama.

When the adverts come on, her father goes into the kitchen and comes back with tea and chocolate.

He hands her hers with a wink. 'Aldi,' he says. 'They do these lovely little bars.'

She goes to bed when her parents do, at half past nine, and lies down in her childhood room, in her old single bed. There's a photo on the wall of her and her dad on her wedding day, standing outside in the park – the afternoon light. That green dress.

Her mother pops her head around the door on her way from the bathroom.

'Anything you need?'

'Thanks, Mum, I'm fine.'

'Hot-water bottle?'

'I'm OK.'

'I know, but it's nippy tonight. And I just thought, for your tummy . . . after everything.'

'I'm fine. Thanks, Mum.'

'All right, love. Night-night.'

'Night, Mum.'

Her mum closes the door softly, and it strikes Hannah, not for the first time, that her parents, whose sphere of life has always seemed so small, so constrained, have mastered the art of kindness. She used to lambast them – the newspaper they read (the *Daily Mail*), the telly they watched (soaps and nature programmes). Their politics. Their religion

(C of E). Their horizons, always so narrow. Their naivety. Their class.

And yet they are kind.

They love their children, and they love one another still. How do they do it? Did they learn it, over time? The slow accretion of habit, of days built from these small, simple acts?

On Sunday morning her parents get ready for church. Hannah watches her mother pull on her winter coat, then tut and fuss at her dad's thin anorak; trying to get him to wear an extra jumper, cajoling him into his scarf.

'Would you like to come?'

'No, I'll go for a walk. Get some bits from the shop. Maybe I'll make some lunch.'

She walks out along the cul de sac: pebble-dash and tiny windows and Union Jacks. It always used to amaze her, how quickly the houses changed, how on the other side of Fog Lane Park you were in Didsbury, where the streets had trees and the houses were huge. Not these little 1930s semis, huddled together as though apologizing for themselves.

She does a couple of laps of the local park, then goes to the Co-op and buys a chicken and some veg. Her parents are back by twelve, and she sees their faces light up at the smell of roasting meat.

Later, when lunch is over and she and her mum are washing up, Hannah turns to her mother. 'How do you pray, Mum?' she asks.

'What do you mean?' her mother says.

'I mean in church, when you pray. How do you do it?'

160

Her mother takes off her gloves and places them on the side of the counter. She rinses the bowl, placing it back in the cupboard under the sink, then turns to Hannah.

'I'm not sure, really,' she says. 'I close my eyes. I listen. I sort of . . . collect myself, I suppose. And then, if I'm praying for someone in particular, I bring them to my mind. If it's for you, I think of you. Sometimes you're like you are now, sometimes you're a little girl.' Her mother's hand takes hers. 'And then I ask. I pray.'

'Do you pray for a baby?'

'Yes, love. I did.'

'You did?' she says. 'And now?'

Her mother steps forward, takes Hannah's cheeks in her palms. 'Now, I pray for your happiness, love. For you to be happy. That's all. Oh, Hannah,' her mother says, as Hannah begins to cry. 'Oh, my lovely girl.'

London

1997

It is August 1997, the summer of graduation, when Hannah arrives in the city.

Tony Blair has been Prime Minister for three months. For eighteen years of Hannah's life there has been a Tory government. They watched the election together, she and Lissa, just before their exams, in an Irish club in Chorlton. They drank Black Velvets until they were reeling. Even her father voted for Tony Blair.

The invitation from Lissa was issued casually, on a postcard from Rome showing the Trevi Fountain.

I have been doing my best Anita Ekberg. It's too beautiful here. I will undoubtedly be bored and lonely on my return. Please come to London soon.

Lissa meets her at Euston, wearing jeans and scuffed plimsolls. She is tanned and her hair is loose. Hannah herself is scratchy with self-consciousness. She has recently had her hair cut in a close bob; her hand moves often to the place where the hair tapers to a sharp point at her neck.

Wow. Lissa greets her on the concourse with a hug. Louise Brooks. I love it.

Really? says Hannah, touching her hand to the nape of her neck.

They wait outside King's Cross station for the bus, and when it arrives Hannah follows Lissa as she runs up the back stairs. The seat at the front is free and Lissa grabs it, swinging her plimsolled feet up on to the rail, chattering away, as the bus takes them through the wastelands behind King's Cross, where Lissa points out warehouses where she has gone to parties, a club that she goes to most weekends. She tells Hannah about her new boyfriend – Declan – an Irishman ten years older than her. Of how he took her to Rome, where he is filming a series, and they wandered the sound stages of Cinecittà, and stayed in an apartment in Trastevere and saw medieval paintings and religious shrines.

Declan says he's going to get me an agent, says Lissa. So I can go up for things in the holidays.

She says this with no particular surprise, just a happy acceptance of her lot.

And Hannah watches Lissa as she speaks and thinks she is more beautiful, if possible, than before. Lissa will be a successful actress. This is clear. She might even be a star. She has talent and looks and insouciance and golden things fall into her lap. And there is no point envying her, for this is simply how it is.

Outside the bus window the industrial land gives way to council estates as the bus climbs a long hill. They get down opposite a Tube station, and Lissa leads the way through streets where tall houses are set back from the road and Hannah can hear music practice through open windows. These streets are quiet, the city softened. They stop at a house with hollyhocks in the front garden and a battered green front door.

Your room's at the top of the stairs at the back, says Lissa, letting them in. You can put your bag up there, if you like.

The stairs are covered with an old Moroccan carpet. There

are things piled on almost every step, either on their way up or down – it is not quite clear. A collection of pictures line the wall: framed cartoons, postcards, and other larger paintings – a big canvas at the top of the stairs of Lissa as a girl. Hannah stares at it; she recognizes the style – there was one in Lissa's room in halls. She puts her bag down in a narrow room with a single bed, which looks out on to a long garden with a greenhouse at the bottom. The sound of a radio comes from somewhere up above.

She sits on the bed for a while then goes to use the bathroom, which is large and grubby and painted a dark grey-green. Magazines are strewn in haphazard piles on the floor. She picks up a wrinkled copy of the New Yorker, *which is open at the fiction page. It is over four years old.*

Downstairs, the living room has been knocked through and one whole wall is taken up with bookshelves. The window on to the street is covered in vegetation and lets in a greenish light; the effect is a little like being underwater. Ashtrays in various states of overflow are set on side tables. There seems to be no order to the books on the shelves: Tolstoy, Eliot, Atwood, Balzac. Hannah takes down one of them, Eliot, Four Quartets. *Its margins are filled with writing, a looping scrawl. There is a movement behind her and she jumps.*

A woman is standing at the bottom of the stairs. She is tall and wears a long brown apron which is covered in paint, and her long greying hair is caught up on top of her head in two combs. She is arrestingly beautiful.

Who are you? the woman asks.

Hannah, says Hannah. Sorry.

Why are you sorry? says the woman, her head on one side.

She looks both curious and dangerous, like a bird of prey. She comes closer, peers at the book in Hannah's hand.

Ah. Eliot. Are you a fan?

Hannah looks down at the text, with its spidery marginalia. What is the right answer?

I think so. I mean – I did The Waste Land. *I liked that. But . . . wasn't he horrible to his wife?*

He was, unfortunately. He was an absolute shit. But he could write.

I'm Sarah, by the way, she says, holding out her hand. Borrow it. But don't worry if you don't enjoy it. Eliot is wasted on the young.

They go into the large, messy kitchen, where Sarah takes over lunch from Lissa, insisting that she is starving and a sandwich isn't nearly good enough. When the food is ready, Hannah watches Lissa and Sarah as they eat, alert to the ease with which they attack their food. The salt is not in a cellar but in a mortar bowl, into which the women reach with their fingers. They pour oil liberally over their salad, then dunk with their bread to mop it up. When the salad is finished they suck their fingers dry. They eat like animals, but in doing so they are more elegant than anything she has ever seen. She thinks of her parents; of her mother in her M&S cardigans, the salad cream poured on to pallid lettuce: their politeness, their serviettes, their insistence on manners.

Afterwards they smoke. Sarah has a similar leather pouch to Lissa's, uses the same dark tobacco papers. Sarah and Lissa speak about films they have seen, plays. There is an edge to these conversations, a competition. When Lissa talks about the art in Rome, Sarah grows silent, listening with her head to one side. *Before she went to Rome, Sarah says to Hannah, Lissa thought a Bellini was a cocktail.*

It is, says Lissa, reaching over and putting out her cigarette in the remains of the olive oil. Art and life aren't mutually exclusive. You taught me that.

Touché, says Sarah, raising her glass.

Hannah feels herself like a plant, tendrils reaching out, hooking on to this house, these women, this life.

You should stay a few more days, says Lissa, when Hannah's time is almost up. My mum likes you. She thinks you're good for me. She's got an exhibition opening next week. Declan will be back. You can meet him too.

Hannah calls her mum, who sounds small and tentative on the other end of the phone. *If you're sure, love? Are you sure they're happy to have you? You won't be in the way?*

The house is huge, Mum.

Oh, in that case. Well, you thank her mum from me, won't you?

It is hot the night of the opening. Hannah wears a slim vest, some wide trousers. She touches her hand to the newly shorn place at the back of her neck. The gallery is tiny, on a cobbled street in East London. Sarah's canvases are displayed in a stark white room. There is wine and barrels of beer. The crowd stands on the street outside, mingling with the crowds from the other galleries.

Hannah looks at the people and thinks, *Here – here is life.* It is as though all along a part of her has been hard at work making a skin for herself in the dark and the silence, and now she is ready to wear it, to step into the light.

She loses Lissa for a while, and when the crowd thins she sees her again, further down the street, speaking to a tall young man in a flannel shirt rolled up to the elbows. Lissa is telling a story, gesticulating, and the man is laughing, leaning in to hear. She watches as they pass a cigarette between them. So this is Declan, Lissa's boyfriend. Hannah feels a strange shifting at the sight of him. A recognition, almost, and a disappointment that threatens to prick the evening's magic and let in something darker. Lissa sees her and waves, and Hannah makes her way slowly towards them.

The tall young man turns towards her and takes her hand in greeting.

Somehow, he does not seem like an actor.

Hey, says Lissa. Hannah, this is Nath.

Lissa

She does not contact Nathan and he does not contact her. Often, though, she replays the kiss in her mind – taking it out when she is alone in bed at night, or in the morning, as she comes to consciousness. She has not heard from Hannah for days. She trusts Nathan has said nothing – still, she hears it, a faint yet shrill alarm, ringing somewhere at the edge of thought.

She throws herself into the life of the play. Klara's approach is starting to work – they are indeed becoming less English, their acting is raw, there is blood in it and sinew and bone. And as Klara grows happier with her cast, the cast, in the way that happy casts do, is becoming a living, breathing entity of its own. The actors arrive earlier and stay later, taking pleasure in watching each other's scenes. They begin to run the play from start to finish, feeling its rhythm, the places where it needs pace, the moments when it needs to slow down and feel itself breathe. When a scene becomes sticky, or does not feel alive, the actors step out of the play text and use the Meisner technique to observe each other, keeping in character, repeating what they see, before moving back into the scene again.

Michael suggests they sing together – an idea taken up enthusiastically by the rest of the cast – and so they learn a

Russian folk song and rehearse it in the morning before they start work, Michael strumming a few chords on the guitar while they sing.

As they move towards opening night, Lissa can feel her own performance improving; her body feels different, there is indolence in it: heat and sadness and sway. Even Johnny is softening. Since the day he made her cry, something has shifted between them, and Lissa finds with surprise that she looks forward to their scenes above all.

The evening before her technical rehearsal, her phone rings – Hannah.

Lissa stares at the name and waits. After a moment there is the buzz of a message. She picks it up, calls voicemail, brings it to her ear.

'*Liss?*' Hannah's voice is soft. '*Can you call me? I need to speak.*'

The alarm in her head sounds louder, more shrill. She rolls herself a cigarette, goes to the kitchen door, and calls Hannah back.

'Hey.' Hannah answers after the first ring. 'What are you doing?'

'Just getting ready. It's my tech tomorrow.'

'Oh shit. Of course.' There's a catch in Hannah's voice. 'Can you come over? There's something I need to ask you.'

Fuck.

'Sure.' Lissa tries to keep her voice steady. 'Now?'

'Please. And Lissa? Maybe – will you bring a bottle of wine?'

She pulls on her parka and makes her way towards Broadway Market, stopping to buy wine and chocolate at the Turkish off-licence on the way.

Hannah buzzes her in through the metal door and Lissa

climbs the old external staircase, to where her friend is waiting at the top. Hannah looks pale, slight in the dusk, infused with a restless, spiky energy. 'Did you bring wine?'

Lissa holds it up. 'Rioja.' She tries a smile. 'Old times' sake.'

Hannah takes it from her, goes inside, to the kitchen counter, opens the wine, pours two glasses and hands one to Lissa. 'Cheers,' she says grimly.

'Cheers,' says Lissa, taking her wine, keeping her coat on.

'Are you cold?' says Hannah.

'No – I can't really stay. I've got to get up early. We've got tech.'

'Lissa. Please. I need to talk.'

She takes off her coat, which Hannah hangs behind the door. Outside, dusk is settling over the park, over the lights of the city beyond. A vase of flowers stands on the table. Small lamps are lit. It is the flat of an adult, and yet sitting before her, on the blue sofa, with her legs folded beneath her, her hair tucked behind her ears, Hannah looks like a lost child.

'What's happening, Han? Where's Nath?'

'Working, I guess. I don't know. We had a row.'

'What about?'

'He doesn't want to do another cycle. The IVF. He said no. I thought he would change his mind. But he didn't. And now he says he wants a break.'

'From what?'

She can feel the way her breath moves, in and out, shallow and high.

'From everything.'

'What does he mean by that?'

'I don't know. I went back to Manchester for a few days. I

thought things would be different, but we've hardly spoken since I've been back.'

'Maybe he's right. Maybe you need a break from it all for a bit. Don't they say that? That it's often when you give up that it actually works?'

'Do you know how many *fucking* times people have said that to me?' Hannah throws her cushion to the other side of the room, where it bounces and falls still. 'Too many.' And then, quite suddenly, Hannah folds in on herself. 'Why?' she says. 'Why is this happening to me? Am I cursed? I feel like I'm cursed.'

Lissa moves towards her, sits beside her on the sofa. 'Hey. Han. You're not cursed.'

Hannah lifts her face from her hands. 'Will you speak to him?'

'I can't—'

'Please.' Hannah grips her arm. 'Get him to change his mind. He'll listen to you, Lissa. Talk to him. Please.'

She takes the bus down to Bloomsbury, gets off at Southampton Row and walks up towards Russell Square, where the trees flare orange and red, the sky an iron grey.

When she contacted him she said she needed to speak to him, but was only free in the morning on Thursday. He texted back immediately: *Sounds intriguing. I'm in uni on Thursday. Come and see me there?*

It took her five changes of outfit to get out of the door. In the end she put on an old faded sweatshirt, jeans and her parka. Trainers. No make-up, hair scraped on top of her head.

At the reception they direct her to the third floor – she climbs the stairs, pushes her way through double doors into his corridor. His door is closed, but as she approaches it opens and a young woman emerges. She is tall, her hair loose. Long limbs in tight jeans. She walks past Lissa without a second look.

There are posters on his door, in the manner of academic offices: one advertises a talk, another a union meeting about the tuition fees. She raises her hand and knocks.

'Come in.'

He is sitting at the desk with his back to her. 'Hey,' he turns. 'Liss.' He looks pleased to see her.

'Hey.' She steps inside, closes the door behind her. The room is pleasant, a high window through which the trees of Russell Square are just visible, a wall lined with books, a small sofa, his desk. Him. He is wearing a soft-blue T-shirt with a wide neckline. 'So this is where the magic happens,' she says.

He smiles and she realizes she can't really look at him, so she goes over to his bookshelves and looks at them instead. They are neat, arranged alphabetically.

'*Coming of Age in Samoa*?'

'Classic. You should read it.'

'What's it about?'

'Sex.'

'Oh.' She can feel herself turning red.

He is grinning. Is he teasing her?

'How's the play?' he says.

'Better. We open tomorrow.'

'That came round quickly. Can I come?'

'Of course. But you need to book.'

'Then I'll do that.'

'Good.'

'Why don't you sit down?'

She sits on his sofa. It is still warm. She thinks of the young woman who was in here before her.

'You look like a student,' he says.

'Thanks, I think.'

'You want a drink? Tea?' He gestures to a small tray, a kettle, cups. 'I have whisky in the drawer.'

'Seriously?'

'Only for emergencies.'

'Student emergencies?'

'Academic emergencies.'

There is a pause, a stillness in the room. She realizes it is her turn to speak. 'I'm here for Hannah,' she says.

'Ah,' he says, 'right. And why is that?'

'I promised her I'd come.'

'Why?'

'Because she seems to think I can influence you.' Lissa looks away, down at her hands. 'And I feel bad. I should never have said that thing, that day in the pub. About not doing IVF. I was wrong.'

'Really? But you seemed quite clear. You told me not to do it.'

'But I didn't mean that.'

'Then what did you mean?'

'I meant *I* wouldn't do it. I only spoke for myself. Not you and Hannah – I didn't think—'

'What? You didn't think what? That you influence me?'

His gaze is steady. He does not flinch. 'Please,' she says.

'Please don't say that. It's not fair. I didn't realize what I was saying. I didn't think of Hannah.'

'You know,' Nathan says softly. 'I have spent most of my adult life thinking of Hannah. Of what she wants. Of how to make her happy. And for most of my adult life, that was what I wanted to do.'

The curve of his cheek, the swell of his Adam's apple as he swallows.

'Why did you really come, Lissa?' he says.

'For Hannah. I told you.'

He nods, then, 'Can I tell you something?' he says.

'Yes.'

'Can I lock the door before I do?'

She nods, watches him stand. Feels her heart, the thrum of her blood. His hands on the key. The sound of the lock. He comes and kneels in front of her. 'Liss,' he says. 'The thing is that lately I keep thinking of what you want. Of what might please you.' He reaches out and takes her hand. 'Your hand's cold,' he says.

'Yes,' she says, although now it is hard to speak.

He takes one of her fingers and puts it in his mouth. His mouth is warm. She can feel pleasure radiating from her fingertip, into her breasts, her crotch, the backs of her eyes. She closes her eyes, leans her head against the sofa.

'Can I do this?' he says.

'Yes,' she says, although it is hard to speak.

She keeps her eyes closed, and now his mouth is on her stomach, very light, and now he is unbuttoning her jeans and easing them down and she is lifting herself, helping him. And now his finger is inside her, and she hears a sound, quite low in the room, and then she realizes the sound is coming from her. And his thumb is rubbing her, and his finger is inside her, and the sound carries on.

'Can I do this?' he says.

'Yes,' says the sound of the voice that is hers. 'Yes, please, yes.'

Cate

'So the second rule of Mum Club is . . .'

'What?'

'We have to do something that scares us.'

They are sitting on a bench in the cathedral gardens, or rather, a flint-walled secret garden in the grounds of the cathedral. Dea had asked Cate to meet her at a small car park on Broad Street, where a small booth was cut into a thick wall, behind which a man waited, and Dea had flashed her university card and the guard waved them through. And it is quiet here, the walls crenellated and fortress-thick, as though the city outside with its traffic and its buses and its shopping and car parks and tourists has momentarily ceased to exist. It is cold, but the sun is out and the sky is blue and clear.

'OK,' says Cate. 'So, what scares you, Dea?'

'Having sex with my wife.'

Cate laughs out loud, and an elderly couple on the adjacent bench turn their heads towards them.

'Don't mock. I'm talking scared on all levels. I'm talking X-rated horror. I'm practically incontinent.' Dea grins. 'What about you?'

176

'What about me?'

'Any incontinence?'

Cate laughs. 'Caesarean, so no, not really.'

'Aha, yes, of course. So, bits intact?'

'Something like that.'

'So, sex then?'

'Not much, no. I haven't been up for it lately.'

'And how's that going down? With your husband?'

'Um. I think Sam might be finding it hard.'

'Tell me about him,' says Dea.

Cate turns to her. 'Who, Sam?'

'Yeah. How long have you been together?'

'Not long. A year and a half.'

'Where did you meet?'

A small hesitation and then, 'Online,' says Cate.

'Go on,' says Dea. 'I love a good origin myth. What was it you fell for?'

'He's funny. Or he can be. He's talented. He's a chef. For our second date he invited me to his flat. He cooked for me there.'

'Nice. What did he cook?'

'Chicken,' she says, 'roasted in cinnamon. He made his own flatbreads.' She smiles. 'That was pretty much the clincher. No one had made me a flatbread before.'

Dea gives a low whistle. 'Me neither. I might have turned, for a homemade flatbread.'

'Yeah, well, they were pretty good. And then he took me to Marseille – he'd lived there for years – and I sort of loved that, the way he knew his way around the city . . . the way he spoke French. And not long after that I was pregnant.' The look on his face when she told him. The unsullied joy. How disarmingly cellular her own response. 'He asked me to marry him, and I said yes.'

'Blimey, quick work. How was it?'

'Which bit?'

'The wedding?'

'Oh.' Cate wrinkles her nose. 'You know – pretty weird. I was huge. It was just a few of us – a registry office, a meal at a restaurant. All I wanted was to have a few drinks, but I couldn't, obviously. My dad flew in from Spain and made a terrible speech. My stepmother got out of it on champagne. It was the first time they met Sam. I just kept thinking that it was all a bit shotgun and entirely unnecessary and wishing I could get drunk. I couldn't work out who we were doing it for.'

'And now you don't want to have sex with him.'

'Yeah. No. Yeah.'

'Well,' Dea grins, 'you know, I think that's entirely normal. I think having sex with a man is extraordinary. All that *penetration*.'

'It's not all bad. Sometimes it's actually quite good.'

'If you say so.'

Cate hesitates and then, 'I was with a woman once,' she says.

'Really? Well I never.'

'Yeah.'

'And?'

'And . . . I think I was in love with her. I miss her.'

'Who was she?'

'Lucy? She was an activist, I suppose. She liked to climb trees.'

'Sexy.'

'It was.'

'Where is she now?'

'I have no idea. The States, probably. That's where I left her. If she's still alive. She was going to be arrested, so she went to ground. I've been looking a bit, lately. Trying to find her again.'

'Okaaay.'

'What?'

'So you don't want to have sex with your husband but you're looking for old lovers online? Sexy, *illegal* lovers online.'

'It's not like that.'

'Really? What's it like then?'

'She was important to me. For all sorts of reasons. Not just sex. Anyway, it's probably good I haven't found her.'

'Why?'

'I'm not sure she'd approve of what I've become.'

'What have you become?'

'Less.'

Dea is quiet, regarding her. That expression she has – curious, amused, alive. It is strange, thinks Cate, but she does not mind being seen by her, being stretched gently on the rack of her attention.

'So, come on,' says Dea. 'Just one woman? Or more?'

'One more. After Lucy. But it was a disaster. It ended very quickly. And I realized I wasn't gay. I just loved a woman. One woman. Once.'

'Aha, the old Gertrude Stein line.'

'Do I have to define it?' Cate says, defensive now.

'No,' says Dea. 'Sorry. Of course you don't.'

Cate watches her face, but there is no judgement, just that same amused look.

'Does he know?' says Dea.

'Who, Sam? A bit, not all.'

'Don't you think you should tell him?'

'I think it might be confusing.'

'Confusing for who?'

Cate falls silent. 'That's a lot of questions,' she says quietly. 'What about you?'

'Me?' Dea rolls her eyes. 'Jesus. Are we going to go into my sexual history now? Now that *is* an X-rated horror. I'll tell you one day. I'll give you the director's cut.'

Cate laughs. 'I'll look forward to it.'

Are they flirting? She can't tell.

'But not now. It's freezing. Come on,' says Dea. 'Let's go somewhere and get warm.'

They stand and Dea threads her arm through Cate's. 'Hey,' she says, as they near the edge of the garden. 'You never said what scared you. If I have sex with my wife, then what are you going to do?'

Cate thinks. 'Honestly? It's my house. Sorting it out. Unpacking the boxes from the move. I still haven't done it. It terrifies me.'

'Well, first of all, let me say that I think the pressure for women to have a perfect home is one of the greatest heists of capitalism. Which I am resisting daily on principle, as I'm sure you've seen from the state of my own house. But, you know, since it scares you so much, I think you should face it. Unpack the boxes. Sort it out. Have a gathering. Invite me round. And Zoe. Get Sam to cook. You never know' – Dea winks – 'maybe we'll all get pregnant again.'

*

Later that evening, when she hears Sam come home from work, Cate gets out of bed and goes down to the living room, where he is already installed on the sofa, beer in hand, computer propped on his chest.

'Hey,' she says, and goes to sit on the opposite chair.

'Hey.' He pulls off his headphones.

'What are you watching?'

'Just some crap.'

'How was work?'

'Tiring. Boring. I'm over it. Really. Plating up someone else's food.'

'I wanted to ask you . . .' she says.

'Yeah?'

'I met someone.'

'What?' He raises an eyebrow. 'Who?'

'Another mum. At that playgroup, the one Alice told me to go to. The one you told me to go to – so I could make friends. And I was wondering if I could invite her over, for a gathering. I was wondering if you would cook.'

'A *gathering*? What's a gathering?'

'Sam. Please.'

'When?'

'I don't know. A few weeks' time. I thought I might invite Hannah down, Nathan. Make an evening of it.'

He frowns. 'I don't know, I have to check my shifts.'

'Sam,' she says. 'You said I should meet people. I've done it. I've met people. Dea, and Zoe.'

'Wait, they're gay?'

'Yes.'

'Canterbury has lesbians?'

'Very funny.'

He takes a swig of beer.

'So can I tell them we'll do it? Will you cook?'

He thinks. 'OK,' he says. 'But let's invite Mark and Tamsin too.'

'Really?'

'Why not? We owe them a dinner. It's been ages since Mark has eaten my food. It might get the ball rolling. Encourage him to invest.'

'Great!' she says.

Fuck.

Lissa

He does not call. She does not call him. He does not text. She does not text him. She looks at her phone. Keeps it in her pocket. Waits for the buzz of a message, but a message does not come.

She has forgotten how this goes. How you cede your power to the man after sex. How this appears to be a fundamental universal law. How you can move from sane to crazy in a few swift moves. Even if they are the husband of your best friend.

The. Husband. Of. Your. Best. Friend.

Think about that for a moment. Examine it. Let it sink in.

Press night goes well. The cast may be a little pushed, a little forced, but the play has its own engine, its own life force, and as they take their curtain Lissa can sense the excitement, see it reflected in the eyes of her fellow actors – it is working, the play is alive, they are part of something good.

The whispers go round the bar after the show that there were plenty of press watching, that they should expect a decent handful of reviews, and this news evokes in Lissa a familiar sense of relief and dread.

By Saturday morning there are four reviews online. The *Telegraph*, the *Independent* and *The Times* are all four stars. The *Evening Standard* carries a five-star review: *Where has Johnny Stone been? With a talent this rare he should be a household name. It's taken an out-of-the-way theatre and a little-known director to give him the opportunity to shine.*

Helen is *a young actress on the cusp of something huge.*

And of Lissa, the reviewer writes that she is *as languid, lost and dangerous a Yelena as I have ever seen.*

She gets a message from Cate.

Saw the reviews! Wish I could come. Having a thing in Canterbury – December 10th. But I think you're performing?

Thanks, Lissa writes back. *But you're right. I'm performing. Hope all's well.*

She leaves her phone in the house and goes for a walk around the park. It is market day, but the weather is cold and the crowds are thin. She feels conspicuous, there is every chance she might bump into either Hannah or Nathan or both of them together – buying bread or bacon or croissants or fish. Are they still having sex? Hannah and Nathan? What are they doing now? She could go round there. Just knock on the door and stay for a coffee. *Hey, Han! Nathan seduced me. Yeah, on Thursday, in his office! Have you ever fucked there? On the sofa? And that thing with his thumb. Is that what he does to you?*

Perhaps he is fucking all of them, she and Hannah and the long-limbed, succulent girls who rise from his sofa and leave it warm. Perhaps none of them knows him at all.

Or perhaps it is she who does not know herself.

She wonders if there is a word for a woman like her, perhaps a Greek word – a special sort of word for a special sort of woman, one who betrays her friend.

Oh, Hannah. Oh, Jesus.

She buys herself a croissant and takes it home and eats it alone, standing up at the sink.

Ticket sales rise in response to the reviews; they are 80 per cent full on the weekdays and then sold out on Friday and Saturday evenings. Their group warm-ups take on a celebratory air. When they have all completed their vocal exercises, their stretches, their articulation exercises and their pacing out of the stage, they gather in a circle and throw a ball to each other to tune up their reflexes. Ten minutes before the first half they sing their Russian folk song. Occasionally the younger men try out Cossack moves, before they high-five each other and whoop as they disperse to their dressing rooms to listen for the call for Beginners on the tannoy.

Only Johnny does not warm up. Instead he sits on the stage on the lounge chair that Vanya favours, wearing his crumpled linen costume, hat pushed down on his head, and does the crossword, looking up occasionally at the antics of the other actors with one eyebrow raised. When they sing he gets to his feet and wanders out for a cigarette.

Lissa is grateful to have something to do, somewhere to go

in the evenings; grateful to have the ritual of performance to hold her, to know where to stand, how to speak, where to put her hands.

She gets a text from Hannah. *Bought tickets! Me and Nath coming a week next Thursday.*

Great! she writes back, as her stomach swills with queasy fear.

The end of the first week, her mother comes with Laurie. After the performance they are waiting for her in the bar. Sarah holds Lissa's face in her hands. 'Wonderful, darling, wonderful – properly good. No review in the *Guardian*, though?'

If a play goes on stage and the Guardian *doesn't review it, does the play really exist?*

'Nothing in the *Guardian*, Ma, no.'

Laurie steps up and hugs her close. 'Best you've been, Liss, best you've been.'

On the Monday of the second week her father comes with his wife in tow.

'Well done, sweetie. You looked beautiful,' he says. 'Reminded me of your mother when she was young.'

Beside him her stepmother nods away like a nervous bird, gripping her handbag beneath her arm. 'I enjoyed it,' she says. 'Not a lot happens though, does it?'

No, Lissa agrees, not a lot happens. When she suggests a drink her father looks willing, but she sees her stepmother touch his arm and he turns to Lissa with a small, helpless shrug.

People's agents come, those with pulling power bringing casting directors with them: The Globe, the National, a TV company. The inevitable whispers pass around the dressing room before the show – *so-and-so is in tonight, so-and-so is in* – and the knowledge of these people watching, people who have the power to change the course of your life, spikes the blood. Now the pecking order shifts and changes, no longer the simple calculation of talent, the meritocracy of the stage. Michael's agent seems to bring half of London's TV and theatre people with him, and Helen's agent comes three times, each night with a different casting director in tow. Lissa sees them in the bar after the show, huddled in a corner as though engaged in vital affairs of state, the industry people leaning in, faces attentive, serious, as they listen to what the young actors have to say.

Her own agent comes finally – unaccompanied by casting directors, in the middle of the third week, when the show is a little flat. She sees her sitting in the back row, a small woman with unruly red hair, and as she is changing out of her costume Lissa gets a text.

Wonderful. Had to get away, speak tomorrow?

The next day she checks her phone often, waiting for a phone call that doesn't come.

Thursday arrives and she spends the day feral with anticipation. She writes Nathan a message. *You coming with Hannah tonight?* She hears nothing back. But as soon as she steps out on stage she sees Hannah, sitting alone, an empty seat beside her, and she is flooded with disappointment and relief.

Afterwards in the bar, Hannah hugs her. 'Amazing, Liss. Loved it. So she was worth it in the end?'

'Who?' She feels strangely disoriented. Her friend here before her, the knowledge of her transgression blazing within her.

'The Polish director.'

'Oh, yeah,' says Lissa, 'I guess she was.' Her eyes rove over Hannah's face. 'Nath didn't feel like coming then?'

'He got held up at work. He sends his love.'

'His love? Really?'

'Hey, did you get a message from Cate?' Hannah says. 'Inviting you to Canterbury?'

'I can't. I'm performing. Are you going to go?'

'I think so. We need to get out of London. Me and Nath. Do something spontaneous for a change.'

Lissa laughs. 'Spontaneity's not your forte, Hannah,' she says. 'If you want to do something spontaneous, go somewhere else. Go to Berlin. Go to New York. Go to Belize.'

Hannah looks at her – a quick, hurt look. 'Well,' she says quietly, 'maybe I'll start with Canterbury and see how I go.'

Lissa smiles, and a strange, bitter taste fills her mouth.

Her birthday comes around – she is thirty-six now, playing twenty-seven. She tells no one in the cast. It is freezing, as she leaves the house to visit Sarah, with a fierce, bitter wind. Sarah gives her the usual handmade card, but there is no present this year.

'I'm just rather busy,' Sarah says in the kitchen. 'The new work's consuming me somewhat. Did I tell you? I've got an exhibition in the summer. The gallery in Cork Street came through.'

'Can I see?' asks Lissa. 'What you're working on?'

'I'm not sure.' Sarah tilts her head, pondering, then: 'No . . . I rather think not.'

When their coffee is finished, Lissa lingers as her mother rises. Outside, the wind has died down, and sunlight strikes the winter garden. 'Do you fancy a walk?' she says. 'It's brightened up. We could go up on the Heath.'

'Work,' Sarah says, already heading for the door. 'You're welcome to stay but I have to work.'

Lissa stays where she is, listening to her mother's footsteps mount the stairs.

On the wall of the living room is one of Sarah's portraits, a picture of Lissa at the age of eight, or nine. She remembers sitting for it so clearly still: it was summer, and hot in the attic, but she didn't mind being up there, Saturday morning after Saturday morning in that old flowered chair. She would sit there with her book – her legs flung over the arms of the chair, the sunlight slanting in from the skylight – as Sarah prepared her paints, set up her easel. Then finally, when everything was ready, she would turn on the radio and start to paint, and Lissa would sense it, the concentration, the way she had all of her mother's attention at last. How safe it made her feel.

Then, one morning, on the pavement outside the school gates, a different sort of painting appeared. Simple white lines, the silhouettes of children drawn in chalk. Everyone standing around, disturbed, as at a crime scene, wondering what they were.

At home that evening, Lissa told her mother about it and Sarah turned to her with a strange smile.

I painted them. Caro and I. We went out, in the early morn-ing, while you were still asleep. They were all that was left. Of the children. In Hiroshima. We painted them so that people would understand.

She remembers the way Sarah spoke, the pride, the par-ticular smile she had, as though she had done something good. When really, Lissa knew, she had done something ter-rible. She had no words to tell her mother how those pictures made her feel. The hollowness of those children who had disappeared.

The day stretches ahead of her, with nothing in it till she must be at the theatre at six o'clock. She heads down to the South Bank, to the BFI, where they are showing a Bergman season. She gets tickets for the longest of the films, then buys coffee and a slice of cake and sits in the window to wait for the cinema to open, watching the faces of the people as they pass. Perhaps he will appear. It is not, surely, beyond the realm of possibility that Nathan might treat himself to an afternoon film. Perhaps that will be how it happens – to bump into him, to let coincidence take care of the plot. Or she could text him again. Tell him where she is. Invite him down.

But of course he doesn't come. He is a busy man. It is only people like her who can sit in a cinema on a weekday after-noon, tasting the equivocal pleasures of time on their hands. She should make a joke of it, she thinks, of Bergman on a birthday. But there is no one to make the joke to.

She is the first into the cinema when it opens, handing her ticket to the usher, sitting in the darkness before the thin safety curtain rises, before the adverts come on.

Hannah

She searches for a hotel in Whitstable for the Friday and the Saturday night, finds one that has only recently opened but has good reviews on TripAdvisor. There is the requisite mention of Egyptian cotton. There are driftwood mirrors in the bedrooms. A neutral palette of white and grey. She calls them up and a pleasant-voiced woman tells her she is in luck, they have had a last-minute cancellation, a room is free but there is a shared bathroom. It is either that or the Travelodge so Hannah takes it. As she hands over her credit-card details she pictures wide skies – walking on the beach on Saturday morning. She books lunch at a restaurant she has heard of further along the coast, an unprepossessing pub with a reputation for spectacular food. She looks at the menu: oysters, salt-baked celeriac, Aylesbury lamb. They will eat oysters. They will walk on the beach. It will all fall into place. She has been wrong. It is the controlled, clinical side of things that has brought them to this. Nathan is right, Lissa is right: they should take a break – let things happen naturally. Maybe everyone is right. The message boards are full of people's stories of conceiving after IVF has failed. It is not the end. It is only the end of the beginning. She has been holding too tight. There is still time, there is still a chance – she just needs to relax. To be spontaneous. It will do them good to get away.

Bras

2008

Hannah is getting married. Nathan has proposed in a cottage in Cornwall. They have been a couple for ten and a half years. She is having a little gathering at the new flat to toast the announcement, with her best women, Lissa and Cate.

It is February, but sunny and mild as Cate and Lissa walk the small distance from the big house, down Broadway Market towards Hannah's flat. They stop at the off-licence on the way. Cava? says Cate, lifting a bottle. Champagne, says Lissa. Let's get a bit of Veuve.

At the bottom of the canal they turn right, where they announce their arrival at a plain metal door and Hannah buzzes them inside. The flat smells both earthy and clean – the interior staircase has been newly covered with sisal. Hannah appears, smiling at the top of the stairs, dressed in simple trousers, a silk shirt. Cate and Lissa take off their shoes and walk slowly up the stairs, the sisal pleasantly rough beneath their feet. The stairs give on to a large, open kitchen and living room, where a long blue sofa lies along one wall.

Cate has seen this flat before – visited often since Hannah and Nathan moved here last year – but tonight it looks different; it is as though the definition has been turned up. Her eyes graze the details of the room: the elegant sofa, a table of lightest wood, a brown jug placed just so upon it, knives arranged by size on a magnetized strip on the wall. They seem to look back at her, these objects, with a cool judging gaze. They seem to ask her how she measures up.

They take their drinks and go through sliding doors on to a large terrace with a view over Haggerston Park where they drink their Veuve and toast their friend.

Hannah carries a particular radiance, this springlike evening, as though she herself is the chief exhibit in this backdrop of her own curating, as though all of this – the terrace and the park and her home glowing gently on the other side of the glass doors, were simply there to reflect her radiance, her status as a bride-to-be.

After a little while Cate excuses herself – she has to go to the toilet. In Hannah's bathroom there is no clutter, there are no bottles on the bath or in the shower. Instead, in the cabinet, there are matching jars of brown glass.

In the hall, on the way back out, Cate hesitates, for Hannah's bedroom door is ajar. Outside there is laughter, the red tip of Lissa's cigarette carving the air as she talks. Cate steps inside. She fingers the linen throw that lies on the large bed, then goes over to the wardrobe, where she takes out one of Hannah's simple silk shirts, feels its supple weight between her fingers, then puts it back. She goes to the chest and opens the top drawer, and here she stops, breath caught – Hannah's bras and knickers are laid out in matching sets. She fingers one of the bras – it is the sort of bra only a woman with very small breasts can wear: two thin triangles of lace with a bright flash of silk on the edge. One is red. One petrol. One is the colour of lightest pink. Cate can feel her heart racing. She did not know Hannah owned bras like this; Hannah, whose exterior is so spartan, whose edges have always been so clear. There is something about the sight of these bras – something insolent and secret and potent – that hits her like a punch to her stomach.

Quickly, furtively, she takes off her jumper and her own bra (large, nondescript), managing to fasten Hannah's on its widest clasp. She turns it round to the front, pulls up the straps, and stares at herself in these two triangles of nothing, edged in petrol-coloured silk. She knows then – she has lost. More than the house and the sofa and the engagement and the knives on metal strips and the jug just so, and the successful ten-year relationship, it is the sight of these bras that tells her that in the fierce, unspoken race she and Hannah have been running since they were children, she has lost.

Over the next days she feels herself slipping, as though happiness were a dance whose steps she has forgotten. She counts her breaths. She counts her blessings, she tries to rationalize – why should it matter what her friends are doing? Why should her happiness be indexed to theirs? But it is. Somehow, it is – she cannot help but take inventory of her life; her lack, at thirty-three years old, of any of the markers that constitute real adulthood. She is beginning to loathe her job, taking the Tube every day to Canary Wharf, going cap in hand to meetings with bankers who believe that in giving you a minute of your time they are changing the world. This job which will never give her enough to buy a home, to buy good clothes.

And Hannah – Hannah who always said she would do something worthwhile and did – who moved from her management training job at the age of twenty-nine and is now senior advisor in a large global charity on a salary twice that of Cate's own. She didn't sell out. She sold in. And it turned out her stock was high.

Cate, who has prided herself on living simply, finds she wants things. She wants a home of her own, a functioning relationship, a child, or at least the possibility of one, money for decent clothes, a knicker drawer that is not a frantic tangle of odd socks and old M&S briefs. Her wants proliferate, metastasize in the darkness inside her.

The other two rooms in the shared house are occupied by people she does not really know. The house, always shabby, feels grotty – the salmon colour of the kitchen, the terrible cheap carpet on the floor. The kitchen is no longer a place to gather. She makes her food and scuttles out again, eats it in her room, at her desk.

Cate tries to speak to Lissa about it, to spin it into humour somehow, but Lissa is preoccupied, on an upward swing. For Lissa there is hope on the horizon. Last week her agent called her with news of an audition. A feature film. A young indie director. A lead role. The director had seen her in a short film she made for no money last summer as a favour to a friend and called about her availability.

Lissa has read the script and it is extraordinary.

Somewhere, she knows, this one is for her.

Declan is away, and so Lissa practises her speech for Cate, while Cate sits on the battered old sofa in the living room, listening, prompting her when she stumbles, which she rarely does. She is good, thinks Cate, she deserves this. Her career will finally ignite and she too will move up and away.

Lissa gives up drinking for the week before the audition, makes sure she drinks plenty of water, sleeps as much as she can. She takes herself off to yoga classes and returns radiant.

The day of the meeting arrives. The director seems as excited to meet her as she is to meet him. He tells her he loved her in the short. She already knows one of the speeches by heart, and she delivers it on camera without looking at her script.

Wow, he says. That was awesome.

She does another speech, equally well. When she gets up to leave the director envelops her in a hug. See you soon, he says.

A day passes. Another. And another. Lissa checks her phone constantly. She checks that it is on. She turns it on and off. Cate watches her face cloud and darken, elation turn to doubt. By the Wednesday she is quiet, by Thursday belligerent.

It's gone to someone else, she says.

Cate watches her take a call from Declan, who is filming somewhere in Scotland.

I'm going to go and see him, says Lissa. I need a break.

Lissa leaves on Friday afternoon. She takes the plane from City Airport to Edinburgh, where Declan has sent a car to pick her up. She sits in the back of the car and watches the city slide by. It is grey and raining. They drive out, up into the country-side, until they reach a castle in large grounds. Behind it there is a large loch. There is no mobile reception. She is relieved.

Cate comes home from work at half past five, locks up her bike, climbs the stone steps and lets herself into the house. There is no one else there. She feels the harsh, grainy texture of her loneliness.

The landline rings. A rare event. It rings and rings and rings and rings off. Then it rings again and perhaps it is an emergency, so Cate goes to answer it; a woman's voice, hectoring, asking for Lissa, who Cate informs her isn't there. Where is she? says the woman, who speaks to Cate like she is shit on her shoe. I don't know, says Cate truthfully. Somewhere in Scotland, I think.

Well, her mobile's not working, says the woman. Tell her, she says, tell her she needs to come back to London. He wants to see her. Again. Monday morning. First thing. Tell her to come back as soon as she can.

Cate puts down the phone. She honestly does not know where Lissa is. She could find out. She could make it an emergency. She could call Sarah, Lissa's mother, who would probably know. She could go into Lissa's room and search the chaos of her desk for a piece of paper which may or may not contain the name of a hotel. Her diary. Her computer. Cate knows the password. It may be in there. She could do any or all of these things, but she does nothing.

On Sunday night she is sleeping when Lissa arrives in the house. It is gone midnight. She barely wakes, she goes back to sleep.

On Monday morning Cate rises and showers and dresses and leaves for work.

When Cate comes home that afternoon Lissa is sitting at the kitchen table, a ball of damp tissues in her hand. Did you get a call from my agent?

Who?

My agent. She said she called here, on Friday. That he wanted to see me for the audition. It was this morning, first thing. She begins to cry. I was asleep. I missed it. It's gone.

Can't you get in touch? Get him to see you again?

Don't you get it? Lissa hisses. It's gone to someone else. It's fucking gone.

Lissa spends the next day in bed with the curtains closed. Cate knocks on her door, but she does not answer.

She does not speak to Cate for weeks.

And Cate is queasy with guilt. She has done something, or not done something – she is not sure which. She should have done more.

But if Lissa had been made to get the part, she would have done so, wouldn't she? It was Lissa's decision to go away to a place in the middle of nowhere. It was Lissa's destiny, wasn't it – to lose out?

Cate

Dinner. Friends for dinner. A dinner party. Supper. Friends for supper. A gathering. However Cate frames it to herself, the thought is excruciating – she is no good at such things. But Sam seems happy about the arrangement. On Sunday, his day off, he brings out his knives and pans. He hands Tom a milk pan and a wooden spoon and Tom sits on the floor, happily playing with them both as Sam flicks through cookbooks.

'I want to do something Kentish,' he says. 'You ever eaten whelks? I could do a ceviche with shallots and tomatoes and lime. And then something with dabs. I could get fish from that place on the coast. They supply the restaurant.'

Cate looks at him in the narrow kitchen, in the grey light of the winter afternoon, sleeves rolled up, and realizes she hasn't seen him so happy for months.

The day of the dinner she spends the morning cleaning. She moves Tom with her from room to room, putting him on the floor with his toys while she scrubs toilets and sinks and vacuums floors. She has the radio on in the background.

Parliament has voted by a tiny majority to increase student fees to nine thousand pounds a year. Large protests in central London yesterday.

When the cleaning is done she turns on the TV and watches footage of protestors on the roof of the Conservative Party headquarters. Placards on fire. Charles and Camilla, their horrified faces as a window of their car is smashed. A close-up of one of the protestors, a young man with his mouth open wide. She knows the look. The war cry. Feels it land in her gut.

Sam is home after his afternoon shift, carrying a bulging bag of fish and vegetables, which he puts in the fridge, along with four bottles of wine. 'I got a good Burgundy,' he says, 'it was on offer in Aldi.'

She can hear him singing as he takes a shower. He comes down in a T-shirt and jeans. 'Come on, little guy.' Sam straps Tom in the high chair, gives him some carrot to play with, then ties on an apron, pulls out his knives and sets to work on an onion. She lingers, watching him, his wide forearms, his skill with the blade, the flash of the knife. When the onion is chopped he looks up. 'What are you looking at?'

'Just – I remember the first time I saw you do that. The first night we met.'

'Yeah.' He smiles, and holds her eyes. 'I remember that night too.' Then, 'Hey,' he says, after a moment. 'I went to check out a premises the other day. It's an old warehouse. Victorian. Backs on to the Stour. It was a grain store. I think it would be affordable.' She can see the excitement in him. 'But let's make this meal great first and then see what Mark says.'

She can hear him chatting away as she moves next door, telling Tom what he's doing – *so you take your onion, and then you sweat it in the oil* – and Tom's burbling responses.

She flicks on the TV again, but it is only the same rolling

pictures as earlier, Charles and Camilla. That same protestor, open-mouthed. She turns it off and texts Hannah: *You still OK for tonight?* Part of her, she is aware, a large part of her, would like Hannah to cancel – would like everyone to cancel – but she gets a text back immediately: *Can't wait!*

Hannah

She decides to work from home, so she can pack and get everything ready in time. 'We have to pick up the rental car,' she says to Nathan as he leaves for work. 'But if we leave at three or so we can get to Whitstable and have some time together before we go to Cate's.'

The weather has eased a little. It is not so cold as it was. She works all morning, then takes herself for a run along the canal, and showers and dresses in her best underwear and a dress that she knows he loves, knee-length, supple black silk – bought for their anniversary last year. She takes time over her make-up. She has bought a good bottle of champagne, which she packs in her bag, then goes online, looking again at the pictures of the hotel, of the restaurant, of the beach at Whitstable. Perhaps this is the beginning of something new. Perhaps they can move to Kent. Walk under wide skies. Get a dog.

At five she receives a text: *Just leaving.* Which means they are going to be late. To calm herself, she goes into their bedroom and begins packing a bag for him, but as she does so she feels a sense of dread – as though their intimacy is suddenly contingent, fraught with a vague peril. She should have gone to get the car herself – she has had the whole afternoon – but the car-rental place is close to the road that leads to the A12, which leads to the A2, which leads to the M2, which leads to Kent. So it made sense, in that way at least. She finishes packing and goes to sit on the sofa, so she will be ready as soon as he arrives.

She is still sitting in the same spot when his key turns in the lock at six fifteen.

'We're late,' she says.

'I'm sorry. There was an emergency meeting. Industrial action. The tuition fees.'

He looks tired, irritable.

'Do you need anything?' she says. 'A shower? A drink?'

'If we're late, let's just go.'

At the car-rental office there are forms to be filled out, driving licences to be photocopied, excesses to decide upon. It is seven before they leave with an ugly Ford Fiesta, and Nathan drives out of London on the A2.

'I think we're too late to go to Whitstable first,' she says.

He nods. She studies his face in the dark. Something she thought she knew by heart has become inscrutable, opaque.

'So shall we go straight to the dinner, then?'

'Whatever you think.'

'Or maybe we should cancel the dinner? Just go to the hotel?'

'Won't Cate be disappointed? Isn't that the whole point?'

'Yes, I suppose it is.' She turns to look out of the window at the 1930s edges of London sliding past. 'I've never been to Canterbury,' she says. 'I only know it from Chaucer. The Wife of Bath. A level.'

He changes lanes. 'I went there once,' he says, 'for a conference.'

'Did you like it?'

She winces. It is as though they do not know one another. Or as though they are following a badly written script.

'Yes,' he says. 'From what I saw. It was nice.'

They fall silent. The script has run out. She feels panic rising in her. 'The hotel looks sweet,' she says. 'There are bikes we can borrow. We can cycle to Margate tomorrow. If the weather's OK.' She lifts her phone and checks the weather, but there is only one bar of reception. 'Apparently it's really up and coming. Margate. There's the Turner. Opening next year. Turner Contemporary. Someone at work went there last summer. Loved it. Sold up and moved.' His face. His shuttered face. 'Or, you know, we could just stay in bed. Sleep. They bring breakfast up to your room.'

What is she? A fucking tour guide? Shut up shut up *shut up*.

She switches the radio on; the news is full of the tuition-fees story. She leans forward and turns it up. 'Do we have to?' he says, leaning in and turning it off. 'It's depressing. I've heard enough of it today.'

They follow the instructions that Cate sent, but they lead only to a large roundabout, which they go around twice as Hannah tries calling to check, but the phone rings and rings and is not answered. 'She's probably busy,' says Hannah. 'With her guests.'

'Right,' says Nathan. 'Well, in the absence of any clear directions, shall we stop the car?' He swings off the roundabout and turns left at a set of traffic lights. There is nowhere to park. She watches the muscle tense in his jaw. 'There,' he says, pointing to the sign for a car park.

They go down into the depths of a multi-storey. What if it closes while they are at Cate's? How will they get to Whitstable? They go up in the lift and do not speak. He looks pale beneath the overhead light. Hannah's phone buzzes in her pocket – she fishes it out. Finally: Cate with the directions.

'She sounds happy,' she says, as she puts her phone back into her pocket.

It is cold on the street in Canterbury, colder than in London. She has dressed too flimsily. She wants to ask Nathan to hold her, but he is hunkered down into his coat. Has she ever had to ask him to hold her before?

He rolls a cigarette and lights it. She bites her tongue. They walk past a small supermarket, and then into a small estate, find number eleven.

She wants to go back to the car. To drive back to safety, to her home, which feels such a long way away. She wants to stop and hold her husband. To shake him until his water runs clear again, until his secrets fall out.

Nathan reaches up and presses the doorbell.

'Hannah!!' As Cate opens the door she stumbles forward. Nathan steps up to grab her elbow. 'Hannah! Nate! Come in, come in!'

Cate is flushed, talking loudly as she pulls them through a narrow hallway, a cramped sitting room, to where expectant faces crowd around a small round table. 'Everyone!' says Cate. 'This is Hannah! And Nate. The best couple in the world!'

Cate

It is going well – surprisingly well – except for the fact that she cannot find her wine glass. She had it a moment ago – did she take it when she went to the bathroom? There it is, on the other side of the table. She reaches for it, but Nathan gets there first and passes it safely back towards her. Mark is talking, something about sailing.

'The coast is so close. Got a friend with a boat, takes me out sea fishing – you should come, Sam. Next summer. We take some decent wine, cook up on deck. He's got cash. If you cook like this, I reckon he might be interested in your food too.'

And Sam is nodding, looking pleased. And the food – they are all eating their food, and it is delicious, really delicious, they are all saying so – and here is Dea, her face intent, listening to something Hannah is saying. And Cate is filled with warmth for Dea – whose idea this was – who turned up bearing cordial, wine-dark elderberry cordial made from her allotment, which Cate stowed in the kitchen for Hannah to drink. But tonight Hannah is drinking – and Cate laughs to herself because it is so good to see Hannah here in her house, drinking wine.

And she looks so beautiful – has obviously made an effort – in that dress, the way her hair frames her face, her face which is flushed from the outside air and the alcohol. And she is so touched that Hannah cares enough to come, to make the journey, that she feels sudden tears in her eyes. She stands up and goes around the table to Hannah, puts her cheek against hers. 'Thank you,' she says.

'What for?'

'For coming here. You look gorgeous, Han.'

And Hannah laughs. 'Thanks. You too.'

And as she circles back to her seat, she catches Nathan and Dea talking together now: 'They've occupied the Senate building. Fifty of them in the War Room. Our VC signed a letter supporting the fees hike.'

And Nathan is nodding. 'It's a shit show.'

Cate puts her hand on Dea's shoulder. 'I saw them,' she says, 'this morning – they were handing out leaflets by the cathedral again. I was looking for that girl. The one with the pink hair, do you remember?'

Dea smiles. 'I do. She's inside. She's in the Senate.'

Zoe leans forward. 'It feels like the spirit of '68 or something. Like these young people are being radicalized overnight.'

'I agree,' says Nathan. 'But don't people always say that? Wheel out the *soixante-huitards*?'

'Well,' says Zoe. 'If my daughter was old enough, I'd want her to be in there.'

'Yeah,' says Nathan. 'I reckon I'd want that too.'

Cate looks around at her table, at her guests, and she feels happy – suddenly and completely happy. There is no future to fear, no past to regret, only this, only a series of moments, strung along, like lit globes on a string – there is warmth, there is food, there is comfort. Upstairs, Tom sleeps. She is grateful. And she sees that the bottles on the table are empty so she goes back into the kitchen and fetches another from the fridge – it is hard to open – and here is Sam, coming in behind her. 'Here,' he says. 'Let me do that.'

She turns around and there he is, her husband – and she leans in and kisses him – not a chaste kiss, and he laughs, pulls her closer, and she traces the rough line of his beard with her tongue.

'Wow,' he says. 'You must be drunk.'

She laughs. She has forgotten this, the fizz of his proximity, this man, this bear of a man. Dea was right. This was what she needed to do.

She helps Sam carry the food and the wine back in. They are configured slightly differently now – Dea and Tamsin are speaking together; Hannah, who is not talking to anyone, is looking over at Nathan and Zoe, whose heads are bent, looking at pictures on Zoe's phone.

'She's with a babysitter,' Zoe is saying. 'I'm pretty nervous but they seem to be going OK.'

'She's gorgeous,' Cate hears Nathan say.

Cate watches Hannah watch them and feels a sudden spasm of protectiveness towards her friend. 'Hey,' she says, nudging Zoe. 'Hey, you two.' Nathan and Zoe look up, startled. Now she has said it she doesn't know what else to say. She claps her hands as Sam puts the fish down on the table.

Hannah

Cate is drunk. She is swaying, holding the plates; Hannah reaches up and takes them from her.

'Here, have some water.' Hannah holds out her glass.

'I'm fine,' says Cate. 'Really, I am.'

Hannah drinks the water herself. She has had two glasses

of wine and her head feels fuzzy. She already has a headache beginning at her temples. She is finding it hard to concentrate on the conversation that is swirling around her; she keeps thinking about the car, about how it will be stuck in the car park and they won't be able to get it out. She needs to call the hotel – she needs to let them know that they will be late, to ask whether that's OK, whether they need to have a special key. She can't remember how far it is to Whitstable. Twenty minutes? Maybe more? It is ten o'clock and they are just eating their main course – at this rate, they will be here till one.

The conversation is getting heated now: Dea, Cate's new friend, and that guy Mark with the big diver's watch, the one who's fond of the sound of his own voice. She recognizes him from the wedding – he was Sam's best man, wasn't he?

'It was needed,' Mark is saying, 'if the markets aren't going to turn their backs on us. You want to be like Greece? Didn't you see the note they left in the Treasury? *There's no money left*. Idiots. Fucktards.'

'Sure,' says Dea, 'and austerity is going to hit the poor the hardest. What about a tax on the banks?'

'They'll just take their business elsewhere.'

'So they are in charge?' says Zoe, leaning in. 'So they dictate policy now?'

Mark turns to Zoe. 'I'm not sure you quite know what you're talking about, love.'

'And why is that?'

'I mean, you're American, for a start.'

'For a start?' says Zoe. 'And what comes after that?'

The temperature has dropped a couple of degrees in the

room. Hannah stands and quickly makes her way to where Sam is sitting. She leans in and thanks him for the food and asks him if he has a landline. 'Sure,' he says, 'it's in the bedroom, first on the left.'

She kicks off her shoes and goes upstairs. In the bedroom she sits on the bed in the dark. She is breathing quickly. There is a tightening in her skull. Something is troubling her. Nathan – the way he was with that woman Zoe. Their heads bent together looking at her phone, his low exclamation at the sight of her child.

There is a noise beside her and she jumps. At first she does not know what it is, then she understands – it is Tom, he is here, sleeping in the big bed. She can see him properly now, in the small light from the landing, his arm flung out to the side. She lies down beside him. He stirs but does not wake. His breath smells sweet. It is so even. He is so deeply asleep.

She curls up beside him and puts her finger in his grip, tracing the small bumps of his knuckles beneath her thumb, her cells fizzing with a longing that might split her in two.

And she understands something, lying here – an understanding that arrives in her cells fully formed. She has lost her husband – or her husband is lost to her. Something fundamental, some deep river that fed them, has dried up.

For the moment – this small moment, with this small hand in hers – this knowledge does not hurt, but she knows there is pain waiting for her, on the other side of this. She knows it will come.

It is quiet, for now, up here, while downstairs there is music, louder now, and Cate's voice raised above it, exhorting everyone to dance.

Cate

'I used to love dancing!' she yells. 'Dea, Zoe, come on!' She pulls them to their feet. Someone needs to change the energy in here – rescue the evening, which is in danger of escaping, of slipping away. 'Where's the rest of the wine?'

There is a bottle by Mark, half full. She goes over towards him, lifts it and pours it into a nearby glass.

'Are you sure you need any more of that?' he says.

'I'm sorry?' Cate turns back to him. 'What did you just say?'

Something in the way he stands – an ancient violence, simmering just beneath the surface. As though on an unspoken cue, Tamsin moves towards her husband. Behind her, Cate can sense Dea and Zoe. Nathan is sitting watching to her side. Sam to her left. Hannah, where is Hannah? Cate lifts the glass to her mouth. The wine is no longer cold. It tastes tacky, overly sweet.

'I think your wife might have had enough. Don't you think?' Mark turns to Sam.

Cate splutters. 'Oh my God, you're not really saying that? *I think you've had enough, love.*' She is laughing hard now. 'Oh, wait – you are?!' She shakes her head. 'You're a joke.'

'Excuse me?'

'You're a fucking joke. Look at you, with that stupid watch. You're not a diver, are you? Wait a minute – shall we see if it works?'

She moves towards him, grabs his hand and turns it over, unclasps his watch, and drops it into her full glass of wine. 'Oops,' she says, as the wine sloshes out over her wrist.

The fury on his face. Tamsin, white with shock.

'You people. Do you have any idea how ridiculous you are? You people,' she says again, waving her glass at Tamsin and Mark. 'You're the problem, do you know that?'

'Cate.' Sam steps forward. 'Mark's right, you've had enough. You're a breastfeeding mother, for God's sake.'

'Oh. Oh, I'm a breastfeeding *mother*, am I?'

'You're tired.'

'Oh!' She bangs the glass down on to the table. 'Oh, that's *priceless*. Of course I'm tired. I haven't had a full night's sleep in almost a year. You know. I'm sorry I haven't got a system, Sam. I'm sorry I haven't got a functioning fucking *system*. It's a form of torture, you know. Sleep deprivation. Did you know that? They break soldiers with it. I mean – you may not be that bright, but at least you can grasp that.'

'I really don't think we need to have this conversation here.'

'Yeah, go on. Shut me down. Shut me up. I shouldn't even be here. I shouldn't even be in this fucking marriage. In this fucking town.'

She looks around at them all, the way they are staring, slack-jawed.

She watches as Mark moves towards Tamsin, as though to protect her, his arm around her, the way she shelters in her husband's bulk. And she understands, in a pure, clear moment that cuts through the wine, that she hates this man. Hates everything he is and everything he represents. She lifts her sleeve. 'Shall I show you what I wear on *my* wrist?' she says to Mark. 'It's a spider. To remind me to keep fighting. Not to capitulate. Not to forget to fight men like you.'

Hannah

She hears Cate shouting from where she lies on the bed. The door banging. Concerned voices. She knows she should go to check, because whatever has happened sounds serious, but she is filled with a great exhaustion, all of her cells heavy with it, as though she has been walking, walking for such a long time, with such a heavy load on her back, and her body is so tired. She just wants to lie here curled beside this child, to feel the warmth of him, and maybe sleep beside him for a while. There are footsteps on the stairs, the door opening a crack.

'Hannah?' Nathan's voice.

'Yes?'

She does not want this crack of light, this light which is sharpening, filling the room, which carries the future within it, cold and hard and unforgiving. She wants to pull Nathan in here, close the door behind them. Lie down in the darkness together with this baby on this bed.

'It's Cate. She's gone. She's pretty drunk. I think she might need finding.'

Hannah rouses herself and comes to stand, then follows him slowly back down the stairs, and out blinking into the living room, where people are scattered in small groups.

'I'll go and look for her,' she says.

'Let her cool off,' says the man called Mark. 'She's pissed. She could do with the air.'

Hannah takes her coat.

'You want me to come?' Nathan says.

'No, you stay.'

Outside it is freezing, and she has no idea where to go. She calls Cate's name and her voice is thin and high. She traces their steps back out to the road, heels percussive on the hard ground, comes to a deserted supermarket car park. She feels vulnerable out here, in these heels, in this dress. 'Cate?' she calls. The road is busy, even at this time of night. She has a sudden terrible thought and she starts to run. 'Cate?' she calls. 'Cate?'

And then she sees her. She is standing on a small hump-backed bridge, leaning out over the river. 'Cate?' she calls.

Hannah is breathless when she reaches her.

Cate's eyes, when she lifts her gaze, are hard and bright. 'I'm leaving,' she says.

Beneath the bridge the cold black water moves.

'Cate,' says Hannah, taking her arm. 'You're drunk. It'll seem different in the morning. I promise.'

'Don't fucking *silence* me. Do you know what you're like, Hannah? You're just like all the rest of them. *Never mind that you feel like shit. Never mind that they cut you open and didn't tell you why. You have a healthy baby. Take some fucking pills and shut up.* You don't want to hear the truth.'

And Hannah feels her own cold fury rising now. 'What truth? What truth, Cate? Come on. Tell me.'

Cate shakes her head, mutinous.

'Well, I'll tell you my truth, shall I?' Hannah speaks quickly, clearly now. 'My husband is leaving me. Because we can't have a child. I lost a child. I had a miscarriage. Have you ever had one of those?'

Cate's eyes in the darkness, all pupil now.

'Shall I tell you the truth of that, Cate? It's like this.' She takes Cate's hand, lifts her sleeve. 'It was about this big. About seven weeks old. A sac to hold a baby. It's fairly monstrous, actually. It's not the sort of thing that's supposed to be seen. It's supposed to stay inside you – to grow and grow and grow until it can't grow any more. You know what that feels like, don't you? A baby, growing inside you?'

Their breath plumes together in the freezing air.

'You didn't tell me.'

'I didn't tell anyone.'

'*Why?*'

'Because you were pregnant at the time. Because I didn't want to upset you. Because I felt ashamed.'

There is a slackening. Cate's hand drops to her side, her shoulders slump.

'I'm sorry,' says Cate. 'You should have told me.' Her voice is thick.

'No,' says Hannah. 'You should have asked.'

It is late when they arrive at the hotel. The room is smaller than she imagined. 'Where's the bathroom?' asks Nathan.

'I was too late to book the en suite,' she says wearily. 'I think it's down the hall.' She is cold. She got cold out there on the bridge.

He nods, goes to his bag. 'Can you tell me where you packed my toothbrush then?'

'It's here.' She takes out her wash bag, hands him his toothbrush.

When he has gone she sits down in the armchair. She sees herself reflected in the driftwood mirror. This stupid black

213

dress. Her make-up, smudged now. All of it broken. All of it over. It is all so absurd.

In the morning two trays are left outside their door. She brings them in and puts them on the table. Nathan sits up in bed, pulls on his jeans. 'I'm going outside,' he says. When he comes back he smells of cigarettes.

She calls the restaurant and cancels the lunch reservation.

There will be no lunch. There will be no oysters or artisan bread or Aylesbury lamb. There will be no children. She kills things before they are even born. He does not touch her. In a way she is grateful. It is as though she has broken into tiny pieces inside, with only her thin skin holding it all together, and if she is touched she might shatter – might never find the pieces to put herself back together again.

They walk along the beach without speaking. They look out at the roiling sea, then they climb back into the car. They drive back up the M2 to London. She pretends to sleep. They drop off the rental car. They take the bus back to Hackney.

They walk up the three flights of stairs into their flat. Nathan packs a bag.

Lissa

It is the final Thursday night, and the play flies. It is the freest she has ever felt on a stage – the lines rise in her as though they are her own.

You have mermaid's blood in your veins, Vanya tells her, *so be a mermaid. Run wild for once in your life.*

As she comes off stage after her final exit, she realizes she has been unaware of the audience; entirely focused on the other actors, out of her skin. She has not thought about Nathan for an hour and a half. As they take their curtain, Johnny turns his face towards her, saluting her with a small nod. Then in the wings, in a gesture of old-fashioned courtesy, he takes her hand. 'Magnificent,' he says.

'You, too.'

He inclines his head. 'We should drink to it,' he says. 'You and I.' He still has her hand in his.

She hurries to the dressing room, aware she is happy, that something has been completed tonight, that a question she asked herself as a young woman has been answered. That she can do this, that it is worth doing. That she has not been deluded or stupid or wrong.

As she is unbuttoning her costume, her phone vibrates and she sees a message from Nathan.

I'm here.

She stares at it, then up at herself in the mirror. She sees her outline there – Yelena's dress for the final act: a long dark coat, the buttons fastening all the way to the neck, her hair pinned up. She sees the way her lips are swollen, the slant of her eyes, her chest moving up and down with her breath. She does not reply to the message; she knows he will wait.

She finishes unbuttoning her costume and slips out of it, hanging it up on the rail, then goes to the sink and splashes water on her neck. She pulls on her jeans and her top. Her make-up she leaves as it is – slightly smudged around her eyes. When she takes her hair out of its clips it falls in waves down her back.

Mermaid's blood in your veins.

She picks up her bag and makes her way out into the bar. Nathan is alone at a table in the corner. She approaches him slowly. He stands before she can speak. His face is a mixture of nervousness and awe.

He is wearing a blue shirt with the sleeves rolled up. She notices this. She notices his forearms. The way his hand moves to his chest as he speaks, referencing his heart. The way his shirt is open at the neck.

She bends her head – she is a queen tonight, and she accepts his tribute. As she sits before him she can feel herself, the parts where her skin touches her clothes, the hardness of her nipples, the tingling of her skull. There is an open bottle of wine on the table and he lifts it, pours her a large glass, and she nods her thanks. Behind the curve of his shoulder she sees Johnny standing alone at the bar, two drinks before him. He looks towards her; she sees his eyes slide over her and Nathan, then back to her, snagging on her with a question. She does not answer it – instead she turns away, to her drink, which is thick and red and looks like blood.

She sees the pulse at Nathan's neck. His mouth, stained a little with the wine. The span of his hands on the table before her.

She drinks her wine and he drinks his and they speak but she is not sure, exactly, of what. When her glass is empty he asks if she wants more. At a certain point the bottle is finished. She looks up and sees that Johnny has left the bar without saying goodbye. She registers this, but distantly. 'We could go back,' she says, turning to Nathan. 'We could go back to mine.'

And like everything else this night, it is surprisingly easy to say.

On the way he makes conversation, but as the train nears her stop the words dwindle and he falls silent. She catches him staring at his face in the window. They walk quickly, without speaking, across the park. In her living room, she paces around, switching on lights, while Nathan stands in the middle of the floor. 'Do you want another drink?' she asks.

'OK.' His voice is low and a little cracked.

She goes into the kitchen, where she leaves the lights off. There is a bottle of whisky at the back of her cupboard and she takes it out, pours a measure into two glasses.

There is a sound behind her and she sees that Nathan has followed, is standing behind her. He lifts her hair from her neck and holds it in his fist. He leans towards her and she feels his mouth at the place where her neck meets her shoulder. Then he presses her gently against the wall. 'Please,' he says, 'don't speak.'

She does not speak. Instead she turns to him and opens her mouth to his.

The next morning, when he has gone to work, she lies in bed and thinks of him. She can feel him still: his weight on her, the look on his face when she was above him, the feeling of him inside her. At the memory she is queasy with desire again, and when she puts her hand to herself she is flooded, swollen, slick with sex.

She goes out for coffee and sits in the weak sunshine, cradling her cup. She knows it is not wise to be out here, feeling this way, only streets from Hannah's flat. She knows the scent of him is still on her, knows she is drenched in it. Men stare at her. She is a battery that has been charged again. It is simple electricity – it is outside of morality. There is a dangerous, shimmering elation to the way she feels.

Hannah

She begins to sleep in the little room. The sounds here are different from those she has been used to – she can hear the wind in the trees, the sounds of the canal: bikes clunking over loose paving stones, the mangled yowl of foxes, the shouts and laughter of drunken kids. She lies awake, staring at the play of light on the ceiling, and if she sleeps, she sleeps lightly and her dreams are full of strange, unknowable things.

In the mornings, for a few moments she is disoriented, lying here in this bed alone, and then she remembers – Nathan has gone, her husband has gone, and for the first time in over thirteen years she does not know where he is.

Outside, the winter city presses on her and she feels flimsy beneath its weight. She forgets to shop and eats little, small mouthfuls of food she has in the cupboards: crackers and butter, a slice of apple. There is no joy in cooking for herself. She is getting thinner. She knows this but does not care; there is nothing to take care of herself for, no future to safeguard, no limits to keep within.

She gets a text from her brother. *She's here! Rosie Eleanor*

Grey. A picture of a small wrinkled bundle of humanity held in her brother's arms. Her niece.

She writes back. *Congratulations!! Can't wait to meet her.*

You're still coming for Christmas? her brother replies.

Yes! Can't wait! she lies.

The next morning she writes to work and says she is ill – a virus, that she needs to rest. The weather has changed again, grown bitter and cold. She puts on the radio, but does not really listen to it. She moves slowly through this place that has all the hallmarks of her previous life – the same rooms, the same furniture, the same books on the same shelves – but is utterly foreign. She has arrived at a destination, but it is an unknown place. She is aware that she hurts, but that the hurt is so large it is beyond her. There is no solace outside, in the sky, the grass, the animals and the trees. She is not like them. She cannot multiply herself – she is aberrant, outside of nature, and she knows it is better for her to be up here, alone.

Sometimes there are children in the park below. From this distance they are small packets of energy, jerky and joyous and untrained. They ride scooters along the paths. They trail after their parents and stop and pick up stones and look at them. She watches the children look at the stones and their parents, more often than not hurrying back to them, grasping them by the wrist and hauling them to their feet. If she had a child, she thinks, she would not rush and pull, she would get down on the earth, she would get down beside them and look at the stones.

Outside the world marches on, and Christmas looms with all its gaudy inevitability. She has said she will go up north, to

Jim and Hayley's, but now she would like to refuse the invitation to her brother's house. But she has given her word, and there are presents to be bought: her parents, Jim, Hayley, Rosie. After work she walks towards Covent Garden, weaving past the tourists, the carol singers, everyone buttoned up against the cold, but she does not buy presents. Instead, she wanders into clothes shops, trying on things she would usually never wear: an ankle-length dress covered with a print of crawling vines, earrings that graze her shoulders, high-heeled boots the colour of blood. Her reflection surprises her – her fringe falling into her eyes the way it does. It is months since she has had it trimmed. Perhaps, she thinks, she will grow her hair long. Perhaps she will shave it all off.

One freezing afternoon, on Long Acre, her eye is caught by a child in a pushchair – a little girl. The child is grinning and giggling, clapping her hands. The buggy stops and Hannah looks up. The woman pushing the child is staring at her, her head on one side.

'I'm sorry,' says Hannah.

'What for?' says the woman. There is something crow-like about her, something unsettling about her gaze.

Hannah pushes her hands into her pockets. 'I just—' The child is chattering to herself, absorbed by her reflection in the shop window beside her. She has cheeks like a child in a picture book. Her hands are large and dimpled and strong.

'Do you need healing?' says the woman.

'Sorry?' Hannah's eyes switch back.

'Do you need healing?' the woman says again. 'Perhaps I can help?'

The woman reaches into the back of her buggy and pulls a printed piece of paper from a small stack. 'Here,' she says, holding the leaflet out. 'Take it.' Her tone is surprisingly brusque.

Hannah obeys, reaching out and taking it, folding it in half.

The woman nods and then, as though it is absolutely in her power, this holding and releasing of the gaze, she looks ahead and walks on.

At the entrance to the Tube Hannah finds she is breathless, as though she has been running. She pulls the paper from her pocket, sees an ordinary-looking flyer – something mocked up on a PC at home. It advertises the healing powers of Lindsay McCormack. There is a photo of Lindsay's sallow face in troubling close-up, and an address, somewhere in the outer reaches of West London. She pushes it to the bottom of her bag. Later, though, back at home, she pulls it out again and gazes upon it in the light of the lamp in the small room – blurred pictures of female forms and trees, text in coloured lettering that is difficult to read. A testimonial from a man who was in chronic pain who feels much better now. All of it badly done, nothing in the least bit compelling about any of it.

And yet.

She picks up her phone, calls the landline number. It is answered quickly. 'Hello?'

'Oh – hello. I saw you. Today. In Covent Garden. You gave me a flyer.'

'Yes?' The woman sounds harassed, and there is the noise of a crying child in the background. 'Yes, I remember.'

'I wondered if you had any space.'

'Space?'

'To see me, I mean.'

'Ah,' the woman says. 'Yes. How about tomorrow morning?'

She tells work she has a dentist appointment – an emergency filling – and then, just after rush hour, takes the Tube out west to the end of the line.

The address is deep in a warren of houses, an ungainly semi with a muddy patch of front garden. A trike rusts on the step, its trailing purple decorations soaked with rain. Hannah rings the doorbell and peers through the frosted glass. At first there is no sound, no movement, and she thinks she may have the wrong house – then the woman comes to the door. She is bundled in a cardigan the colour of porridge, her hair pulled back into a scruffy bun.

'Come in.' She leads Hannah through a dark hallway to a small back room with a table and two blankets. 'Hop up.' The woman pats the table.

The room is chilly, uninviting. 'Would you mind,' says Hannah, standing in the doorway, 'if I visited the loo?'

A flicker of irritation crosses the woman's face. 'It's just out the door on the right.'

Hannah locks herself in the toilet and stares at her reflection in the mirror. Her cheeks are flushed, but her lips are pale and set in a tight line. What is she doing here? She has a strange, uneasy sense that she has been summoned here, or that she has summoned the woman from the depths of her subconscious mind – that this woman holds some unearthly power, that if she goes back into that cold room, she might never come out again, might never leave this cheerless place. She uses the toilet, flushes, and washes her hands with the small hard sliver of soap. In the hallway she hesitates – there is still time to run.

But the woman is waiting. She holds out her hands for Hannah's coat, which she hangs on the back of the door. 'Hop up then,' she says again, gesturing to the table.

Hannah slips off her shoes and complies. It is cold. Should she tell her how cold it is in here? The woman is wrapped up in her cardigan, but Hannah is only wearing her work dress. She pulls the blanket around her knees. It crackles and sticks to her tights.

'So,' says the woman, her head on one side. 'What brings you here?'

Hannah's lips are dry. She licks them. 'It was strange. For you to approach me – and – and – this is unlike me, very unlike me, but I just felt compelled to call.'

The woman nods. 'I sensed it,' she says.

'Sensed what?' says Hannah.

'Your need.'

'Need for what?'

The woman pauses, shifts in her seat. 'A child.'

'Ah,' says Hannah, and then falls silent, her skin prickling with anticipation, with fear.

'Tell me,' the woman says.

'I – we've been trying. For a long time. For three years, and nothing. And then we started IVF. And I got pregnant. And lost the baby. And then we tried again. The IVF. And now my husband has left.'

The woman nods, as though none of this surprises her.

'Sometimes,' says Hannah, 'I feel cursed. I don't know why I should be cursed.' She is babbling now, gibberish. 'I try and be good.' The woman is staring. Hannah is silent a moment, then, 'It's cold,' she says.

The woman gets up and turns the radiator dial a notch. 'I have the heating off in the day.'

'Don't you heat it up? When you have clients? Patients?'

'They usually like the blankets,' the woman says.

'Oh.'

'Would you like another?'

She looks down at the shiny, unpleasant blanket over her knees. 'No. Thanks.'

The woman rolls up her sleeve. She takes Hannah's calves in her hands. Her palms are not warm. 'All right,' she says. 'I'm going to work on you now.'

'Work on me?'

'Just lean back and relax.'

The woman's eyes begin to roll back in her head. She nods to herself, as though her suspicions are confirmed by the feel of Hannah's feet, her calves. The woman's eyes are closed now; she seems to be listening.

'Mmmmm. Mmmmm.' The woman is making a low humming sound. 'Mmmmm. Mmmm. Mmmm.'

Hannah looks out of the window at the dreary little garden.

'Am I cursed?' she says to the woman. 'Can you tell me if I'm cursed?'

But she is not sure if she has spoken or not, if she has uttered or only thought the words.

Lissa

On the last night the cast club together and buy salmon and dill and cream cheese and crackers and vodka, and one by one, when their final scenes have finished, they go into the men's dressing room and down shots – *Nostrovia!* By the time of the curtain call they are all tipsy, and when the final curtain has been taken they pile back into the dressing room, all of them in their costumes still, making Johnny and Helen – the last of them left on stage – drink three shots each to catch up.

Klara comes and finds them, hugging them all in turn. The technical staff drink beer and cider while the actors sink more vodka, singing their Russian song over and over again – until even the technical staff join in. Someone puts on dance music, and the dressing room becomes a shebeen as the noise level increases to a roar.

Lissa checks her phone. She has had only one message from Nathan since Thursday.

No regrets.

At first she read it as a question, but then realized it was a statement, and replied: *None.*

The music has changed – Greg has got hold of the stereo and is playing old dance tunes from the 1930s – and the actors have coupled up to turn each other around the floor.

'Lissa.' Johnny is before her, hand outstretched. 'Would you like to dance?'

She takes his hand and he pulls her to her feet. She is drunk, she realizes, and she leans on him for balance as he moves her around the room. She closes her eyes briefly, enjoying his proximity, his warmth, his smell of tobacco and soap.

'I'm sorry,' she says into his chest.

'What for?'

'The other night. Standing you up at the bar.'

'S'all right.' Johnny's voice rumbles against her ear. 'He your boyfriend then?'

She gives a gesture, part shrug, part shake of the head. 'It's complicated.'

'Ain't that always the truth.'

They stop moving and he steps back a moment, holding her at arm's length, regarding her. He reaches out and tucks a piece of her hair behind her ear. 'It's been a pleasure, love. Here.' He takes out a piece of paper, scribbles a number on it. 'Just so you've got it,' he says, handing it to her. 'Look after yourself, won't you?'

'I'll try.'

'None of my business,' he says quietly. 'I know.'

Then he lifts her hand in that same courtly gesture, his lips to her knuckles, and turns away. She watches as he slings his black leather bag over his shoulder and slips out of the door without any elaborate goodbyes.

On the other side of the room, Michael and Helen are kissing, their hands in each other's hair. Lissa checks her phone again. The sand is running out – soon the magic will dissipate and the play will truly be over. Soon the night will end and there will be nothing but the flat and the call centre, and she will no longer be a queen.

Mermaid's blood.

She lets herself out of the dressing room, walks down the darkened corridor. After a few steps she stops and calls Nathan. He picks up on the second ring. 'Liss?' Wherever he is, it sounds quiet.

'I want you,' she says. 'Can you come here? Now?'

There is a pause and then: 'Where are you?'

'At the theatre.'

'How long will you be there for?'

'An hour. Maybe more.'

'I'll come.'

She clicks off the phone, holds it lightly in her palm. Hears her breath in the corridor. It is as though she has taken half a step outside her skin, to a place where things are weightless, where there is only the logic of desire. She feels no guilt, only interest. She wonders if it would be this easy to murder.

At half past eleven, her phone buzzes in her pocket and she slips out of the room without being seen, making her way through the bar, where the bar staff are clearing up, to where Nathan is standing waiting outside on the street, hunched into his winter coat, smoking a cigarette, smoke pluming in the cold air. It has started to snow, and flakes tumble from the sky. Already an inch or two has gathered on the pavement.

She steps towards him, reaching and taking his cigarette from him, bringing it to her mouth. The smoke hits her bloodstream, mingling with the alcohol, meeting the cold, making her reel.

'You're her still,' he says.

She looks down at herself – her velvet coat, her boots. She had forgotten she was wearing her costume. 'Yes,' she says, and she can see how this pleases him – how it excites him. 'Yes, I'm still her.'

He takes her wrist and pulls her to him. His mouth tastes of smoke. She can feel him against her, already hard. 'Where can we go?' he says.

'Here,' she says. 'You can come in here.'

She leads him back through the bar to the dark corridor to the women's dressing room, which is empty, the lights turned off. Soon the women will be back, changing from their costumes, moving out into the night, but for now they are occupied – she can hear the party continuing, the men Cossack dancing; she can hear the thump, thump of their heels on the floor.

She sits on the table and lifts her long, heavy skirts, feels the cool air on her thighs. Nathan bends towards her, and puts his mouth on her flesh. There is the cold shock of his cheek, the warmth of his mouth, his tongue. When he stands before her, she opens herself for him, and he spreads her wide.

Hens

2008

Hannah is getting married. She does not want a hen do. Instead, she wants to go on holiday with Lissa and Cate. Since she is getting married in May, she decides Greece would be perfect in late April. She clears the dates with the others and spends hours searching for a place to stay – finally booking them a villa for a week on one of the islands, close to the beach with its own pool. It is expensive, but not hideously so. She has recently had a promotion at work – since she knows neither of her friends is earning much, she does not ask them for any money towards the cost. And she gets a thrill from this, from treating her friends, her best friends, her best women, Lissa and Cate.

They have fun in the airport. They try different perfumes and sunglasses. They drink champagne at the champagne bar. They make jokes about the gaudy horror show of late capitalism but they enjoy it really. They are so busy enjoying it that they almost miss their flight.

The villa is beautiful. They each have their own room, their own bathroom. The towels are thick and the thread count is high. Hannah takes pleasure from watching her friends squeal like young girls as they run around the tiled floors, opening cupboards, finding chocolates and wine and fruit. They are all implausibly touched that the owners have left them a bottle of cheap wine. They drink the cheap wine from the bottle and they put on their swimming gear and jump into the pool.

They sleep late. They eat long breakfasts of yoghurt and honey and nuts and toasted white bread and strong coffee. They angle their chairs towards the sun. It is twenty-two degrees at ten o'clock. By noon it is twenty-five. There are wild flowers everywhere. They agree this is the perfect time of year to visit Greece.

In the afternoons they go to the beach, a short walk along a rocky path that is fragrant with thyme. They take books and rent loungers and swim in the blue sea.

They put cream on each other's backs, exclaiming gently over the softness of each other's skin. They eat lunch at beach tavernas which are knocked together with driftwood and serve inevitable but delicious Greek salad peppered with oregano. They drink sharp retsina served in small glass jugs, misted with condensation in the heat.

In the evenings they go out to restaurants. They try several and then settle on one they like and go there every night – a small pretty place with tables overlooking the harbour. They dress carefully for these outings, even though the restaurants are only village tavernas – they wear dresses and put on make-up, they thread earrings in their ears.

They grow peaceful on this holiday. They go to bed early. They soak up the sun. They remember how well they live together. It does them all good to get away.

But as the week comes to a close, happiness grows gritty and begins to chafe. Lissa thinks of the call centre, realizes she has forgotten to book shifts for the week of her return. Which means she will not have enough for her rent. Which means she will have to ask Declan again. And Declan is growing tired of these requests, she knows. Just as he is growing tired of her.

On the final morning, Lissa regards herself in the mirror in the early-morning sun. She knows she is beautiful, has always known this, but now, in her thirties, this beauty that once was something abundant, something she threw away on cigarettes and alcohol and late nights and coffee and no real exercise to speak of, lately this beauty has come to seem a finite resource, one she must attend to, take better care of. And this care, it would appear, takes money, money she does not have. More than once, lately, she has come to find herself standing at the counter in Boots or Selfridges or Liberty's holding an expensive face cream in her hand. More than once she has considered slipping the expensive face cream into her bag.

Last week, her agent dropped her.

These chances, Lissa, her agent told her on the phone, they come along once in a blue moon for people your age. I'm sorry. I just don't think I can represent you any more.

In the mirror, Lissa's mouth is set in a straight, tight line. She is angry. Angry with Cate. Cannot help but blame her for what occurred. And angry too – though she knows this is unfair – with Hannah, all this generosity, this villa, this holiday. She wishes it were her, able to be generous, able to treat her friends. But Hannah is good. Hannah is dutiful. Hannah works hard, and so is justly rewarded. Whereas she is broke. Perhaps it is her beauty that is to blame. Her beauty, this unasked-for gift. Perhaps it has warped her – made her lazy. Made her expect too much.

Last week, before coming out here, she bought a dress in Liberty's, on her credit card, a wrap in silk crêpe de Chine. It has a print of Japanese flowers. She has brought it out here but she knows she won't wear it. It stays at the bottom of her suitcase. It is the outfit of someone who has achieved things she has not. Who is living a life she is beginning to expect is not destined for her.

On the last evening of the holiday, Lissa insists they go for cocktails. There is a little bar she has seen tucked down an alleyway. They all go out to the bar and drink Kir Royales and champagne cocktails in its dark interior. They have three cocktails each but they do not feel drunk, just merry, as they make their way down the cobbled streets to the harbour and to their restaurant. It is their restaurant now. They order wine and drink it quickly, and then have more. They eat bread dipped in olive oil and salt, and drink more wine. They start to feel drunk.

So, says Lissa, lighting a cigarette. What happens next? She is speaking to Hannah.

What do you mean?

Well, after you get married. You going to have kids?

I suppose so, says Hannah. Yes.

Does Nathan want them?

Yes. I think so.

You think so?

Yes, says Hannah. He does.

Right. Lissa nods.

What? says Hannah.

Nothing, says Lissa.

What? Why are you making that face?

I just, it's quite a big deal, isn't it? Having kids. Don't you think you ought to think about it a bit more than that?

I have thought about it, actually. I've thought about it a lot. And I want children. What about you? Do you want kids?

No.

No? Just no?

Yeah.

Don't you think you ought to examine that a bit more? What if you regret it?

Sure, says Lissa, blowing the smoke of her cigarette out into the evening air. I'll examine it. I don't want kids because I think you should really, really want kids to have them. And if you want to do anything else in your life, then maybe you should do that instead. I saw enough of that with my mother.

What do you mean? says Hannah.

I was in the way. Of all of it: her art, her life. Her fucking activism. *She should never have had me. Everyone would have been a lot better off.*

Oh, for God's sake, says Hannah. Don't be ridiculous. Your mother is amazing.

Is she? says Lissa. Of course. Of course she is, Hannah, and you would know. Since you know my mother so well.

Hannah stares at her friend. She has rarely seen this side of Lissa before. This drunken curdling. This bitterness.

Leave it, Lissa. Cate leans in. Give Hannah a break.

Oh? Give Hannah a break? Lissa turns to Cate, her teeth bloody with wine. What about me? What about giving me a break, Cate? Cate the moral compass. Showing us all the way. You think you're so fucking squeaky clean? Whose fault is it that I didn't get that part?

Not mine, says Cate.

Fuck you, Lissa spits.

Hannah watches Cate reel back as though she has been hit.

Then – I'll tell you why you don't want children, Lissa, says Cate, leaning back into the fray. Because you're fundamentally selfish. Because you're never going to want to put another person before yourself.

They have never argued before, Cate and Lissa. Not like this. It is exhilarating. With the wine and the cigarettes and the balmy spring night, it is like a drug. They want more. They could imagine brawling in the street. Tearing each other's hair out. Taking bites out of each other's skin.

Hannah watches them. There is something erotic, she thinks, in their arguing. She feels strangely bereft.

People look towards their table. These three English women with their quirky clothes and their loud voices and their empty bottles of wine. How rude they are. How incontinent they all seem.

Cate

Since the dinner Sam has refused to meet her eye. He is asleep in the mornings, waking late and hurrying out of the house to work, then stays out later and later after his shifts. Still, she is often awake herself when he comes in at one, two, three o'clock. She does not go to him.

She has called Hannah but Hannah has not picked up. She has sent her messages – *Can we talk? Call me when you're ready. Han, we need to talk, call me. Please.* Hannah has not replied.

She remembers Hannah's face on the bridge. The cold, clipped way she spoke. The razor-sharp edges of her hurt.

She wants to say sorry, but she wants to say, too, that it is not fair. That Hannah did not tell her – did not give her the chance to do the right thing.

The only person she has heard from is Dea.

Emergency Mum Club? Whenever you're ready. Just say the word.

She has not written back.

The days are short and bitter and she stays inside, the heating on too high. Tom is fractious, picking up on her lack of ease, and her patience with him is thin and frayed. She shouts at him often and often he cries. And then she shouts some more. When she does go out, the pavements are icy and treacherous. There are carol singers raising their reedy voices to the spires in the centre of town. They are selling Christmas trees in the garages of Wincheap – trussed in plastic. The students are still in the Senate building. The wet black branches of the trees.

At the weekend Sam rises early and dresses Tom himself. They come in to where she lies in bed, Tom dressed haphazardly in an ill-fitting jumper which barely covers his belly. 'We're going out,' he says.

'Where?'

'Mark and Tamsin's. Mum'll be there.'

'Right,' she says. 'I don't suppose I'm welcome then.'

'No, I don't suppose you are.'

When they have gone she takes out her computer. Checks her emails. Searches again for Lucy Skein. Nothing.

She leaves the curtains drawn and burrows back into bed.

The sound of the front door wakes her in the late afternoon. She pulls on tracksuit bottoms and a sweater, makes her way downstairs, sees Tom asleep in his buggy in the hallway, finds Sam in the kitchen, sitting at the table, a small zippered bag in front of him.

'Are you leaving?'

'You should be so lucky. They're from Tamsin. For Tom. Jack outgrew them.'

Cate unzips the bag. A pile of clothes, neatly folded. They smell aggressively clean. 'That was nice of her.'

'Yeah, well. She's pretty nice. But you could always give them back. I mean, we wouldn't want too much of my family. Contaminating the air.'

'Sam—'

He holds up his hand. 'Wait,' he says. He leaves her, goes upstairs. She hears his footsteps above her head. When he comes back down he has the prescription bag in his hands. 'What are these?'

'They're pills,' she says flatly. 'Anti-depressants.'

'And are you taking them?'

'No.'

'Don't you think you might need to?'

'No. Yes. I don't know.' She shakes her head. 'I'm sorry,' she says.

'For what? For marrying me? For saying I'm not that bright?' His face is twisted.

'I just – I think I've been confused.'

'About what?'

'Me. You. Everything.' She looks at the floor. 'There's someone—'

'Someone else?'

'Not like that.'

'Like what then? Like what?' He bangs the table in front of him. 'Come on, Cate. You might as well tell me now.'

Behind her in the hall, Tom stirs, grizzles, then is quiet again.

'Someone I used to know,' she says. 'A long time ago. I've been thinking about her. A lot. That's all.'

Sam nods. 'OK. A woman?'

'Yes.'

'So, what, you're gay now?'

'No. I mean . . . I was. I wasn't. It was just her. Just Lucy. I just loved her.'

He looks at her for a long time. 'OK,' he says. 'When was this?'

'Eleven years ago.'

'And where is she now?'

'I don't know.'

'But you want to?'

'I don't know.'

He looks at her for a long time, then nods, as though something has been decided. Then he stands, takes a can of Red Bull from the fridge. 'I'm late for work,' he says. 'I'll see you later tonight.'

The next afternoon, when Sam comes home she is screaming at their son. Tom is wailing, some half-eaten food on his high chair, the rest on the floor. 'I'm calling Mum,' he says, going to pick up Tom. 'She can take him for the day tomorrow.'

Alice arrives with Terry the next morning, and Cate hands Tom over. It is a cold clear day, the sun low in the sky. They exchange few words. She thinks she can see the relief on her son's face. When they have gone, she closes the door and cries. When the crying has stopped she goes upstairs to the bathroom, pulls out the bag of pills, and sits on the floor of the bathroom with them between her legs. In her pocket her phone rings. Dea. It rings and rings, then stops. The buzz of a message is loud in the silence of the house. She lifts the phone and listens.

I've got a bonfire needs tending. What are you doing right now?

Cate lifts her head to the window, sees the thin sun, calls back.

The allotment is surprisingly close, just on the other side of the river. There are a couple of other figures dotted there, bent to the cold earth, but she sees Dea immediately, standing alone on a plot halfway down. A small fire going, a pile of bracken and leaves beside it.

'Wow,' says Dea as Cate approaches. 'You look terrible.'

Dea is dressed in faded canvas dungarees, a parka, her beanie on her head, and a large mug in her hands.

'Thanks.'

'Is this still the aftermath of the other night?'

Cate shrugs. A couple of old camp chairs sit around the fire. At the back of the plot stands a rickety-looking shed with potted marigolds in front of the door.

'This is nice.'

'Yeah, well, I like to keep my end up.' Dea looks down at herself. 'Lesbian allotment-holder. Dungarees. I'm ticking a lot of boxes right now.'

Cate raises the ghost of a smile. 'Where's Nora?'

'With Zoe. Her family are over already for Christmas. They're great, but they're loud. And the house is small. Where's Tom?'

'With Alice.'

'Well,' says Dea, raising her mug. 'It was a great dinner party. Thanks.'

'Please.'

'No, really, it's the most excitement I've had for a while. I particularly liked the line about the breaking soldiers.' Dea raises her mug. 'And that guy Mark. I liked seeing you stick it to him.'

'I'm glad you had a good time.'

'You want a tea?'

'Sure.'

'Chuck some brambles on the fire,' Dea calls as she heads to the shed. 'They're extremely satisfying to burn.'

Cate eyes the pile, then goes and lifts a prickly armful, throws them on the flames, watching them twist and buckle in the heat. Dea comes back out with a mug of tea. 'Lemon balm,' she says, handing it over.

'Thanks.'

'The food was great, though. He's a talented man, your husband. You were right.'

'Can we stop talking about it now?'

'Sure.'

Cate sips her tea, which is green and gently fragrant, and stares into the flames. There is the sweet smell of woodsmoke. Gulls calling in the high thin sky.

'I went up to the Senate building today,' says Dea. 'To check in on the students. They've turned off the heating in there. The university authorities.' She shakes her head. 'It's barbaric. I took them a couple of blankets. They're asking for more.'

'They should come out,' says Cate sullenly.

'Oh?' says Dea. 'Why's that?'

'What are they going to change? What does anyone ever change?'

Dea looks at her.

'You know how it is.' Cate shrugs. 'Young people become older people. They'll compromise. That's what we do. We stop fighting. We capitulate. We become part of the problem.'

'Right.'

240

'The vote's over. The Tories have won. If the students are cold, they should go home. See their parents. Have Christmas. Get warm. Don't you think?'

'No,' says Dea. 'I'm not sure I do. I'm not sure you do either.'

She goes over to the pile of bracken, taking an armful of brambles and feeding them to the fire, regarding Cate through the flames.

'Have you compromised then?' she says. 'Is that what's going on?'

When Cate does not reply, Dea crouches to poke the fire with a stick, rearranging it, raking the burning embers. 'I meant to tell you,' she says, after a while. 'There's a job going. At the university. It's just maternity cover, but I thought of you.'

'What sort of job?'

'Outreach – all over Kent. Going into schools, helping kids get into higher education. We've got some of the poorest areas in Britain on our doorstep – Sheppey, Medway. I'm sure it would suit you. It could be quite creative, if you gave it some thought.'

'Right. So poor kids can go to university and be thousands of pounds in debt when they finish?'

'What would you rather? That they didn't go at all?'

Cate is silent.

'Anyway, they're interviewing early in the New Year – they want someone to start in the spring.'

Cate turns back to the fire. 'Who are you? My careers advisor?'

'No,' says Dea, throwing a stick into the flames. 'Just a friend.'

241

Hannah

In the car on the way to Jim and Hayley's, she sits in the back seat, behind her mother, her head leaning against the window as the edges of the city give way to villages and then the villages to moorland, to dry-stone walls, all of it with a thick covering of snow. Every so often, her father brakes for a grouse or a sheep in the road.

Her dad sings tunelessly, happily, to the radio, banging the steering wheel to the beat, while her mother chuckles and tuts and shakes her head. They are excited, on their way to visit their son, their granddaughter: grandparents at last.

She always used to sit on this side, on family holidays – Jim to the right of her, this exact view of the back of her father's head. Often they would bicker. Once, she remembers, on the way to a campsite in Wales, her dad finally lost his temper and stopped the car, ordering them both out on to the grass verge. He pulled away and left them, and they were silent, horrified, for a full five minutes until he drove back around. Now her little brother is a father. Soon he will be driving on family holidays of his own.

They pull up outside a stone cottage on the edge of a village; it has thick walls and small windows. As they climb from the car Jim appears in the driveway to meet them. He is bigger than Hannah remembers – has put on weight – but it looks well on him. Somehow he manages to be everywhere at once – opening the door for their mum, carrying on a conversation with their father about Christmas traffic and the weather and enveloping Hannah in a hug. 'How are you doing, sis?'

His vowels. She always forgets how northern he is. She would like to shelter here, in his arms, in his vowels for a while. 'OK,' she says into his shoulder. 'I'm OK.'

He leads the way inside, carrying their luggage into a narrow hall, a Christmas tree in the corner. 'The bedrooms are all up there. You and Mum are first on the right,' he says to their father, 'and you're at the end, Han. But Hayley's up there napping with the baby.' He claps his hands together. 'Right then. Who's for a drink before they wake up?'

He serves them all – gin and tonic for their mum, a glass of wine for Hannah, and ale for their dad, and she sees how proud he is, her brother, how proud to be witnessed by them: householder, father, host.

Later, when they have been through the tour of the house, they sit in the living room, where peanuts and crackers wait in small bowls on the tables and a picture of Jim and Hayley's wedding hangs above the fireplace. Hannah and her parents sit, slightly stilted, slightly hushed, perched on the edge of sofas – an audience waiting for the main actor to take to the stage. There is the creak of the stairs and there she is, Hayley, standing in the doorway, plump with sleep, creamy-cheeked, a tiny parcel of humanity held in her arms. For a moment, no one moves; the tableau is too perfect: the soft-faced Madonna and child. Then: 'Oh.' Hannah's mother gets to her feet. Hannah watches as she sweeps the baby up from Hayley's arms, her face beatific, transformed. 'Rosie,' she breathes. 'My lovely little Rosie!'

Hannah stands, makes her way over to the group, and sees James's features on a tiny old woman's face peering out from beneath layers of blanket. 'Oh.' She stretches the tip of her finger to touch the baby's cheek. 'She's so lovely, Jim. She looks just like you.'

Soon the baby starts to cry, and Jim gets to his feet. 'You sit down, love,' he says to Hayley. 'I'll do the feed.'

He comes back from the kitchen with a tiny bottle for his tiny daughter. Hannah watches him take her, the care with which he lifts her, the love and absorption on his face as Rosie takes the bottle and feeds. They are all silent, watching, listening to the sounds of suckling.

'Never did that in my day,' says Hannah's father.

'Don't know what you're missing.' Jim looks up with a grin. 'The oxytocin. It's incredible.'

'Oxy what-what?' Their father beams.

She goes to bed when her parents do, at ten o'clock. On Christmas morning she wakes early, stands at the window and looks out at the snow-covered fields. The rise of the moor beyond. The baby is lovely. The house is lovely. Jim and Hayley are lovely. It is exhausting, how lovely they all are. She can feel their compassion, their concern whether this is all right for her: Hayley's gentle, almost apologetic movements with her daughter. Their eyes on her when she takes the baby for a cuddle. Their collective in-breath, hoping Rosie won't cry in her aunty's arms. No one has asked her about Nathan. Have they decided amongst themselves that they will not?

This house, with its thick stone walls, its low lintels, its view of the fields and the moor and the steel-grey sky, its family sleeping in the room next door, oppresses her. She does not want to be here. She imagines walking out, through the garden, on to the high, snow-flecked moor. The air would be pure and clean and scouring. She wants to be scoured.

But she would need boots and waterproofs – she has not packed the right clothes.

She wonders how quickly she can get away – whether she can take the train back to London on Boxing Day. She checks the services, but they are scant and expensive, and she already has a ticket for the twenty-seventh. Two more days then, two more days to bear.

She thinks of the books she read as a child – all those maiden aunts, the illustrations showing the glasses and whiskers and good humour and cheer. Always in chairs. Always in the corner. She used to be in the centre of things. She is an edge dweller now.

She is aware that there are different, competing Hannahs within her: the polite Hannah, the good Hannah, Aunty Hannah! who is happy with the invitations to stay, who smiles and sits quietly, and parcels up her pain. And the bad Hannah, who is capable of poison, of madness – the one who wants to stand up, to upend the table, to take the baby and run away with her, to claim what should have been hers. To scream, *It should have been me.*

It should have been me!

It should have fucking been me.

Lissa

The front door is hung with a homemade wreath; woven willow studded with mistletoe and holly, taken from the bush in

245

the garden. Lissa lifts the knocker and lets it fall. Sarah answers the door in her apron and takes Lissa's face in hands that smell of turpentine and spices. 'Happy Christmas, darling.'

'And to you.'

Lissa has brought gifts: a mug, speckled with a brown glaze like freckles, two beautiful new pencils and a vase to keep them in. Sarah coos and smiles and is pleased. Lissa opens her gift from her mother: a scarf, hand-knitted in fine green wool. 'It's beautiful, Mum,' she says. And it is.

Sarah has made food – seasonal but not traditional, something she excels at, that she invests with an almost moral purpose. When Lissa was small, she used to feel hard done by for the lack of tree – *a Victorian invention* – the absence of chocolate, of all the *tinselly baubley nonsense* her friends' homes were filled with. But now the times have caught up with Sarah, and each corner of the house contains something beautiful: leaves salvaged from walks on the Heath, a table decoration made from raffia and twine. Small glass bulbs are suspended over the table. Candles stand ready to be lit.

Lissa sits in the low armchair; Ruby pads over towards her and she lifts her on to her lap. They drink wine mulled with cloves and cinnamon and star anise. 'So tell me, any more meetings?' says Sarah from the stove.

'One. For Salisbury.'

'Oh darling, that's great. Any joy?'

'No.' Her agent had called her, apologetic. *You're just not quite what they were looking for.*

In truth, she had known the part was not hers as soon as she read the script: a blowsy blonde in an Ayckbourn comedy.

246

'I don't mind,' she says, stroking the cat. 'After *Vanya* it's hard to imagine doing something like that.'

Sarah brings over the soup, which is a vibrant orangey yellow – there are toasted cumin seeds and yoghurt to spoon on top. 'Squashes from the garden,' says Sarah.

They eat in companionable silence, until Sarah puts down her spoon. 'I wanted to say, darling. You were really wonderful in *Vanya*. I haven't seen you be better. There's a quality you have. A radiance. It's rare.' Her mother sounds surprised, as though it has occurred to her for the first time.

'Really?' Lissa looks up. 'Why do you say that?'

'What do you mean?'

'Why now?'

Sarah's brow creases. 'Because it occurred to me. Because it's true.'

'Oh.'

'Darling, I'm trying to be nice.'

'Trying?'

'Oh God, Lissa.' Sarah puts down her spoon. 'Don't.'

'Don't what?'

'Don't turn a compliment into its opposite.'

'I just think it's strange you choose to be complimentary about my choice of career now.'

'What do you mean? What's different about now?'

Lissa looks at the clock – she has been here for an hour. There is no one else: no brother, no sister, no father, no child. Only she and her mother, grinding away together like an unoiled axle.

'I'm seeing someone,' she says quietly, curling her spoon around the last of her soup.

'Oh?'

'Yes,' she says. 'Someone lovely.'

'Oh, darling. Oh. But that's *wonderful*.' Sarah leans forward. 'Who is he?'

'He's a . . . friend.'

'Anyone I know?'

'I don't think so.' Already she regrets speaking. Already she is somewhere dangerous. She did not mean to say this – she is a fool. 'He's someone I met . . . online.'

'Oh. Well, everyone meets there now, don't they? The internet.' Sarah waves her hand. She makes it sound like the village green. 'It would be stranger if you hadn't, in a way. So.' Sarah's face is hawk-like, hungry. 'Can't you tell me anything? Does he have a job? A name?'

'He's called – Daniel.'

'And what does he do?'

'He's an academic.'

Sarah's hands come together in an involuntary clap. 'Well. Well. You must bring him around,' she says, reaching over and gripping Lissa's hand. 'Bring him over for supper soon.'

'Yes,' says Lissa, as her mother stands and clears the plates. It has grown dark outside, and when Sarah comes back with plum pudding, she lights the candles on the table. They reflect the room through the dark, gleaming surface of the window, and Lissa sits there, in her borrowed robes, and she shines.

He comes to her flat on Boxing Day. It is sunny, and the snow has started to thaw. They undress quickly and do not speak.

She pulls herself on top of him and makes him stay still, watching him, moving very slowly. When she comes she cries out. And when he comes she leans down and takes his lip in hers and sucks it, feeling him judder and fall still.

'Melissa,' he says to her afterwards, his hand tracing the curve of her hip, 'of the Melissae. The guardians of the honey.'

She leans in and kisses him and it is true – with him her core is molten and sweet.

When the evening comes she finds she is ravenous, and he stays in the flat while she goes out to the Turkish shop and buys food: noodles and vegetables and beer.

She cooks for him – she is hungry: for food, for sex, for life, and this hunger is beautiful, voluptuous. They eat noodles and drink the cold beer and she watches him eat, loving to watch this man eating this food she has prepared for him, listening to the low, resonant hum of his voice. She reaches across for his wrist, catches it, kisses him there.

'Are you happy?' he asks her.

'Do you mean now? Or generally?'

'Both. Now.'

'Now, yes.'

'And generally?'

She shrugs. 'Is anyone? Are you?'

He looks at her. 'How come you don't have a lover?' he says.

'I do,' she says, watching the complexity of the emotions on his face.

'I mean – you know what I mean.'

'I don't know.' She pushes her plate away. Outside it is dark already. 'It's harder than it looks, finding a good man. So many are so disappointing.'

'That's sad.'

'It's true.'

'I always hated Declan,' he says.

'Yeah,' she sighs. 'He was a bastard. You were right.'

'I've boycotted his films on principle.'

She laughs.

'I'm loyal,' he says. And the way he says it makes her stomach contract.

'Thank you,' she says, although she knows he is not. For if he were, he wouldn't be here at all.

'You never wanted kids?' he says softly.

She looks up at the ceiling. 'Not with him.' She levels her gaze with his and she feels it – loosened, filling the room, leaving space for nothing else. If they were to go back to bed now, she knows, if they did not use protection, she knows in her body that she would conceive – that this is how children are made, this desire, this drenched desire.

'You could stay the night,' she says. 'No one would know.' She watches his face, sees the struggle there.

'It's worse,' he says.

'What do you mean?'

'For Hannah. Me staying. It feels – worse somehow.'

'Really?' she says. 'Worse than us fucking?'

He flinches.

'Hannah doesn't know,' she says softly. 'Hannah doesn't have to know.'

He looks down at his hands, then back up at her. 'Sure.' He leans to her, a clumsy kiss that lands on the side of her mouth. 'I'd love that.'

Outside, it is cold. Inside, the room glows, golden. Time is somewhere else. She could live here, she thinks, and – in this moment – she could love this man.

Hannah

She is grateful to get home, back to the flat – grateful for these in-between days – between Christmas and New Year. The pendulum has stopped swinging, time has stalled and pooled, and she is here, held in the lees of the year. Still, she feels restless. There is something rising in her, some itch, some need.

She takes to buying wine. She drinks most evenings, one glass, then another. The sales are on and she goes back to the clothes shops in Covent Garden, where she buys the boots the colour of blood and the dress that is covered with creeping vines.

On New Year's Eve, she dresses for herself in the dress and the red boots, and puts on music and dances, turning slow circles in the room. She drinks red wine, one glass and then another, and then her eye falls on to a pouch of tobacco Nathan left. One cigarette. What would be the harm? She slides out the papers – black liquorice papers – and rolls herself a cigarette. She lights it from the stove, then steps outside on to the terrace, where the air is crisp and a handful of stars are visible in the high black sky. She brings the cigarette to her lips, and immediately the taste of sugar paper makes her think of Lissa.

And then, suddenly, the knowledge arrives – hitting her body before her mind. It spikes her blood, makes her heart race, her palms damp.

Lissa.

Nathan and Lissa.

She holds on to the terrace rail, then she throws the cigarette into the park below. She goes back into the flat, picks up her phone and calls Nathan.

'Lissa,' she says when he picks up.

'What?'

'What happened?' she says.

'What do you mean?'

'With you and Lissa?'

He hesitates a moment too long. She holds the phone away from her ear. Feels her stomach heave into her mouth. Hears his voice, speaking to the cold empty air.

Cate

At New Year she gets an invitation from Dea for dinner, and accepts, since Sam will be working.

We're going up to the Senate building first if you'd like to come? Dea writes. *There are five students still holding on inside. I think they're freezing. There's a vigil for them at sunset. Bring a candle and something for them to eat.*

Cate brings some mince pies and wine, and takes Tom up the hill to the university, where Dea and Zoe and a small group of others are clustered round the Senate building, candles in their hands. They talk in low voices and pass food parcels in via the security guards. Afterwards they walk back down the hill to Dea and Zoe's for food.

'I downloaded the application form,' Cate tells Dea, as she helps her tidy up after the meal.

'Really?' says Dea. 'Glad to hear it. Are you going to fill it in?'

'Yeah,' says Cate. 'I suppose I am.'

At nine o'clock she straps Tom into the car seat and drives him home. She knows Sam is due to finish work at eleven. She goes over to her computer, prints out the form, and begins to fill it in. The time goes quickly, but half past eleven comes and she is tired, and Sam is not home so she puts on the television and wraps herself in a blanket with a cup of tea.

She is dozing when her phone rings, and she jumps awake to see Hannah's name on the screen.

'Han?' She snatches the phone to her ear. 'Hey! Happy New Year!'

It is a while before she can make out any words, because at first there is only weeping, weeping that sounds as though it has been happening for a long while already – thick, clotted, exhausted sobs. 'Hannah?' she says softly, waiting for her friend to find her voice.

'Lissa,' says Hannah eventually.

'What about her?'

'Lissa and Nathan.'

'What?'

'Together.'

'No,' says Cate, sitting up on the sofa, wide awake now. 'No, Han, that's impossible.'

'Don't tell me what's possible,' hisses Hannah. 'I know it's true.'

On the television people are singing together, 'Auld Lang Syne'. There are Scottish pipers in bearskins and serious faces. She mutes the sound. The room is dark, only the light of the screen. She is silent. A strange taste fills her mouth.

'Hannah,' she says. 'Is there anything I can do? Do you want to come here? Can I come to you? Are you in the flat? I can drive – I'll put Tom in the back and leave now.'

'No. No.'

'Is there anyone near by that can come and be with you?'

She almost says *Lissa* – Lissa who lives moments away – and stops herself in time.

'No,' says Hannah. 'Are you there? Will you stay there? I might – I might call again.'

'Of course, Han. I'm here.'

When the call is finished Cate stares, stunned, at the television screen, where people are holding hands and dancing. She is aware of several conflicting and equally powerful emotions – of shock and disbelief, and a strange sense of inevitability, the last of which makes no sense at all.

She is sitting in the same spot when Sam returns home two hours later. She has stayed awake, but Hannah has not called again. She watches him come in, take off his jacket and hang it on the peg with careful deliberation. He takes two beers out of the pockets of his coat. 'I got these, they were giving them out at work – you want one?'

'Sure.'

He opens them with his lighter and passes her one, coming to slump on the sofa beside her. He looks tired, she thinks, tired and drunk.

'I just spoke to Hannah.'

'Oh?' His eyes are unfocused.

'Nathan cheated on her.'

'What?' He looks at her, mouth agape, beer bottle halfway to his mouth. 'Who with?'

'Lissa.'

He sits forward. 'You're joking?'

'No. At least, Hannah's convinced of it.'

'Fucking hell.' He takes off his cap, runs his hands through his hair. For a moment he looks horrified, and then he starts to laugh. She stares at him, appalled, and then she starts laughing too. They put their hands over their mouths as though they might be overheard, as they shake and shake with strange twisted exhilaration, until, abruptly, they stop. Cate feels the guilt swilling around her body.

'Shit,' says Sam, shaking his head. 'Poor Hannah. Shit,' he says again.

Cate puts down her beer. 'Sam,' she says.

'What?'

'I'm sorry. I'm sorry about Mark.'

'Yeah, well. He probably deserved it. He's always been like that. Even when he was at school.'

'Will they forgive me?'

'It's not them you need to worry about,' he says. 'It's me.'

She goes over to him. 'Will you forgive me?' she says.

'That depends.'

She slides her hands into his palms. 'Can I kiss you?' she says.

He says nothing. She lifts her lips to his. He lets her, but does not respond. Then he turns his face away.

'I need to tell you something,' he says. 'I asked you to marry me because I fell for you. And I thought you felt the same. I'm not here to be your consolation prize, Cate. I want to be chosen. Not settled for.'

And he slides himself out of her hands, stands, and leaves her where she sits on the floor.

Lissa

She lies in bed late on New Year's morning. She wears only a T-shirt and knickers. He is coming to see her – there is no need to get dressed.

She jumps up at his knock, but as soon as she opens the door she sees that something is wrong.

'She knows,' he says.

She puts her hand to her mouth.

'Come in.' She sees his hesitation. 'Come in,' she insists, taking him by the wrist.

He steps over the threshold into the kitchen, where he stands, his coat still on. She turns on the light, the ugly old electric ceiling light, and his face is pale beneath it. 'I said nothing,' she says.

'No. I didn't imagine you had.'

They fall silent, and the silence is painful and inert. She wants to fill it, with desire, with violence. She crosses towards him and takes his hand in hers. He looks down at her hand, then back up at her face. 'I'm sorry,' he says.

'What for?' She puts her hand over his eyes, tenderly, as though shielding them from the sun. She feels him close them – the eyelids flickering beneath her palm. She reaches behind her and turns off the light again. She moves her hand away gently, running her fingertips down his cheek, his neck. His eyes remain closed as she gets to her knees before him and begins to unbuckle his belt.

'What are you doing?' he says.

He is hard already when she takes him into her mouth,

and she holds him there for a moment. She moves her mouth against him and he pulls her up to standing, then he turns her around and pulls down her knickers and pushes himself into her, roughly, and she gasps in pain. He pulls out of her. He cups himself, pulls up his jeans, turns away from her. 'Sorry,' he says. 'I'm sorry.'

She turns around to him. He is still wearing his coat. It is a strange sight, him in his coat, cupping himself like that – she could almost laugh.

'It's OK,' she says, pulling her knickers back up. But it is not OK. Not really. Not at all. 'It's OK,' she says again.

He pulls up his jeans, buckles his belt. 'I'm going away,' he says. 'I'm going to go away for a couple of weeks. I need some space.'

'You need some space,' she repeats. Her voice sounds strange. She wants to cry, but she knows she has no right. She can feel it coming towards her, like a wave, a wave that will flatten her. And how afterwards there will be nothing left, nothing left to say what this was, how this felt. How no one will be interested in her version of events.

'I won't contact you,' she says.

He nods. 'I think it would be best.' He reaches out and his hand lands briefly, gently, on her cuff. He touches her as he might a child.

And she is furious now. And she sees that he wants it to be easy. He wants the water to cover this over, for the bubbles to rise to the surface and disappear, for the smooth surface to give no sign of what was underneath. 'It wasn't worth it,' she says.

'What?'

257

'The sex.'

She sees the shock on his face. He steps back into the room. And his expression has changed. It is needy now. Now she has hurt his ego. He wants something from her – she sees that, despite it all, he wants her to tell him it was good. That he was good. How pathetic, his need. How desperate the pair of them are.

'Lissa,' he says, holding out his hands in supplication.

'It wasn't worth it,' she says again. 'None of it.' And she gestures as she speaks, at herself, at him, at the sudden painful squalor of it all.

Hannah

She dreams of violence, of Lissa's face lacerated with a thousand tiny cuts. Of holding Nathan's severed head, his blood soaking her lap. Sometimes the violence is chasing her and she is running from it across a wide open space. It is gaining on her and there is nowhere to hide – a dark presence, its long fingertips touch her neck.

At night, sleepless, she travels over the roofs to Lissa's house, to where she lies in her guilty bed. How does she sleep? Does she sleep?

Finally, she sleeps herself, and when she wakes, when the world assembles itself in the dawn light, she understands it is a new world – the old one blasted to shards – and that this new world is a place that operates by different physics, different laws. She imagines them together, her husband and her friend – their hands, their lips, their naked flesh, the parts where their flesh has met. The secret, beloved places on his body that she had come to think she owned. How did he touch her? Was it animal and nothing more? Or was it, is it, more?

She may not ever know. And this fact – the knowledge of his subjectivity, these experiences of his to which she will never have access – feels more violent, somehow, than the betrayal itself. What she feels when she thinks of this is beyond pain; it is close to delirium – colours seem brighter, sounds louder. Many, many times she lifts her phone, or goes to her computer – to curse him, to accuse her – but each time she turns away, puts down the phone; for what words could she find that would encompass this?

She avoids the park, no longer walks down the market. She walks to the bus stop and then back, that is all. She makes sure there is little chance of seeing Lissa in the street. Still, she thinks she sees her often – a tall fair frame ghosting at the edge of sight.

Winter turns, becomes spring. It stays cold. She has annual leave to spend. Two weeks of it. She has no real idea of where to go.

She clicks through pictures of cottages, of white-sand Scottish beaches, of lochs that look deep enough to drown a city in. Of places where she knows no one, and people are few. She is hungry for something that she cannot quite name – some elemental nourishment, something wild. She wants to taste salt water. Be scoured. Feel wind and weather on her skin.

One day, riding the Tube home from work, she sees a poster for Orkney. Sea and wide skies and wildlife. She goes home, and within minutes has booked planes, and a hotel and a car. She will go in March.

At night she dreams of running fast across open country. She wakes breathing quickly, the room altered, the silhouette of the tree's branches thrown starkly on to the wall.

Epithalamium

2008

It is Saturday, which is market day. It is late spring, or early summer. It is May, and the dog roses are in bloom in the tangled garden at the front of the house.

They take turns in the shower, Lissa and Cate, then dress quietly in their rooms. It is cool and overcast, but the forecast for later in the day is good.

As Lissa dresses she thinks of Nathan. Her friend. She knew him first. And she has always suspected that all those years ago, when they met again after university, had she been more available, he might have wanted to be with her. Would he have been hers now? Somehow, today of all days, she wants him to notice her, notice her beauty. She would not admit it to herself, but she wants to outshine Hannah, she wants to be seen. So she cuts the tags off the silk dress from Liberty's which she definitely cannot afford, and slips it on. She outlines her eyes in green kohl. She wears heels that make her over six feet tall.

Over in her morning flat, Hannah dresses. Her mother and father are with her. Nathan has spent the night away, at his brother's house. Her mother knocks on the door to come in.

Oh, Hannah, she says, when she sees her daughter in her dress. Oh, Han.

*

They stand waiting in the largest of the municipal rooms in the registry office. It is, they all agree, for a couple like Hannah and Nathan, the best possible place to get married – its very utilitarian nature invests it with a sort of magic.

Nathan waits at the head of the room. Lissa watches him, his face, his blue suit, asking his brother for the third time to check his pocket for the rings, and as she watches he looks up, catches her eye and smiles.

The music starts, they stand, and Hannah appears on the arm of her father. She is wearing a simple green dress, her eyes shining, and at the sight of her, Lissa is chastened – how could she have thought she would ever outshine her? This woman that she loves. Here, in her green column of a dress, walking slowly towards Nathan, Hannah is mythic, archetypal. And Nathan here, standing at the front, has eyes for no one else, his face eager, lit, waiting for his bride.

As Hannah and her father pass her, Cate is thinking of her own father, and trying to remember when the last time was that she touched him – years ago now. And how she wants him here, in this moment, wants nothing more than for her own father to hold her like this – wants her own father to look at her like this, transfigured with pride and with love. Perhaps it is only for this that weddings are made.

And Cate thinks of Lucy, and where she is – and whether she ever thinks of her. And whether she is alive or dead, and whether she will ever love anyone like that again, and how time is passing and they are all getting older, and she is crying, standing here, thinking of Lucy and of Hannah and Nathan, of her mother and how she misses her, of her father and love and of time, and how it is all so beautiful and so impossible, really.

And Hannah looks at Nathan and thinks of how she loves him. And how she is happy. And when the serious-faced woman who is holding the ceremony turns to her and asks her if she will take this man – Yes, she says, yes. I will.

Afterwards, when the wine has been drunk and cake has been eaten and speeches have been made, Hannah finds her friends. She takes Lissa by the hand and threads through the crowd in the pub to find Cate, and takes Cate by the other hand, and leads them outside, into the May sunshine, through the gate, into the park, into London Fields. The cherry tree by the gate is heavy with blossom.

The forecast was right: it is a beautiful day. They walk out on to the grass, and as they walk, in this golden, tipsy light, the world feels full of love, of possibility. Hannah brings her friends towards her, presses her forehead against theirs. I love you, she says. And, their heads bent to hers, Cate and Lissa murmur their love back, for this is what marriage does – it flows out beyond the couple, engendering love, engendering life, making us believe, even for an afternoon, in a happy ending, or at least, at the very least, in the expectation that a story will continue as it should.

2011

Lissa

'You can change behind the screen,' says the teacher. 'Or go to the toilets.'

He is young, younger than her anyway, short and wiry, dressed in a striped woollen jumper and jeans. Expensive-looking glasses. Mild grey eyes.

Lissa nods. She knows the drill. She doesn't bother to tell him she has done this many, many times before. They don't want to hear you speak.

She takes her bag and walks down the corridor to the women's toilets. There are high shelves on either side, the smell of paint and clay and turps. She locks herself in one of the stalls and takes off her coat and T-shirt and bra, her jeans and her knickers. She folds her clothes and puts them back in her bag, then puts on her kimono, keeping on her socks, as the floor is chilly. She pees quickly. The last thing she wants is to need a pee before the first break. The first break is not for forty-five minutes.

She makes her way back down the corridor, and pushes open the heavy door of the studio. The students are here already, busy preparing their easels. A thin, clear light falls from high windows. She makes her way over to a raised plat-form in the middle of the room.

'OK, Lisa,' says the teacher.

'Lissa,' says Lissa.

'Right, Lissa. So – when you're ready, just take whatever pose you like. We'll do some short ten-minute sketches, and then move on to the longer poses later in the morning.'

Her toes are already cold, but there are a couple of heaters, which are on. She slips out of her kimono and sits down.

The teacher looks at her for a moment, then: 'Actually – what about we begin standing?'

She stands, finds a pose, one foot in front of the other, arms behind her back.

'Right,' says the teacher to his students. 'Charcoal or pencil. Ten minutes. Let's go.'

There is the scribble of charcoal and pencil on paper.

So, thinks Lissa, here she is again.

She has managed to eke out her savings from *Uncle Vanya* by living on soup mix and porridge, rarely going out, spending her days watching old films on her computer, feeding her melancholy, and now she is down to the last two hundred pounds in her account.

She always thinks that somehow she won't be back here. She's always wrong.

For a long time she waited, bracing herself for Hannah's fury, but when weeks had passed and she heard nothing she wrote her a single message – *I'm sorry. I'm here if you ever want to talk*. It was weak at best, craven at worst.

Nothing from Nathan. Not since New Year's Day. Not since the scene in her flat. She wrote him a letter, then burned it. Wrote him another, then burned that too.

In the break she goes out to use the loo, and on the way

265

back she casts a look at some of the students' sketches. Her haunches. The rise of her breasts. The shortness of her hair.

In the early spring, she took herself to the hairdresser and told him to cut her hair. He approached her warily – an inch? he asked. More, she said. He cut off two. More, she said. And then he capitulated, sliced it, sheared it, and they both watched the locks fall silently to the floor. And she cried when she saw herself in the mirror, for she did not know herself any more, and he looked at her in horror. I'm sorry, he said. I thought it was what you wanted. It is, she said. It was.

'OK, Lissa.' The teacher comes over to her. 'So, now we're going to do a longer pose.'

'I know.'

'So, just make sure it's something simple – something you can hold for forty-five minutes.'

She sits down on the raised platform, still in her kimono, and finds a pose, one knee up, the other leg bent beside her. She clasps her knee in her arms to brace against. She has a small repertoire of longer poses. There are some people who can sit for hours in the most contorted of positions – dancers usually, acrobats. She is not one of their number.

After a few minutes the room settles down. They are painting now – there is the sound of brush on canvas, the teacher's footsteps as he moves quietly from easel to easel. Sometimes he says nothing, sometimes he leans in – *Good*, he murmurs, or *See this – the line here?* He traces his hand on the paper, lifts it, moves it through the air.

She looks down at herself – her lower legs, the stubbled hair which she forgot to shave this morning. The heat in here is patchy – part of her lower calf is turning mottled and red. She can smell the scent of herself.

She is aware that she has lost much, so much that she cannot quite comprehend its scale: she has lost Nathan, she has lost Hannah. She has lost Cate, who will not return her calls.

But she has lost much more than that, as though loss were a black hole, pulling all the potential futures, all the things you might have been, all the successes, the loves, the children, the self-respect you might have had, down into it.

'We want to capture something,' the teacher is saying. 'Some essence. It is not our job to interpret. We want to *transmit*.'

Her left buttock is already growing numb. There are pins and needles starting in her foot. She shifts slightly, hears a tut from the teacher.

'Lissa,' he says. 'Please try to keep still.'

There is a cough and she looks up into the eyes of a young woman. She is twenty or so. Beautiful in a precise way. She looks like a serious little doll.

She imagines the young woman's body beneath her clothes, smooth like alabaster. What does she think when she looks at her?

Does she think of why she is doing this job still, at her age?

Does she look at the curve of her belly? Does she wonder if she has had children?

She looks back at the young woman, who is staring now at her thighs, making larger strokes with her charcoal. Her doll-like, impassive face.

All I am, thinks Lissa, is a collection of lines. There is nothing real inside. Like those bodies her mother drew, all those years ago on the pavements of Tufnell Park. As though it were prophecy – this hollowness. There is only the outline left. She feels dizzy suddenly, and she moves again. There is an audible groan from the other side of the room.

'Excuse me,' she says. 'I don't feel well.'

She stands up, wraps herself in her robe, goes out into the corridor and lays her cheek against the cool, hard surface of the wall.

Hannah

Gatwick, early morning, and she is an oyster, newly shucked. The wide world presses upon her; the women in their heels and coats, the people who walk quickly because they have somewhere better to be. She feels at once invisible and far too visible in her waterproof jacket and walking boots.

Thirty-six. She is almost middle-aged. Is it worse if men look at her, or not? The tip of her thumb nudges the space left by her wedding ring, a small groove, a ridge of callused skin, and then an absence. The callus has almost disappeared now, although her thumb still returns to it, like a tongue to the gap where a tooth used to be.

At Aberdeen, she has a wait of an hour before the connecting flight. The airport is full of men. Men with the look of squaddies – although less fit, many of them are huge, red-faced, balding, tucking into breakfast and pints at the bar. She avoids them, browsing the stands at Smiths, thinking to buy a magazine, but they all seem faintly ridiculous, so she moves to the book stands. She has read nothing for months.

What used to be an innocuous activity is now trip-wired; she wants nothing about love, nothing about children, nothing about infidelity. She lifts guidebooks and puts them back again. She does not need a guidebook. She is capable of navigating by instinct. She is capable of spontaneity. In the end she buys a copy of *Emma* and a bottle of water. She has read it before. She is pretty sure there are no babies in the book.

The Orkney plane is tiny. Rain laces the window panes. She stows her bag beneath the seat. People greet each other as old friends. Just as the door is about to close, one of the men from the bar climbs aboard, breathing quickly, as though he has been running. He says hello to an older lady on the other side of the aisle from Hannah, before taking his seat a couple of rows in front. His hair is short and neat. He moves with the exaggerated precision of someone who knows it is still morning, and that he is drunk. The first glimpse of the islands is through a break in the cloud – choppy sea and then the low-lying grey-brown of the land. As the plane banks she sees rain, and almost-empty roads.

It is not yet midday – too early to check into the hotel – and so she collects her hire car and decides to drive up the island. The sky has lifted a little. She knows the main concentration of sites is forty minutes or so away; burial chambers, standing stones. She might as well see them while the rain holds off.

She passes through the town: a large red-bricked cathedral, stone-fronted houses, a huge Tesco on the route out to the north. The landscape is sodden, unpromising. The radio in the car is tuned to Radio 2 – some inane chatter, some cheesy songs. She tries for something else but gets only static, and so turns it off. This was not what she expected, when she booked this holiday, in the quiet of her flat. She expected something craggy, magnificent, some sort of scale to dwarf her interior landscape, but there is barely a hill or a tree to be seen, only tussocky grass and pebble-dashed bungalows. It is, if she is honest, all quite bleak.

She parks at a set of three huge standing stones and climbs out of the car. A large sheep with a broad face stands in the middle of them, cropping the grass. The sheep is remarkably ugly. So are the stones. They look like a piece of Brutalist civic architecture – something an overeager county council might have thought was a good idea some time in the 1970s. She walks around them dutifully. She stands in the middle. The sheep eyes her suspiciously. She waits to feel something but feels nothing other than mildly self-conscious.

At the far north of the island is a Neolithic village. Her internet searches have told her it is five thousand years old. As she climbs out of the car, the clouds are feathered overhead. She can smell the sea. The track towards the village is studded with stones, each one marking an event: a man on the moon, the French Revolution, the fall of Rome, leading all the way back to when the village was built, at the same time as the pyramids of Egypt. The gift shop is stocked with Viking hats, the sort made from hard plastic with two plaits of synthetic hair hanging down on either side, with Fair Isle sweaters and stuffed puffin toys.

A pleasant man behind the desk in the gift shop sells Hannah a ticket, and tells her she must watch a short film first before visiting the site, which she duly does, sitting behind an older couple in matching waterproofs. She is then funnelled through a small exhibition, each one of whose cases she reads diligently, learning about the food the villagers would have eaten (fish and deer and berries), the pots they made, the strange, lovely balls they carved; and it is not without interest, this exhibition, if you are a schoolchild, or a historian. Or someone with nothing better to do. Outside the museum is a replica house – she ducks inside, sees two beds, a dresser made from stones, a stone-bordered hearth.

When she comes out and goes to explore the village proper, it starts to rain again. She walks around the houses, peering down into their interiors, and they are impressive, moving even, and yes, it is easy to imagine these people going about their lives, inhabiting their houses, with their beds for children and their beds for adults and their stone dressers, as though from an episode of *The Flintstones*, carving their jewellery, eating their trout and deer and berries, and loving and fighting and fucking around the hearth. She turns away from the houses and looks out at the sea, a wide, gently shelving bay along which the rain is coming in hard now. She feels a fresh wave of anger and pain. What is she doing here? What was she thinking, coming to the edge of things, to stare at hearths and homes and places where families lived and loved, and only feel more of what she does not, will not, have?

She wanted something wild, something that exists only unto itself – nature without audience. Must everything be made human-size? She does not want the domestic. The domestic is what she came here to escape.

Tesco is the size of a large aircraft hangar and she is grateful it exists.

She wanders the aisles, letting the supermarket's white noise wash over her.

She buys a bottle of Rioja and some cheese crackers and crisps.

The hotel has been billed as one of Orkney's finest. It is tired, and has not been decorated for years. There are queasy swirls of colour on the carpet, and a smell of fried food and burnt coffee seeps from the restaurant. Her room is pleasant enough, despite the pictures of lurid purple flowers on the walls. The bed is huge but uncomfortable – two beds pushed together. The pillows are unspeakable. She twists off the top of her wine and pours a third of a bottle into her tooth mug.

By six o'clock she is hungry and has almost finished the wine. There is no answer at room service and so she goes downstairs to the restaurant. 'Can I order food here?'

'Aye,' says the young woman behind the bar. She has a small, heart-shaped face, make-up, a pretty mouth.

'Can you deliver it to my room?'

'I'm the only one on right now. Do you mind waiting? You can take it up yourself?'

Hannah looks around her at the near-empty restaurant. She is alone apart from an older couple who look as though they are on a business trip, their heads bent over a computer screen. 'OK.'

'You can have a drink on the house,' says the young woman with a wink, 'seeing as I'm in charge.'

'OK,' says Hannah. She looks over the menu. 'I'll have fish and chips,' she says.

'Perfect,' says the young woman.

'And a glass of wine. What wines do you have by the glass?'

'Just the Merlot.'

'A glass of that then.'

'Perfect,' the young woman says again, taking a large glass and filling it almost to the rim. 'There you go.'

Perfect?

She takes it to a seat in the window. A vase of plastic flowers stands on the table before her. Outside, the harbour is rain-washed. Shafts of fading sunlight pierce the drizzle, then disappear again, leaving steely grey light in their wake.

'Tomorrow's better. Weather-wise.'

She turns and sees a man beside her. It is a moment before she recognizes him from the airport, from the plane. She nods in response. He looks as though he has sobered up, whereas she is on her way to being drunk. He takes a seat at the next table, diagonally opposite her, and she feels a vague sense of annoyance. Now she will either have to make conversation or ignore him. She looks in her bag, finds the paperback she bought at the airport, slides it out on to the table. She takes a sip of her wine, opens the book. *Emma Woodhouse, handsome, clever, and rich—*

The young woman comes over, puts a pint down in front of the man. 'There you go.'

'Thanks.'

The murmur of the couple in the corner – something about a meeting. Something about figures. The world of work. The man lifts his pint and drinks. 'That good then?'

She looks up. The man is large, but not overweight; her age, or a little older. He looks ruddy, as though he has recently showered. The hair at the back of his neck is damp.

'Your book?' He gestures towards it. 'Is it good?'

She holds it up to him. 'I'm on page one.'

'Ah,' he says.

'But I've read it before.'

'Right.'

'They all learn lessons. And live happily ever after.'

'Ah,' he says. 'Right enough.'

She looks back down at the page, but the words are dancing now.

'You up here on holidays then?'

'I suppose.'

'You suppose?' He gestures to the chair in front of her. 'Do you mind if I join you?'

'I'm just waiting for my food. I'll be gone soon.'

'Then you won't get bored of me.' He lifts his pint and takes the seat opposite her, his back to the woman behind the bar.

'Cheers.' The man lifts his pint and drinks. His fingers are thick, the skin chapped and red. There is a wedding ring on his hand. His phone is beside him on the table. She sees a picture of a woman and a child on the screen. 'So what is it then? If it's not holidays? You here on work?'

'No,' she says. 'Not work.'

'Mystery,' he says.

'Something like that.'

'I'm from here,' he says, as though in answer to a question she has not asked. 'Grew up here. I work on the rigs. Off Aberdeen. Two weeks on, three weeks off. I stay up on Papa Westray when I come off. Work a farm up there.'

She has a vision of a cottage. A view of wind farms and the

sea. A wife and child. The woman on his phone. Managing alone while he is gone.

'You?' he says to her. 'Where are you from?'

'London. Manchester. London.'

'That's a lot of places.'

'Manchester.'

He nods. 'There's some lads from Manchester on the rig.'

'Oh?'

'They don't sound like you.'

'Well. I've lived in London for years.'

He leans towards her. 'What's that like then?' he says. 'London?' There is something about him, his energy, something untethered. Something hungry in his eyes.

She leans back. 'Oh,' she says. 'You know.'

'I don't get on with cities,' he says.

'No.'

They fall silent. He turns his phone over on the table, so the blank back faces upwards and the picture of the woman and the child has gone. 'What have you seen then, today?'

She shrugs. 'I saw the main sights. Apart from that burial chamber. Maeshowe. I suppose I'll go there tomorrow.'

'Did you like the main sights then?'

'Not really. I thought Orkney was . . . something else. I thought it would be wilder. It's all a bit . . . polite.'

'Polite!' He throws back his head and laughs.

The diners at the next table look up, then down again at their food.

'You should go south,' he says.

For a moment she thinks he means the South: the hot South. Sun and sea and warmth on the skin.

'Go down to Ronaldsay,' he says, 'see the tomb there. The Tomb of the Eagles. On the cliffs there. That's wild. That's a good one to see before you go.'

She looks down at her hand, fiddles with her ring, but her ring is not there. The man looks at her finger, then back up at Hannah's face.

She is aware, in the moment, that an invitation has been extended. Aware of a conflicting set of emotions, the answering leap of desire.

Is this how it was? With Lissa and Nathan? Was it spoken or unspoken? Did they think of her, before they crossed the line?

'Is that your wife?' she says.

'Where?' He looks startled.

'There.' She reaches in, takes his phone, turns it over and presses the button on the side. There she is, a young woman, squinting into the light, a child of four or so before her.

The man looks down at his phone, back up at Hannah. 'That's her,' he says.

'So what are you doing here?' She is furious now, hissing her words. 'Talking to me?'

He takes the phone from her, looks at the photograph briefly.

'She's dead,' he says. 'She died a year ago.'

'Oh.' It is as though he has kicked her in the stomach. 'God.'

'It's all right,' he says. 'It's not your fault.'

He looks away, to the rain-washed harbour, then back again.

'Anyway,' he says, 'I didn't come here to talk about my wife.'

She is silent. And then, without anything more being said, something is agreed.

They ride up in the lift. She watches his hand press the button for the second floor. His thick fingers. His wide palms. He leads the way down the corridor and she follows, half a step behind. He opens the door, then steps back to let her enter, and for a moment she feels a sharp slice of fear – he could be anyone – but then the fear dissolves. He goes to put the key in the socket but she puts her hand on his wrist. 'No,' she says. 'Keep it dark.'

The visitors' centre at the Tomb of the Eagles is staffed by a soft-voiced woman. The woman speaks about the tomb, about how it was found on her father's land, a mile or so from where she and her family live today. About the human remains that were found there – no skeletons, only jumbled bones, thousands upon thousands of them. About the eagle talons found in amongst them. About the theory that the bodies were left out to be eaten by the birds. Like the sky burials of Tibet. How only the clean bones were saved.

'Excarnation,' the woman says in her soft voice.

'Excarnation,' says Hannah, tasting it. A new word.

When the small tour has finished, the woman tuts at Hannah's jacket and boots, and kits her out in proper waterproofs. When she is ready, Hannah laughs.

They go to the window and the woman points the way to a hunkered mound in the distance. 'Come back along the cliffs,' she says, 'that's the best way. You might see the seals then.'

The track is muddy and rutted with puddles; Hannah walks through them, not around them. When was the last time she wore wellington boots? A scrap of song comes to her and she sings out loud. A dog bounds out of one of the farm buildings, weaving through the fence ahead of her, trotting back to make sure she is keeping up, then running ahead again, chasing the swallows, who skirl and dive, loving the wind. Primroses stud the path and she bends and picks them, and then is unsure what to do with the picked flowers, stowing them in the pocket of her coat.

The chamber looks like nothing so much as a heap of rocks, almost indistinguishable from the shelved rocks around it. The entrance is covered with a trolley. She feels a tremor of fear, but moves the trolley away and gets down on her hands and knees, crawling along the tunnel before emerging into a small, chambered space. It is not dark – small skylights have been built into the ceiling – nor is it cold, or eerie, even; it is simply rock and earth and a deep insulated quiet. Outside, back through the tunnel, she can see the wind in the grass, the white spray on the sea.

She sits there for a moment, uncertain what to do. There is a scrabbling in the tunnel and the dog appears, coming close to her, panting. She holds him to her, feels his heart, the warmth of his flank. 'Hey,' she says. 'Hey there.'

Ahead of her, leading off from the chamber in which she sits, is a smaller, darker space. From here it is impossible to see just how far it extends. A torch lies on the ground and she reaches for it and switches it on, flashing it into the chamber, which is revealed to be small, but big enough for a person to lie within.

She turns off the torch, crawls under the stone lintel and lies on her belly, her cheek on the cold ground. It is strangely comforting – lying like this, she can feel her heart beating in her belly, her chest, the rush of her blood. The distant thump of the sea on rocks. The soft sound of the dog, breathing close by.

She thinks of the bones that were piled in here for so long, thousands upon thousands of them.

Soon enough her flesh will be no more.

She thinks of the night before. The shock of his body: the difference of it, the shape of it. His smell. The places where she put her mouth. And she was different. Her body different. The way they moved together. The strange animal noises they made. Afterwards, lying in the dark with this familiar, unfamiliar man, she thought of Nathan. Of how she had forgotten to see him as separate. Forgotten to feel his unfamiliarity. Forgotten to acknowledge the animal inside him. Lissa would have kindled the animal in him. And with this thought comes something else: a sort of grief, for her own animal nature, for its own wild desires.

She turns on to her back, switches off the torch, and there is only the darkness – the low, intimate sound of her breath.

After a long while she crawls back out to the main chamber, and then pushes herself out into the brightness of the day. The dog follows her, and they walk along the rocks back to the car. The clouds have lifted, the wind has stilled, the day is clear.

She drives back up the island, past a strip of white sand, the sea gentle beside it, and she is seized with a desire so strong and immediate that she stops the car. She climbs down and walks back along the sand until she is no longer in sight of the road, takes off her clothes and runs into the sea. She lets out a sound, a shout – of cold, of joy, of exhilaration – as the water lifts her off her feet and slaps her skin.

Cate

Spring arrives early, and the city turns green. She takes her bike out of storage and cleans and oils it, and then she cycles up the hill to work – watching the trees come into bud and then leaf, the candles of the horse chestnuts that stand by the side of the wide road.

At first it makes her breathless, the climb – she has to stop and wheel her bike several times to make it up the hill. But soon she is feeling fitter, feeling her muscles respond, the air flood into her lungs.

The ride is lovely, but it is when she is driving that she sees it most – out on the B roads, between Canterbury and the coast, the radiant springtime sweep of the land.

Dea was right; the job fits her – two days a week in the office and then a day a week visiting schools. Sam has dropped a day at work, and so they manage the childcare between them, she and Alice and Sam. She likes the teenagers she meets – their attitude, their sass. They give nothing for free. She is working on a scheme to get kids from a school in Sheppey to visit the campus, working with the Creative Writing department to publish an anthology of the teenagers' work.

Tom is almost walking now. He likes to pull himself up to standing, cruising around the living room in his tights, delighted at his new-found mobility. Cate watches him, fascinated. It is extraordinary, she thinks, this urge to stand, to walk; extraordinary to watch the human animal evolve before her eyes. Everything he comes across he puts in his mouth: pencils, elastic bands, scraps of food from the floor. He becomes enamoured with putting pencils in holes. She buys plastic guards for the power sockets. It becomes imperative to get out of the house.

On a sunny Sunday in March, a week before his birthday, he takes his first steps across the living room; one, two, three and then he sits on his bottom. She applauds, calling to Sam, where he sleeps upstairs, and he rushes down, rubbing his eyes and blinking. They coax and wheedle and Tom manages another few steps. Sam brings out his phone and manages to catch it, sending it immediately to Alice. Cate sends it to her dad.

Often, at the weekend, she straps Tom in the buggy and walks over to the allotment, where he and Nora toddle on the ground, amateur naturalists investigating stones and eating earth, while she and Dea dig over the beds for the new season's planting. She likes the work, likes the way it makes her sweaty, likes the sweet smell of the soil.

She goes for walks. Sometimes she goes with Dea; sometimes, if she is alone, while Tom naps in the buggy, if the weather is fine she simply sits on a bench in the sun. When he wakes there is often a short gap of time in which he comes to himself, in which he looks out at the world from his seat, not looking for her, not looking for anyone. She sits behind him, letting him have this moment, a minute when she is not immediately there hovering over him. It occurs to her that it begins so early, this process of letting go – of not inserting yourself between your child and the sun.

They are tentative with each other, she and Sam, but they have grown easier, grown closer. Still, they give each other plenty of space, as though whatever small fire has been rekindled will be smothered with too little air. But Tom sleeps in his own bed now, and sometimes, in the quiet of the night, it is easy to turn towards Sam, curling into his frame, waking with her arm over his chest.

She texts Hannah every day, just a single line to check in.

One morning in early April, she cycles up the hill to the

281

university, arrives in the office and opens her email. She sees it immediately. A message from Hesther – subject line *Lucy Skein*.

Cate begins to shake. She looks up and out at the room, but no one is watching her – the sun slants in through the window. It is still the same morning that it was.

She opens the email.

Hesther is sorry to have taken so long to reply; she has been away – travelling for work. It is lovely to hear from Cate after so long. Cate's eyes travel hungrily over the words, down to the bottom two lines.

I haven't seen Lucy for years, but funnily enough I bumped into her when I was in Seattle for work last year. She seemed really well. Seems she changed her name. I have her contact if you'd like it.

And below, an email address. A name.

She types it immediately into her search engine. And she is there before her. Dr Lucy Sloan. Dept of Int. Development. University of Oregon.

Her face. The way the lip curls up when she smiles.

A relic from a different life.

Lissa

You must bring Daniel, Sarah says to Lissa on the phone and, in the subject heading of the email that contained the exhibition invitation, she put in bold letters – *Bring Daniel! Excited to meet him.*

In the end, in desperation, Lissa texts Johnny: *Got a plus one to an art opening. Don't suppose you'd like to come?*

I'd be delighted, he replies, almost at once.

They meet at the Tube. He is dressed as always in black with his black leather bag, but his shirt looks new, and he is wearing a smart jacket. He is freshly shaven and looks well. She is surprised by how happy she is to see him, to have him lift her hand in that courtly, gentle way he has. 'Hiya, sweetheart,' he says. She has forgotten the soft Scouse rumble of his voice.

'You look good,' she says. 'Very natty.'

'I'm working. Got a bit on *Doctors*.'

'Ah ha.'

'And,' he says, half apologetically, 'I seem to have scored a season at the RSC.'

'Whaaat? That's great!'

'Don't get too excited.' He holds up a hand. 'It's small parts mostly, but then Enobarbus in *Antony and Cleopatra*. It's set in Liverpool in the sixties. Don't ask. They'll probably mangle the fuck out of it, but hey ho.'

'Johnny, but that's proper!' She finds she is unconditionally happy on his behalf.

'You'd be a good Cleopatra.'

'In another life.'

'What about you? Any meetings?'

'Not really. Actually,' she says, 'I'm thinking of giving up.'

'Hush, child,' he says.

'No, really.'

'Come, come,' he says, taking her by the arm. 'Less of that.'

'When do you start?'

'May,' he says. 'Apparently they're all quite civilized, the Stratford lot. Voice classes together every morning – that sort of thing. A year's worth of the mortgage too.'

'Well,' says Lissa. 'You deserve it.'

'So whose exhibition is this then?' he says.

'Oh,' says Lissa. 'It's just my mum's.'

'Blimey,' he says with a wink. 'Then I'd better behave.'

The gallery is busy, thronged with faces she has not seen for years. Her mother is surrounded by people. It is a month or so since she has seen her and Sarah has lost weight, but she looks extraordinary – regal in a long red dress. It is she who should be Cleopatra, thinks Lissa, not herself.

The pictures are few; there are no more than seven. In each one the painted area takes up only a third of the canvas, then there is an expanse of white space around it. They are hung without frames, so the effect is of the image being suspended in space. As the eyes adjust to the canvas, objects emerge. In one there is a young girl wearing a cotton dress, half turned away, her face in profile; she is stooping to look at something on the ground, but the ground is not there, has disappeared into blankness beneath her feet. The face is smudged, but Lissa knows it is her.

In the largest of the canvases, which takes up most of one wall, a smudged line suggests a figure, or a creature, walking on the horizon, thinning to nothingness; it could be the Bolivian salt flats, it could be the surface of the moon. There are few distinguishing features, but Lissa knows the figure is Sarah – her mother with her back turned – walking away.

The canvases are not cheap – between two and five thousand each – but there are already three red dots on the cards tacked to the wall.

'She'll sell the lot at this rate.'

Lissa turns to see Laurie beside her. The older woman threads her arm through Lissa's. 'I think she knew when she started these, don't you?'

'Knew what?'

'How ill she is.' Laurie gestures at the paintings. 'It's as though everything inessential has fallen away.'

And Lissa feels something falling away from her – the ground, her stomach. She looks down at her hands, which Laurie is squeezing.

'And you, Liss?' Laurie is saying. 'How are you? How are you coping with it all?'

'Fine,' Lissa hears herself say softly. 'I'm doing fine.'

By the time the gallery owner climbs on to a crate to stand above the crowd and speak, the place is packed. Lissa has walked around the block, decided she will leave – decided she will come back again. She has smoked four cigarettes, drunk four glasses of wine. She has lost Johnny, found him and lost him again. She hangs back as the crowd makes a tight circle around Sarah and the gallery owner, silent while Sarah says a few brief words, but Lissa hardly hears above the hard thrum of her anger, and when the crowd parts, she pushes her way towards her mother and takes her by the arm.

'Why didn't you tell me?'

'Tell you what?'

'Laurie told me. She thought I knew.'

'Oh,' says Sarah. 'That.'

'*That?*'

'I didn't want to concern you.'

'You didn't want to *concern* me? How ill are you?'

'Fairly ill.' Sarah wipes a hand over her forehead. 'I have stage four cancer.'

It is hot – hot everywhere, inside and out. 'And how long have you known?'

'Since Christmas.'

'*Christmas?*'

'I refused the chemo.'

'Of course you did. And you didn't think I might have something to say about that?'

'It's my body, Lissa. My life.' Her mother looks weary, cornered, and Lissa senses the people behind her – knows they are being observed.

Sarah's face changes. 'Is Daniel here?' she says quietly. 'Did you bring Daniel?'

'No,' says Lissa, her voice rising. 'No, he's not. Do you know why? Because he doesn't exist. Or he does – but he's Nathan. Hannah's Nathan. I fucked Hannah's Nathan and I told you he was someone he wasn't and now he doesn't speak to me. And nor does Hannah. Because my life is a mess. Because you never taught me how to love.'

Sarah reels as though she has been hit. Lissa steps in for more, grabbing her mother's arm. 'You're so selfish,' she says to her mother. 'So fucking selfish. You know that? You always have been and you always will be.'

Sarah steps away, a small, elegant parry.

'Goodness me,' says Sarah. 'And you say *I'm* selfish? Dear

me, Lissa, I know you wish you were more often on stage, but for once, please can you spare me the drama?'

'Hey.' There is a steady hand on her arm. 'Hey, love.'

Lissa turns to see Johnny beside her. She sees Sarah surrounded, Laurie between them. 'Time to go home, Liss.'

'Come on,' says Johnny, as he beckons her into his arms.

Hannah

It is, apparently, the warmest spring in years. The cherry trees on her walk to the bus stop are in full blossom. The Georgian cafe on the corner has its tables and chairs on the street.

She gets up with the dawn and crosses the park to the lido. It is fairly quiet at this time of the day. Only the serious swimmers in their lanes. She goes into one of the small changing rooms, puts on her costume. Takes her cap and goggles. The morning air has a chill but the water is warm. She swims, long fifty-metre lengths. She takes pleasure in her strokes. She watches the light ripple and refract on the water. She remembers Orkney, the horizon, the light. As she swims, her thoughts change. They become less jagged. In the water there is no past and no future. By the time she comes out of the pool her body is tingling and her mind is clean.

She takes to walking everywhere. She walks to work. She walks back along the canal in the afternoons, savouring the light – the changing sky. She sits outside on the terrace, feeling warmth on her skin. She buys herself flowers, each Sunday at the market. One Sunday morning her eye is caught by some plants, which she buys and puts in terracotta pots and arranges on the windowsill in the little room, where it is sunny and they will receive the light. The evenings are lengthening; it is light now at seven o'clock.

The heat increases as April passes; by the end of the month it is as hot as July. Each morning, before work, she rises early and goes to the lido and swims – further and further every day. Work is fine, but she knows she is ready for a change. She thinks she might apply for a different job – swapping Farringdon for Lisbon perhaps, or New York. All those jobs she didn't apply for, all those opportunities she didn't take, back when she was waiting, treading water. She has no ties – can do anything, go anywhere she likes.

After work, in the still of the flat, Hannah pours herself water and stands at the sink and drinks it, then goes into the little room, takes off her clothes and lies naked in the evening sun. She closes her eyes and lets the light play in purple and red and green across her lids. She feels full, although of what exactly she cannot say.

One evening, lying like this, her phone buzzes with a message.

She lifts it, sees the name – Nathan.

Need to collect some stuff. Is that OK?

She stares at it while long seconds pass. She does not reply. Half an hour later the phone buzzes again.

Would it be OK to come round later?

She puts the phone down, picks it up again.

What time?
Soon? I'm close by.

Her heart beats faster.

OK. Come. I'll be out.

She stands and pulls on knickers and an old black summer dress; one that has been worn so often it cleaves to her. She leaves her phone behind, in case she is tempted to change her mind and call him, then takes her keys and walks towards the canal. It is still warm. The bars on Broadway Market are full, but she walks away from them, following the canal towards Victoria Park. She takes her time, doing a lap of the evening grass, moving between the lengthening shadows of the trees, and then makes her way back home in the gathering dusk.

She knows he is still inside as soon as she turns her key in the lock – a difference in the quality of the silence, a slight disturbance in the air. She does not see him immediately, as she kicks off her sandals, standing at the doorway in her bare feet. A small sound comes from the little room. She walks over the wooden boards, down the hall, where she pushes open the door. He is standing staring out of the window at the tree.

He turns to her. 'I couldn't bring myself to leave.' His voice is hoarse. There is a small bag at his feet.

She should feel angry, she thinks, but anger is far away.

'You changed things in here,' he says. 'You painted.'

'Yes.'

'It's nice.' He gestures to the plants on the sill, the print on the wall. 'It's funny we never touched it, isn't it? This room. All that time.'

'I suppose it is.'

Outside there are the sounds of running footsteps, the percussive slap of trainers on pavement, of children playing in the street.

'How have you been?' says Nathan.

'All right,' she says, and she leans against the wall behind her, sliding slowly down to the floor. She brings her knees towards her, clasps her arms around them. She can feel her breath coming shallowly, in and out. The evening sun is an oblong slice on the carpet between them. 'Bad, for a long time. Better now.'

Nathan nods.

'What about you?' she says.

'Han,' he says softly. He takes a small step towards her, but she puts her hand up to stop him.

'No,' she says. 'Don't come any closer.'

And so he stands there, unmoored, in the middle of the floor.

There are many things she wants to say:

How could you do this to me?

How could you ever show your face here again?

But what she finally says is,

'How was it?'

'How was what?' he says.

'With Lissa.'

'Han.' His face contracts. 'Don't.'

She puts her head back on the wall and looks at him. The

sadness on his face. How is it, after all of it, that she feels so strong, but sitting here, like this, he looks as though he will break? 'Tell me,' she says. 'I want to know.'

She has been in the fire, all this time – this is how – she has been tempered by the fire.

He turns away. Puts his hand on his bag, lifts it, puts it down, takes his hand away. 'It was . . . It felt dangerous,' he says. 'And it felt wrong.'

'And that was good?' she asks.

'Yes,' he says. 'In a way.'

'Did she come?'

'What?' He looks wretched.

'You heard me. Did she come?'

'Please,' he says. 'Don't do this.'

'It's my right,' she says. 'Isn't it?'

'I don't know.'

'Did she come?'

'Yes.'

'Was she loud? What noise does she make when she comes?'

'She wasn't loud,' says Nathan. 'No.'

It is as though she is drilling down into something hard and deeply satisfying. 'How does she fuck? Did she turn you on?'

She slides the straps of her dress off her shoulders; slowly the fabric falls to her waist. Her nipples are hard.

For a long time she does not move, until she slides out of her dress, and now she is just in her knickers. 'Do you want me?' she says.

He nods, and his face is slack with desire.

'Do you want me as much as you wanted her?'

'More.'

She stays where she is, in the sun, on the floor. The animal in him. The animal in her. 'Say it again,' she says.

'More,' he says, then slowly crosses the floor towards her. When he reaches her he kneels before her, his head on the ground. Then he lifts his head, pushes her knickers to the side, slides his fingers inside her, and she arches to his touch.

Lissa

They speak little on the train as it makes its way through the western edges of London. They are in an uneasy truce – this trip a peace offering of Lissa's, accepted by Sarah, the first day they have spent together in weeks. Once they leave Reading the land opens up and there are wider skies, smaller villages. The summer is in full, glorious bloom.

Sarah dozes, her hat beside her on the seat, a novel open on her lap. Lissa studies her mother's face. She does not look ill – she looks, if anything, more beautiful than ever. The weight she has lost serves only to display more clearly the fine architecture of her face – which in sleep has none of the slackness of age. Her hair is as long and thick as it ever was.

Her mother opens one eye, latches it on to Lissa, and Lissa turns away.

They get down at a country station and cross a river. Sarah walks slowly, leaning on her stick, a red scarf trailing jauntily from her wide-brimmed hat. There are swans in the river – two cygnets that have not yet turned white. They swim closely to each other's side, their parents close behind. Cows meander in the opposite field. It is lovely, but in the way of certain country roads there is no pavement, only a thin grass verge, and the traffic is fast and loud and harries their backs.

'Hang on, Mum, wait a sec.' Lissa puts a hand on her mother's arm to halt her, then turns back to the road and reaches out her thumb. A man in a Range Rover stops almost immediately. He is pleasant and hearty, and Lissa senses her mother's silent relief as he drives them up a hill towards the Common, dropping them in a car park, where Lissa helps her mother down. Sarah walks to the fence, where an old control tower still stands. Lissa wanders over to a board, which tells a little of the history of the Common, of the airbase, of the flora and fauna to be found. *Greenham Common*, it says, *restored to lowland heath.*

Past grazing by commoners' livestock has enabled a rare heath plant-life to develop, consisting of heather, gorse and other acid-loving plants.

The removal of the runways and the erection of fencing allows commoners to once again exercise their grazing rights.

She squints. In the middle distance is a concrete pathway – the old runway – where two girls, young teenagers, stand playing aeroplanes, their arms out to catch the breeze, their laughter high on the air.

'This way,' Sarah says. The sandy gravel crunches beneath their feet; heather blooms in all directions, star-like white flowers studding the grasses by the path. They walk parallel to the old runway, past a pond, a fire hydrant. Sarah's head turns this way and that, occasionally nodding to herself, as though things are falling into place. 'That was the Blue Gate,' she says, pointing with her stick, 'over there.'

Cyclists pass them, families lumbering along together, older men in packs of three or five, wearing their wrap-around sunglasses, their helmets. Sarah tuts at them as they shoulder their way over the path. It is warm, getting hotter. Lissa takes water from her bag, offers it to Sarah, who takes it and drinks deeply.

'There,' Sarah says suddenly, her eyes fixed on something behind Lissa. 'There they are. The silos. Where the missiles were held.'

Lissa turns. They are huge, grass-covered. They look, she thinks, like nothing so much as burial mounds, the sort where Bronze Age kings would be interred with all their loot. They make their way slowly over the Common towards them. Triple barbed-wire fences still stand in front of them; some-one has painted over them in red paint.

Pussy
Cunt
Fuck
You

A sign still stands amidst overgrown vegetation – *Ministry of Defence*.

Sarah rattles the fence with her stick. 'Bolt cutters,' she says proudly, 'made short work of this.' She smiles. 'We always had our bolt cutters on us.' Then she throws her head back and begins to make the most extraordinary noise – a ululation – at once utterly earthed and utterly unearthly. Lissa sees some walkers look up, wondering. When Sarah stops there is silence; she smiles a wicked smile. 'It frightened the daylights out of the soldiers,' she says. 'They didn't know what to make of us.'

'I'm not surprised. I'd have run for my life.'

'Did I tell you we danced?'

'Where?'

'Over there.' Sarah gestures with her stick to the silos. 'We cut the fence, put ladders up, climbed over and danced in the moonlight. It was New Year's Eve. We made our own music. We danced beneath the moon.'

She is a witch, thinks Lissa, as Sarah begins to sing again, softly this time. *My mother is a witch*.

She wanders a little away, to where brambles crowd the path. The blackberries are ripe, and she plucks a handful and brings them back to Sarah; an offering held in her palm. 'Delicious,' says Sarah, 'thank you.' She has found a feather from somewhere, and put it in the band of her hat. 'We should pick more. Take them home and make a crumble.'

They do so, Lissa lifting the brambles so Sarah can reach in and pick the darkest, ripest berries from the middle of the bush, taking the sandwiches she has packed for later out of their box and filling it instead with the glistening fruit. When the box is full they walk on, through a small, thick copse, where birches and sycamores dapple the light and bracken is chest-high and the silos are invisible. 'Ah, yes, this way,' Sarah says, 'I know this path.'

They reach a tree with many trunks, and Sarah steps off the path towards it, reaching her hands up to it. 'Hello, old lady, I remember you. This is where I camped,' she says, 'just beside this tree.'

'I remember,' says Lissa. 'I was there.'

'Yes,' Sarah turns to her. 'Of course you were. For a short time. I always forget.'

They walk on slowly and emerge again into the sun by a gate. A section of perimeter fence still stands, a concrete panel set behind a newer fence. It is painted with serpents, with a simple green butterfly – they are crudely done, little more than daubs, but they have an eerie power to them. It is like coming across forgotten cave paintings. Beneath the rusted metal, green paint is still visible, flaking with sun and with age. The air feels close, the vegetation pressing at their backs.

'I remember this,' Lissa says, threading her fingers through the gate. Tarps slung up in the rain. Women's ruddy faces. The smell of wool and fire and bodies.

'Thirty thousand people,' says Sarah, 'hand in hand around the base. They came and dragged us from our tents. Told us we were unnatural' – she laughs – 'as though it were natural to keep missiles of death on common land.'

'I remember them coming.' Lissa's hands close on the wire of the fence. 'Taking you from the tent. It frightened me. I hated it. You being here.'

'Why?'

'I thought I would lose you. That you would be shot.'

Sarah turns to her. 'The world is a fearful place,' she says evenly. 'It was not my job to lie about that. It was my job to try to make it safer. If you had your own child, you'd know.'

The comment lands. Twists. Does its work.

'I was pregnant once,' says Lissa quietly. 'With Declan.' She turns back to the fence, where a tiny insect crawls across the flaking green paint. 'It wasn't easy. The decision. I thought it would be, but it wasn't. But I couldn't have done it. Not with Declan. Not on my own.'

'My God. Why didn't you tell me?'

'I felt stupid for letting it happen, I suppose.'

'And why didn't you keep it?'

Lissa exhales. 'I was young and selfish and I wanted to have my life. I wanted to work. I didn't want a child who felt in the way.'

Her mother is silent, then she says quietly, 'Is that how you felt? Is that how I made you feel?'

'Sometimes. Often. Yes.'

Sarah shakes her head. 'That was never how I felt about you.'

'Really?'

'Truly.' Sarah regards her, steadily. 'But I had to live my life. All my life. Otherwise I would have been no mother at all.'

Lissa nods. 'I understand,' she says. And standing here, her hands threaded through this fence, she finds she does.

After a moment she speaks again. 'I'm sorry,' she says, turning towards her mother.

'What for?'

'That you're not a grandmother. You would have been a wonderful grandmother.'

And she would – she would have been magical. That would have been the right distance to love her from. To have been loved.

'Thirteen,' says Lissa. 'My child would have been thirteen.' And she finds she is crying, properly crying, her shoulders heaving, the sobs coming in shudders. Her mother steps towards her and folds her into her arms.

After a long moment, Lissa pushes the heels of her palms into her eyes and Sarah takes her arms away. Then they turn and walk back through the copse on to the Common and Lissa is glad of the space, the fresh air. In the distance a herd of cows is visible on the flat land. As they grow closer it is clear that they are in the middle of the runway, some standing, some lying. 'Look at that.' Sarah chuckles. 'You wouldn't get many warplanes past those ladies.'

The wind is high now. Sarah's hat is whipped off her head; Lissa runs to fetch it from where it has landed in a nearby bush.

As she walks back slowly towards her mother, she thinks, *It is here – the catastrophe. My mother is dying. I am losing my mother. Soon my mother will be gone.*

'Hold it a moment, would you?' says Sarah.

And Sarah steps on to the runway and turns to face the wind, eyes closed, her arms outstretched as though she is flying, and Lissa comes beside her, and does the same, feels the wind beneath her as she lifts her arms.

Hannah

She is tired. The spring has given way to early summer and the heat. Then the weather changes; it grows cooler and begins to rain. She feels tired still.

One day, when she is at work, she puts her head on her desk and falls asleep. When she gets home she climbs into bed and pulls the covers over her head and sleeps deeply. She wakes in the middle of the night thirsty, and goes to get water.

I'm pregnant, she thinks, standing by the sink. The thought seems to come from above her, beyond her.

She goes to the bathroom; in the back of the cupboard there is a box of old tests. She pees on one and sits in the darkness. She does not have to wait long; almost immediately a strong line appears in the second box.

She looks at it. She looks and looks and looks.

It is a fizzing in her blood.

It is anxiety.

It is great piercing shafts of joy, joy so pure she has to stand and hold on to something and wait for it to pass.

It is fear.

She has lost before. She knows how losing looks and feels, and what it leaves you with.

She tells no one. Not Nathan. Not her mother. Not Cate. She knows it may not last.

At the weekend she sleeps late, and wakes full of dreams. She lies in the bath and looks at her toes.

Cate

She takes the train to Charing Cross, the Underground to Bethnal Green, and then the old bus route up Cambridge Heath Road, gets down on Mare Street and walks along the canal, past the gas tower, past the gate to Sam's old studio, right down Broadway Market. It is a Thursday, and the road is fairly quiet, although the tables outside the deli are full. At the top of the road she turns left, following the terrace of Victorian houses to the end, where she stops, looking up at the tall house, the high windows, then walks on, through the park, where the London planes are in full splendid leaf.

The cafe was Lissa's choice – a bakery in one of the arches by the train station – and Lissa is waiting for her already, sitting outside. She stands hurriedly when she sees Cate approach.

'I got you a coffee.' She gestures to the table before her.

'Thanks,' Cate says, sitting down.

Lissa is dressed soberly, jeans and a plain T-shirt, no make-up, her hair caught on top of her head. She looks different. Her face, for so long seemingly immune to time, has begun to be claimed by it. There are greys in amongst the blonde of her hair.

'I wasn't sure you'd see me,' Lissa says.

'I wasn't sure I'd come.'

'Do you mind if I smoke?'

Cate shakes her head, and Lissa takes out her pouch and rolls.

'I went past the old house,' says Cate. 'On the way here.'

'Oh?'

'It was funny. Looking at it and not going in. Are you still in the basement?'

'Barely. I can't really afford it. I think I'll have to move.'

'Then it really is the end of an era.'

'Yes, I suppose it is.' Lissa lights her cigarette, blows the smoke away from them. 'How's Tom?' she says. 'And Sam?'

'He's good. Tom's walking now.'

'Do you have pictures?'

Cate takes out her phone, bringing up a couple of recent photos as Lissa leans in. 'He looks like a sweetheart.'

'He is. Sometimes.'

'How's Hannah?' asks Lissa softly.

'She's OK, I think. As far as I know they're still apart. I'm seeing her later. I guess I'll know more then.'

Lissa nods, turns to look out into the street. 'I won't bother to defend myself,' she says.

'OK.'

Above their heads, the rumble of a train, the squeal of its brakes. The hiss as it opens its doors.

'It's funny,' says Lissa, turning back. 'I've been thinking, lately, about that audition. That film. Do you remember? Before we went to Greece?'

Cate's stomach tightens. 'Yes.'

'And how I couldn't forgive you for it. I've sort of hated you, I think. Ever since. For not telling me about it in time.'

'Lissa—'

'No.' She holds up her hand. 'Let me finish. I know you have your own version of events. I just wanted to say that, lately, I've come to understand that I'm capable of things I didn't ever imagine. And I wanted to say that, whatever happened, I forgive you. That I wish you well.'

Cate opens her mouth to defend herself, then closes it again. 'Thank you,' she says. 'That means a lot.'

There is the rattle of the train leaving the station above, bound for Liverpool Street, or for the north, for far reaches of the city.

'Sarah's ill,' says Lissa. 'She has cancer.'

'Oh God,' says Cate. 'How far?'

301

'Stage four.'

Cate puts down her cup. 'I'm very sorry to hear that, Liss.'

Lissa's hands move to her hair and back down again. 'Yeah,' she says, 'it's all a bit shit.'

'Is she having treatment?'

'She refused it.'

Cate waits for Lissa to speak.

'I sort of admire her for it,' Lissa says, 'but I'm angry too – I mean, I'm fucking furious actually.'

Cate nods.

'And . . .' Lissa looks up. 'I know you went through it with your mum, and I wanted to ask you what to expect?'

She has the afternoon to herself, until she needs to be at Hannah's at six, so she wanders down to the bookshop, where she finds a picture book for Tom. The tables outside the deli are still full. Everyone sitting at them seems terribly young. As she queues inside for salad she watches them, these young people in their summer clothes, the self-consciousness of the way they sit, as though ready to have their photos taken, with their lemon water and their flat whites, starring in the movie of their lives. The way you do, when you are twenty-four or twenty-five, and you only see yourself from the outside in. She buys her salad and takes it into the park, where she sits beneath the old tree at the back of the old house and eats it, and then lies in the dappled sun.

At quarter to six she takes the back route to Hannah's flat. Hannah buzzes her in and she climbs the three flights of metal stairs to where her friend is waiting at the top.

Hannah looks well – she is tanned, wearing a short-sleeved

dress, her hair a little longer. Cate doesn't know what she expected, some lingering sadness perhaps, but the flat feels lovely, homely, the way the light catches the flowers on the table. Hannah makes tea, which they take out on to the terrace and drink in the last of the evening sun.

'You look good,' says Cate. 'How are you, really?'

'I've been swimming,' says Hannah. 'Every morning. It helps. And you? How're you and Sam?'

'OK, I think. Good.'

'That's good.'

'I heard from Hesther,' says Cate.

'Who?'

'Hesther. From Oxford. I wrote to her to ask for Lucy's address. A while ago. In the winter. She wrote back. Sent me her contact.'

'Oh Jesus, Cate. Really?'

Cate looks out, at the sun, setting now in the trees. She thinks of the days after the email – the letters composed, scrapped, written again. And then waking one morning in early summer, dressing Tom, dropping him off at Alice's, cycling through the morning to work, and knowing, or understanding what she had known, really, all along. There was nothing to be gained from writing. There was much to be lost.

'I didn't get in touch,' she says lightly, 'in the end.'

She hears Hannah exhale. 'That's good.'

She turns to Hannah. 'I did see Lissa, though.'

'Lissa?'

Cate sees the momentary shock on her friend's face. 'We met up this afternoon.'

'To talk about me?'

'Actually, no. Not really. Although she asked about you. She seemed different. Sad. We talked about Sarah.'

'Sarah. Why Sarah?'

'She's dying. She has cancer. Lissa asked to see me, to ask me about it. About how it might be.'

'Oh,' says Hannah. 'Sarah? Oh no.' For a long while she is silent, then she leans forward and puts her face in her hands.

'Han . . .' Cate puts her hand on Hannah's arm, worried she has punctured her frail bubble of happiness, but when Hannah looks back up her face is unexpected, shining.

'I'm pregnant,' she says, quite quietly.

'What?'

Hannah laughs, puts her hands to her face.

'Oh my God,' Cate says. 'Who—?'

'Nathan. He came to the flat. To collect some things. It was quick. So quick.' She shakes her head. 'All that time, and then . . .' She makes a gesture, her palms upturned, and Cate sees the surprise still, on her face.

'Does he know?'

'No.'

'Are you going to tell him?'

'Yes. No. I don't know. Not yet.'

'You have to tell him, Han.'

'I want to wait. Wait to see if I'll manage to keep hold of it. If it will stay.'

'How many weeks are you?'

'Eight, or nine. I'm not sure. I've got a scan booked at the end of the month.'

Cate watches her hands move to her abdomen, rest there. 'Can I come?'

'To the scan?'

'Yes. Can I come with you?' Cate reaches across, takes hold of her friend's hand.

Lissa

It was suggested that Sarah might want to move downstairs, to the old study at the back of the house, but she has refused. *I'll die in my own bed, thank you very much.*

Laurie has moved in, taking the bedroom beside Sarah's, the one that faces out on to the street. They have established an easy rhythm, Lissa and Laurie; they are solicitous with each other, taking turns to sit with Sarah while the other cooks or cleans, or sleeps.

Sarah is a surprisingly easy patient – whatever pain she is in, and Lissa knows it must be great, she rarely complains.

Sarah's friends visit. Some of them Lissa hasn't seen for almost thirty years: June and Caro and Ina and Ruth. They congregate round Sarah's bed. Lissa leaves them to it. Some-times the laughter is raucous and wild. Sometimes they sing.

While Sarah sleeps they gather around the kitchen table. They take over. They make Lissa sit and drink wine, or tea. They take Lissa's face in their hands and cry and kiss her cheeks and tell her how much she looks like her mother, and when they hug Lissa to their chests in their embrace, she knows that they have lived through illnesses and lived through children and lived through no children and that they are a tribe, these women, with their battered bodies and their scars.

305

She is awed by them, these women of her mother's gener-ation; they appear to her shining, like a constellation that is setting in the west. These women, these caretakers. What will happen to the world when they have gone?

When they are gone the house is quiet.

She cycles back along the canal to Hackney in the summer sunshine, and packs up the flat into boxes, which she loads into a rental van and drives to a storage facility on the North Circular. She goes back to the flat and cleans the oven, washes the windows. Has a last cigarette on the wide stone steps. She posts the key through the letterbox of the house of the estate agent in Stamford Hill then she takes a taxi to Tufnell Park with three small bags of her stuff.

She moves into the attic, where she sleeps on a futon on the floor. She likes it up here, though it is hot at this time of year, at the top of the house. The old chair is still here, and she sits in it and reads, while Sarah sleeps downstairs. She roams her mother's bookshelves, reading at random – Carson McCullers, Zola, Katherine Mansfield. Many of the books have her mother's notes in them; some from her time as a teacher, some from earlier, from her university degree. There is some-thing moving about reading like this, alongside her mother, feeling the youthful energy in her mother's scrawl, keeping her company while she sleeps downstairs.

One afternoon, as she sits there reading, an idea comes to her, a surprising one, and she lets it settle in her body, feeling its contours, trying it out for size.

In the early mornings she takes the battered old hose and douses the garden – *It must be early when it's hot like this,* Sarah tells her, *so their leaves don't burn.* Lissa stands in the greenhouse at the bottom of the garden inhaling the musky tang of the tomatoes and green growing things, and looks up at the house, at Sarah's bedroom, where the curtains are still drawn and her mother sleeps. She is starting to have her favourites: the lady's mantle, which cups the water like mercury; the sweet peas, racing up their trellis. Sometimes she bends and takes the tendrils in her fingers and strokes the ends of them, watching them reach out for life. She attempts to cut the lawn with the ancient mower, whose teeth are rusted and saw at the grass.

In the long, light evenings, they sit in Sarah's room and read to her. She loves to be read to; poetry mostly – *more bang for the buck,* she says, *no time for* The Brothers Karamazov *now.* She sends Lissa and Laurie to the bookshelves over and over again – knows where each book stands on the crowded shelves, knows its neighbours, can direct you to a volume in the dark. She treats poems like medicine and knows what she needs.

She asks for Shakespeare, and Lissa and Laurie take it in turns to read the sonnets. One sunny Sunday, Lissa calls Johnny, who comes to join them, arriving freshly shaved, bringing flowers and pastries and good coffee and wine. They read *Antony and Cleopatra* all the way through, taking it in turn to read the parts. It takes all day, and is one of the nicest days she can remember. Sarah has her eyes closed for most of it. Sometimes Lissa sits beside her, takes her hands, which Sarah squeezes now and again.

Later, Johnny helps to carry Sarah down to the garden. It is the first time in a week since Sarah has left her bed. When Lissa and Johnny make a hammock with their hands and lift her, she is noticeably lighter. Laurie disappears into the kitchen to roast a chicken, waving them all outside.

'Fetch my sketch book, would you?' says Sarah, when she is sitting in the chair. Lissa does so, bringing it, and her tin of charcoals. Then she retreats to the bench behind her, watching her mother's charcoal move over the paper, the garden spring to life beneath her hand: Johnny dozing in a deckchair, Ruby stretched belly up in the sun.

Later that evening, when the chicken has been eaten and Sarah is asleep in bed and Johnny has departed, Lissa and Laurie stand by the sink, clearing the last of the plates.

'Is he your lover?' says Laurie.

'Who?' Lissa looks up, startled.

'Johnny?'

'No.'

'He'd like to be. He's a lovely man.'

'I don't need a lover,' says Lissa. 'Not now.'

Laurie nods.

'And he's complicated.'

'We're all complicated,' says Laurie. She stows plates in cupboards, wipes down surfaces. It is the tidiest the kitchen has ever been.

'I'm giving up acting,' says Lissa. 'I realized that earlier, when we were reading. I don't want to do it any more.'

'That's a shame, Liss,' says Laurie softly.

'No,' says Lissa. 'It's not. I never want to go to another audition again.'

She feels this land, the certainty of it. The relief.

'Do you know what you're going to do?'

'Sort of.' Outside, the light lands in the pear tree. 'I've been thinking. I'd like to train to be a teacher.'

'Really?'

She nods. 'An English teacher.'

'Like your mother.'

'Like Sarah, yes.' She turns to Laurie. 'But I'm not sure. I'm going to go away first. To make up my mind.'

'Where?'

'I don't know.'

It is hard, hard to think of a destination that does not seem contrived – she does not want to find herself. Or perhaps she does. Perhaps that is exactly what she wants.

A few days later, when Sarah is dozing and Laurie has gone for an evening walk on the Heath, Lissa goes downstairs to feed Ruby. While the cat is busy at her bowl, she fills the old watering can in the dim kitchen, goes outside and drenches the beds with water. The garden is full of the smells of evening – the jasmine, the honeysuckle and the lavender – and the low humming of the bees. As she makes her rounds, she feels how her mother loved her garden – easily, simply, without rancour or friction or pain. She feels her mother's choices, her mother's care, her mother's subjectivity, like a veil hovering over this small patch of earth, merging with the night. Perhaps, she thinks, this is what remains.

She thinks of smoking a cigarette but does not. Instead she goes back into the house, puts the kettle on the stove and makes herself a cup of tea. She takes it back up the stairs, her eyes adjusting to the lack of light. As soon as she enters the room she senses it. She puts down her tea and walks slowly over to where her mother lies in her bed. She lifts Sarah's hand, which is cool, and she rubs her mother's thumb with her own.

At first she wants to rub and rub, to rub the life back into her mother, the way you would rub warmth back into someone who is cold, but then she understands that she cannot – that the time for that is passed – and so she stops, and holds her mother's hand instead. She reaches over and brushes her hair gently from her forehead. Someone has shut the window – it must have been Laurie – and Lissa stands and opens it. Then she comes back to sit beside her mother, to hold her hand.

The morning after Sarah's death, Ina arrives. She is a hospice nurse and knows what to do. Lissa watches as Ina unpacks her bag beside Sarah's body: small brown bottles with stoppers, scissors, string, muslin squares. Ina is small and steady and purposeful. 'Can I watch?' she asks her.

'You can help,' says Ina. 'If you like.'

First Ina straightens Sarah's limbs, then takes her head in her hands and moves it gently from side to side, placing it down on the pillow, placing another pillow beneath her jaw. 'We'll clean her now,' says Ina.

Lissa fetches boiled water from the kitchen, and Ina adds lavender oil and sage, and soaks swabs of muslin in the fragrant water. The women clean Sarah's armpits, her chest, her legs. Ina swabs in between her legs. She takes a fresh square of muslin and folds it, placing it in a pair of clean knickers.

'She might leak,' she says matter-of-factly. 'We all leak.'

These bodily fluids, this defilement, this shit are what life withstands, hardly and with difficulty, on the point of death.

She misses Hannah. She wants to talk to Hannah.

'Here,' says Ina, moving around Sarah's body. 'We need to

wrap the fingers, to take off her rings. The fingers will swell and then we can't.'

Lissa watches as Ina wraps Sarah's fingers with cotton thread, massaging in oil, moving the fluid gently down towards her mother's wrist so the rings might ease off. She does the same for the rings on her mother's left hand. 'That's it,' says Ina approvingly. Then, under Ina's instruction, they place Sarah's hands gently on her chest. 'It's better that way, so the blood doesn't pool.' She is like a midwife, thinks Lissa, in her gentle, certain ministrations; a midwife for death.

'Can I have a moment?' she asks Ina.

When Ina steps outside, Lissa takes her mother's hands. She lifts her fingers to her face, as though her mother might read her – read the Braille of her daughter's features, even now, even beyond death. Then she slowly places the hands back down on the sheet.

Hannah

Cate is waiting for her outside the hospital. Hannah sees her scanning the car park, watching for her.

'They'll think we're together,' says Cate as Hannah approaches, and she laughs. Her hands move like birds, unsure where to land.

'Well,' says Hannah, threading her arm through hers. 'That's all right.'

They are the first couple there and they do not have to wait to be seen. A sonographer in jeans and a T-shirt calls them into a small dark room.

She gets up on to the table. The monitor faces away from her. Her heart. Her breath coming quickly.

The sonographer glances at Hannah's file, then turns to Cate. 'And you're the partner?'

'No,' says Cate. 'I'm just a friend.'

'Well,' says the woman gently, 'why don't you go and sit down there.' She gestures to a chair at the head of the table.

The woman puts cold gel on to Hannah's stomach. Hannah catches her breath as the sensor rolls over the tautness of her skin. She looks at the woman's face. The woman is silent, staring at the screen, at the dark places inside her – her face impassive. She is a seer, a diviner of meaning, a reader of the runes. But why is she so silent?

A wave of fear and nausea breaks over Hannah. 'Is everything all right?'

The woman looks up. 'So far,' she says.

Hannah clenches her thumbs into her hands.

'Just taking measurements,' the woman says.

The woman rolls a ball, the keyboard clicks, and then, 'Here,' she says, turning the monitor around to face them, 'here's your baby. Everything looks fine.'

A creature is projected there, waving its limbs. A heart flickering, flickering, beating faster than Hannah's own.

Lissa

All week Sarah's friends, her colleagues, her ex-pupils, all those who knew and loved her, are encouraged to come to the house and write their messages on scraps of cloth. Lissa and Laurie make coffee and tea, they give out glasses of wine and of water, put crisps and toast and soup on the table, and listen.

She imagines this is a little like it must feel after the birth of a child: this liminal space where time behaves differently, is gentled and held.

There are middle-aged men whom Sarah taught as teenagers, who tell of her classes, of her importance in their life. Younger women with their children in tow, who stare at the house – at the books and the paintings in it – and nod, as though it is exactly what they had expected, or hoped. Sarah's dealer comes, bearing a spectacular bouquet, leaving a trail of expensive scents in his wake.

Johnny brings his oldest daughter, a tall girl of seven, with straight brown hair that hangs past her shoulder. 'This is Iris,' says Johnny. Iris is dressed in high-tops and a hoodie. She stands hand in hand with her dad. 'We're going for ice cream,' says Iris. 'Do you want to come?'

'Sure,' says Lissa.

They walk the streets and the streets are strange – it is the first time she has been out properly in days. 'Is your mum dead?' asks Iris.

'Yes,' says Lissa, 'she is.'

Johnny reaches out and puts his arm around Lissa, and she lets him, and his daughter watches them and she does not seem to mind.

She sleeps in her mother's bed – the bed she died in – and it is not eerie, but comforting. Her mother had the death she wanted, she thinks. She understands now what a gift that was. How many people can say the same?

*

313

The morning of the funeral Lissa puts on a yellow sundress. It is October, but unseasonably warm. Johnny and Laurie arrive to help – they wind the fresh flowers through the weave of the wicker basket.

Don't call it a coffin, darling. It's a basket, that's what I want, a basket filled with flowers.

The basket is indeed filled with flowers, dried ones and fresh ones, and posies of herbs and the ribbons of cloth covered with messages to send Sarah on her way. As she and Laurie and Johnny lift Sarah into the back of her old van, which still smells of turps and canvas and coffee, the ribbons lift and flutter in the breeze.

Sarah joked that she wanted to be buried under the pear tree in the garden, but they take her to Islington and St Pancras Crematorium instead.

Which is actually in Finchley, Sarah had said with mild disappointment, when she looked at the map.

The room is packed; there are hundreds of people there. When the ceremony is over, one by one the mourners come to speak to Lissa to say goodbye. Her dad is there, with her stepmother, and he holds her for a long moment before releasing her again. It is then that she sees them – Hannah and Cate. They must have been here all along.

'Oh,' says Lissa, looking at her friends. 'Oh,' she says again.

Hannah reaches her hand to Lissa and Lissa takes it.

'You're pregnant,' she says, and it is only now that she begins to cry.

'Yes,' says Hannah.

And now she is nodding, grinning stupidly in this sun.

'Look at you,' she says. 'You look wonderful.' And it is true, Hannah does; she is a fine ripe fruit.

'I came for Sarah,' says Hannah. 'I came to say goodbye.'

'Yes.' Lissa nods. 'Thank you.' And then, 'I'm sorry,' she says. 'I'm so sorry. Please, forgive me.' And then, for she cannot truly believe it, 'You're pregnant,' she says again. 'Can I? May I?' She holds out her hand.

Hannah nods, lets her place her hand there.

And now Lissa is laughing, standing in the sunshine with her hand like this, on the taut skin with the life beneath, laughing and crying and shaking her head.

The house is quiet. Laurie had offered to come back with her, as had Johnny, but Lissa refused. *I'll be fine*, she said.

There are books left open on the tables, and she lifts them gently and closes them, placing them back on the shelves. The kitchen has their breakfast things still sitting in the sink. She rinses the bowls and puts them on the side, then props open the door to her mother's garden. Sunlight pools on the floor. She pours herself a gin and tonic and rolls a cigarette.

She lifts the drink to the urn, which rests on the kitchen table. On Monday, as promised, she will go to Greenham with Laurie and Ina and Caro and Rose, and leave some of her mother's ashes by the tree. The rest Sarah has asked her to scatter in the garden, *wherever you like*. She'll do it tomorrow, alone.

In her inbox is a ticket to Mexico. Her flight is next week. She has no plans, only a vague destination – a town on the

Pacific coast. It is not an ending or a new beginning. Or perhaps it is. But if it is an ending, it is not clean, or neat – it is simply the part where one pattern joins another. It is made of blood and sinew and bone.

When she has finished her cigarette, Lissa shuts and locks the door. She comes over to the table. How many hours spent here? How many breakfasts and lunches and dinners? How many times was she put here, with drawing materials or crafts, and told to look after herself?

Once, she remembers not being able to sleep, hearing voices in the kitchen, coming down to find her mother and her friends here, sitting around the table. 'What are you making?' she had asked.

'They're cranes,' her mother replied. 'Here, look.' Sarah lifted her into her lap and showed her how to fold the paper to make the origami birds, and explained they were making them to mark an anniversary, of a bomb dropping in Japan, that they were a sign of peace, a sign that nothing like that should ever happen again. They sat around the table, the women, speaking in low voices, as Lissa followed her mother's instructions and a bird emerged, like magic, like something beautiful being born.

The women murmured to each other, and there was the soft, susurrating sound of their voices, the ripple of their occasional laughter, the warmth of her mother, the smell of her, of turps and of spices, the feeling of being allowed to stay up, of being held, the whiteness of the paper and the pleasure in folding and in making something fine.

She remembers all this, standing here in the evening kitchen – the peace there was in this room. She remembers the sense of peace.

Hannah

It has not been easy to sleep, these last nights. Even with all the pillows she cannot find a comfortable place to lie.

The baby wakes her often. She lies there, feeling the baby move her limbs in the small space left to her. Hannah thinks she feels a heel bone, an elbow. She touches the baby through the skin of her stomach. The baby is a selkie. An underwater swimmer. An habitué of the dark.

The baby is a girl. At first, this knowledge troubled Hannah. A boy felt simpler somehow. How to be a mother to a girl?

But now the thought of a girl is wondrous.

Now she is impatient to meet her.

There is a line to be crossed first. A birthing. She is not scared, she thinks, of pain. It is only the surrender, perhaps, that frightens her.

She speaks to Nathan sometimes. He has a room in a flat close by. He visits and when he visits he is quiet, solicitous. He cooks for her, soups and risottos. He makes a large pan and he leaves it for her on the stove. Sometimes they walk together, along the canal. Sometimes, when she is tired, she takes his arm. Sometimes, before he leaves her where she sits, huge on the sofa, she catches him looking, catches the look on his face.

He asks for little, but he has asked to be present at the birth. She has not said yes to this. She does not know if having him there will make things easier or harder. There are many things that she does not know. And this not knowing, in these cold January days lit from a warmth within, feels OK somehow.

Cate stays one night a week. Hannah looks forward to her visits, when they will sit and talk and laugh. She has asked Cate to be her birth partner, and Cate has said yes. It will take her an hour and a half to drive from Canterbury, two hours at the most.

Hannah wakes in the night.

It is very late, or very early. It is four o'clock. It is the time at which people are born and the time at which people die. It is dark and she is wet – the bottoms of her pyjamas are soaking. She reaches for her phone and calls Cate.

'She's coming,' she says.

She feels the leap of her heart, the beat of her blood in her ears.

She is coming. Here, in the darkness, a new story is beginning.

Her girl is on her way.

London Fields

2018

It is Saturday, which is market day. It is late spring, or early summer. It is mid-May, and the dog roses are in bloom in the tangled garden at the front of the house. Lissa sees them as she passes, on her way to the park.

It is warm. She is dressed simply, in faded jeans, an embroidered peasant blouse. Her feet are in thin sandals and she carries a canvas bag on her shoulder – inside it: good tomatoes, bread, Rioja, a goat's cheese covered with ash.

As she enters the park, she pauses on the path, looking over towards the back of the big old house with its crumbling garden wall, the old tree beneath which they used to love to sit. Today, the grass beneath the tree is packed with bodies, the air filled with the scent of barbecues and cigarette smoke, the blare of competing sound systems. It looks like a festival for the young. She looks up once more at the house, at the open windows, at the distant, shadowy figures that move around inside, then turns and walks on. They have arranged to meet on the other side of the park – close to the lido – the side where the families go. Here the grass is quieter and still green. She finds a spot and puts down an old rug and kicks off her shoes. The grass is lovely beneath her feet. She is nervous. This meeting was her idea – she wrote to them both, on a whim, one morning from the balcony of her small flat in Mexico City, telling them she was coming – a rare visit to England, to London, for Laurie's funeral, asking if they might want to see her again, after all this time. She was surprised, and pleased, when they both replied and said they would.

Presently she hears a shout and looks up to see Cate, dressed in a light summer dress, and a young girl of five or so coming over the grass towards her. Lissa sees Cate pause, bend to the girl and point, reminding her, no doubt, who this tall woman with the short fair hair is, for Lissa has never met Cate's daughter, born the year after she left for good.

This is Poppy, says Cate, when they have hugged hello. She's been excited to meet you. I told her you used to be an actress. She loves to perform.

Ah, says Lissa, yes, a long time ago. And she kneels beside Poppy, a round-faced, smiling child, and asks the right questions, listening as the girl chatters about her ballet classes, about the play she did last Christmas at school.

Another call, and they turn, and here is Hannah, come from the lido, with her own daughter walking beside her – a tall six-year-old, another child that Lissa has never met, a girl with the look of her mother – the same sleekness, the same dark hair, the same graveness of expression. Clara, says Hannah, this is Lissa. Hannah and her daughter take their places on the rug and the food is brought out and smiled over and tucked into.

The talk, though, is only small talk, and Lissa, who has been imagining this moment for weeks, for years – feels a creeping sense of disappointment. Somehow she had hoped for more. But what, truly, can there be to say to each other, after all this time? Small talk is small, but the inroads to intimacy were savaged years ago. And who is to blame for that?

But then, as the afternoon deepens, as the wine is drunk and the light thickens, the women start to relax. They talk about the old days. They raise a toast to the old house. Hannah asks Lissa about her life in Mexico and Lissa tells her about her job, teaching English in a language school, about the city she has grown to love, the mornings when she takes herself to a cafe with her laptop and sits and writes. Small moments, really, but they make her feel alive. And as Lissa talks, carving the air with her hands, Hannah feels a part of herself unfurl, just as she did that first time she met her – Lissa carries colour in her, she always did, and Hannah feels herself draw a little closer, warming herself at the small fire of her old friend.

When Cate and Hannah talk, they talk about their children mostly – talk through them, even, reaching for them, touching them often, smoothing their hair. And their children talk, too – they know each other well, it is clear; they tell Lissa about a holiday they all took last summer to France. As Lissa watches, she feels a familiar ache. She will be forty-four next birthday. As the years in which she might conceivably conceive have diminished, she has felt a corresponding, surprising sadness rise. It is not that she wants a child, not really, she is happy with her life, with her apartment in a cool-tiled building in Coyoacan, with her partner, who is a kind and gentle man. She and he sleep late on the weekends. They have their lives to themselves. It is just that sometimes, lately, on the way to work, or walking through the weekend markets, she will stop, made suddenly breathless at the sight of a baby. And Mexico is full of babies. But mostly, most days, she is fine. Her partner has a son, a boy of fifteen, who lives with his mother nearby. He spends every other weekend with them. Lissa likes him. He is *kind and studious and funny, like his father. He likes to sleep late, too.*

Hannah's daughter talks about her dad – who is coming to pick her up later, as she is staying at his house tonight – and the mention of Nathan hovers dangerously in the air between the women, but as the girl chatters on, oblivious, the moment loses its charge, is lost in the next moment, and the next.

They look at each other, these women, as the girls talk, noticing the ways in which they have aged. They are not the same women they were.

They worry. They worry about their parents – their fathers mostly. Hannah's father, who forgets things – more and more, it seems – who no longer meets her on the platform at Stockport station when she travels north. Cate's father, in Spain, who drinks too much, and is lonely. Lissa's father, who seems to have no joy in his life at all.

They worry about summer, which is coming earlier and lasting longer each year – a worry that taints their enjoyment of this beautiful May afternoon like a dark drop of ink swirled in clear water. Most of all they worry about the future, about their children, about the world they will inherit, a world that seems so fractured and fast and ever more splintered. They worry about how their generation will be judged by those who come after, and if that judgement will be hard, about whether there is still time to rectify this, because, more and more these days, they would like those who come after them to look back and be proud.

Sometimes it seems that the list of their worries is endless, that they are corroded by worry, hollow with it – they and everybody else they talk to, these days.

But long, too (although sometimes harder to name), is the list of things for which they are grateful: for small mercies, which no longer seem so small. For moments. Like this morning, for Cate, saying goodbye to her husband and her son, knowing they will be there to meet her again this evening, when she returns, knowing there will be food to eat, a table to sit around, the talk of her children. Her husband's continued steady presence in her life. And for Hannah, the pride she still takes in her work, the fact that she is still friends with the father of her child, the ongoing, unceasing miracle of her daughter's presence – a love so strong and fierce she feels no loneliness and no need for another, for she has found the love of her life. For Lissa, the quietness of her flat in the morning, when she rises early, and feels the warmth of the day to come in the air, and sits in the cool dawn and writes and feels sufficient unto herself.

They are grateful for these things because they know that old age and illness are not, perhaps, so very far away, and are not kind. They have seen this already, understood this, been humbled by it. They are humbled often, these days.

At a certain point in the afternoon, when the two girls have picked at the picnic and eaten their cake and are full of sugar and spiky energy and impatience, they jump up and move away from their mothers and from the other, blonde woman they do not know and whose name they will soon forget, on to the grass – called by the sun and the sky and by something else, something within that tells them they must move, right now. The same impulse, perhaps, that calls the seed to push up from the earth and reach for the light.

And Hannah's daughter takes Cate's daughter by the hand

and they spin round and round, round and round, and the women watch them, caught by their clumsy grace, the assertiveness of their small bodies in space, filled with a joy that is close to – that might, in fact, also be – pain. And the girls whirl on, laughing – glad to be free of the blanket, of the weight of their mothers' attention, of their mothers' need for them, of the looping, dipping, hard-to-follow thread of the women's conversation – giddy with movement, their hands clasped tightly together, round and round, round and round, in this spun-gold moment, dizzy with, drunk with life.

Acknowledgements

If it takes a village to raise a child, then it takes a very special village to raise a child *and* support the mother while she writes a novel. While writing this book I was fortunate enough to move to such a place – thanks to all my family in the Shire, but especially to Judith Way for deck therapy, to Cherry Buckwell for the walking cure, to Kate Christie for goddess-mother love, to Fionnagh Winston for wit and wisdom, to Rebecca Palmer for a home from home for my daughter, to Kelly Tica for boundless love, support and chicken soup, and to Rachael Stevens for sorting my life out, on so many levels, more times than I care to count.

Thanks to Ben and Toby for great chats about Seattle and LA – even if they didn't make it into the finished book.

To Olya Knezevic, who told me to watch *Autumn Sonata*.

To Judith, for taking me to Canterbury, lending me her library card and sharing her love of the city.

To the lady who opened the Tomb of the Eagles on a wild and wet day in November and gave her time so gently and generously.

To Philip Makatrewicz, Thea Bennett and Cherry Buckwell, who read the book in early drafts and whose clarity and enthusiasm were incredibly helpful.

To Josh Raymond and his legendary skinny black pen, whose edits are worth an ISBN number in themselves.

To the Unwriteables, still going strong after a decade of love and support.

To Naomi Wirthner, who called me in to her *Seagull*, and wove the magic round us all.

To my mum, Pamela Hope, whose activism inspired and shaped me, and who came with me on a memorable walk to Greenham Common.

To Dave, for making it work somehow.

To Bridie, for hearing the call, and answering with your wild bright wondrous self.

To my wonderful editor, Jane Lawson – she who understands what an ending must be.

To the inimitable Alison Barrow. I feel so lucky to have you on my team.

To my agent Caroline Wood, whose dedication to this book and desire to see it be all it could be were unwavering. Caroline, you have helped more than anyone else to bring this book into being – thank you so much for your rigour, enthusiasm and support.

And finally to the beautiful women who have shaped my life, the horizon watchers, the fierce dancers, the van converters, the river swimmers, the caretakers, the ones who know the old ways. Thanks for all you've taught me and all we've shared. More, please, more.